GW00993505

Mavis Road Medley

Fifty-four Mavis Road is an address that will linger long in the reader's memory. Its story is a medley of people, races, attitudes, ideas, friendships, love, and linking them all, music . . .

MAVIS ROAD MEDLEY

Goldie Alexander

Margaret Hamilton
Sydney
1991

Dedication

For David
And to the memory of my father who arrived in
Australia on 1 April 1929 'just in time for the Depression'.

 **Publication assisted by the Australia
Council, the Australian Government's
arts funding and advisory body.**

First published in 1991 by Margaret Hamilton Books Pty Ltd
PO Box 28, Hunters Hill, NSW 2110 Australia.
© Goldie Alexander, 1991
National Library of Australia Cataloguing-in-publication entry
Alexander, Goldie.
Mavis Road medley.
ISBN 0 947241 24 8.
I.Title.
A823.3
All rights reserved. No part of this publication may be reproduced
or transmitted in any form or by any means, electronic or mechanical,
including photocopying, recording, or any information storage and retrieval
system, without written permission.
Enquiries should be addressed to the publisher.
Typeset in Goudy 11/12pt by Silver Hammer Graphics.
Printed in Australia by Globe Press.

CONTENTS

1. Old Things In The Cellar

WHEN THE FALCONERS moved to fifty-four Mavis Road, all the family, apart from Didi, was pleased.

One Saturday Tom appeared in the kitchen doorway to announce, 'Remember that old metal trunk in the cellar? You'll never guess what's inside.'

'It's about time you cleared up the mess down there,' Jane said without looking up. 'Wait till I've balanced these figures.'

Kate kept on reading. Only Didi was curious enough to ask. 'What are you talking about, Dad?'

'The old trunk. I prised off the lid. It's filled with blankets and clothes. I thought you might find them interesting.'

Didi laughed uncertainly. Tom's sense of humour was quite often perverse. 'Oh, come on, Dad. Why should I be interested? I wouldn't wear someone's smelly old things.'

'Did I say anything about wearing them?' Tom cleared his throat, a sure sign he was getting irritable. 'I thought you might have a look. Some of the old newspapers go back to the early 'thirties.' He gave a raspy cough, closed the kitchen door and headed downstairs to the cellar.

Didi glanced at her mother, still absorbed in her accounts, closed the dishwasher door and followed her father to where he was laying down his collection of wine.

In a recent renovation the outside walls of this double-storeyed terrace had been painted dusty aqua, the cast-iron lace-work a shade darker. The leadlight pattern on the front door, the marble fireplaces, ceiling roses and 'wedding cake' cornices had all been carefully restored, and some ramshackle sheds out the back replaced by a large family-room. The rear glass doors led to a miniscule swimming pool and the front garden was replanted with ivy, ferns and a weeping willow.

But the cellar was left unchanged. Icy, dark and dank. The true age of the terrace could be seen in the number of old crates, newspapers and grime left behind. Didi halted on the bottom step and stared about in dismay. Hiding all this junk in such a smart house was, she decided, rather like discovering your favourite pop star wore false teeth.

Although the Falconers had moved in three months ago, Didi had avoided coming here alone. She wasn't always like this. Jane often told of the Easter when three-year-old Didi wandered alone into a huge shopping arcade. Or the family picnic when, following a smelly old wombat, she was lost for hours in the bush. Her curiosity increased with age. Tom's harsh comment, 'We'll tattoo your forehead "Explorers Unlimited" and warn people off,' was once warranted. But out in the bush there were no elusive shadows to wheel one about, no dank smells she preferred to avoid.

Tom was shifting cartons about.

'Isn't this a mess?' His gesture took in the rubbish piled into the centre of the room, the cartons heaped by the far wall. 'It'll take ages to clear this junk away.'

Just looking at Tom's stocky frame stripped to shorts and singlet made Didi feel cold. 'Say, Dad,' she asked, thinking how the streaks of dirt on his face looked like Indian warpaint, 'where are those old clothes?'

8

Tom pointed to a shabby metal trunk, the sort once used by passengers on long ocean voyages. Cobwebs still clung to the rusty hinges and Tom's fingerprints showed clearly in the dust. Didi opened the lid and peered inside. A musty smell, a curious combination of mildew and naphthalene rose up to meet her. 'Phew,' she cried, backing off.

Tom grinned. 'Bit high, isn't it?'

Nose wrinkled in self defence, she began pulling out the contents on to the floor. The blankets, half a dozen or so, she placed on top. Their pile was worn, yet the colours, varying shades of brown and orange, seemed as fresh as if woven yesterday. She burrowed further inside. The clothes Tom mentioned were spread between layers of newspaper. One glance at a black woollen skirt told her it was her size and, apart from that awful smell, still wearable. Though slightly apprehensive about spiders and cockroaches, she rummaged inside and unearthed a black jumper, hand-knitted in a pretty lacy pattern, several pairs of yellowing cotton panties, a cotton petticoat, a roomy pink and white nightie tied with pink ribbons at the neck and wrists, and two neatly folded pairs of thick, flesh-coloured stockings.

The woollen dress was right at the bottom. Navy. Didi admired the hibiscus flowers beaded on to the bodice, the skilfully draped skirt and the tiny buttonholes at the back. She wondered who had been silly enough to leave these lovely things behind. Turning to Tom, she cried, 'I reckon I could wear some of these.'

'Thought you'd change your mind once you saw them. You know,' he murmured half to himself, 'I've always wanted a cellar...'

'But Dad.' Didi frowned. 'We're only renting this place.'

'Next best thing.' Tom took another bottle from the carton and studied it. Something about the label must have displeased him for he turned to Didi, who was repacking

9

the blankets, and growled, 'Aren't you supposed to be stacking the dishwasher? You can't expect your mother to do everything.'

'But you told me to come and look.' A tiny whine crept into her voice. 'Anyway, why doesn't Kate ever help? She gets out of everything. It's not fair, it really isn't fair.'

'You keep forgetting Kate's doing Year Twelve. When you get there—mind, after your last school report I'm not too sure you will—you'll be relieved of some of those chores.' And by turning his back Tom showed Didi the conversation was over.

'Hmmmmpph!' She crossed the room, climbed the ricketty stairs and paused on the landing. 'Those clothes... Can I take them upstairs?'

Tom cleared his throat. Didi fled rather than risk another outburst. She would return later on. Closing the stairwell door, she tiptoed past the kitchen and up the stairs to the blessed privacy of her own room.

There, she switched on the stereo and curled up on the carpet. Two minutes later, *Dontchaknow, Diamonds are a girl's best friend...* was interrupted by a terrible pounding.

'For Christ's sake, turn it down,' Kate yelled. 'You know I'm trying to work. Honestly Didi, do you have to be so inconsiderate?'

'Piss off, stupid old cow!' Didi called. But mildly. In no mood for a fight. Crawling to the bookshelf, she flipped a few tapes and selected one at random. As James Reyne commiserated, *When I wake up in the morning, And get out bed, Yawning and scratching my head...* Didi sat at the desk, opened her diary and began writing.

Saturday, 13 April.

Today Dad found some old clothes in our cellar. He thinks they belonged to the 'thirties, but some of them are still OK... Chewing the end of her pen, grateful to be alone, she continued, *My sister Kate has hair the colour of autumn leaves, a perfect heart-shaped face, terrific features and a smashing figure. She's clever, gets high grades at school and has heaps of friends. Everybody likes her...* Then she printed in large red capitals: *EXCEPT ME.*

She read what she had written, looked up at the mirror and scowled. Nothing had changed. Her best feature, curly, shoulder-length hair tied into a loose pony tail, seemed drab and ordinary. She studied herself from a different angle. Her face seemed rounder than ever.

Certainly Didi's features weren't perfect. While Kate took after Jane, Didi looked too much like Tom. There were the same greenish-brown cat eyes, the same stocky shape. Kind people described Didi's smile as appealing, but her nose was too snub, her cheekbones too high.

Fed up with examining her reflection, Didi turned to the room. She hated the high ceiling which shrank her bed, bookshelf and desk into Hobbit size, but at least the walls were right. They were painted the same dusty aqua as the exterior of the house, but she had covered them with posters. Billy Idol beamed behind wrap-around glasses, Rick Astley smiled warily, and Marilyn Monroe laughed as her dress billowed out like an umbrella. INXS and Crowded House shared another wall. The prize piece was a print, a gift from her best friend Helene Schaeffer. It showed the sun setting behind an old-fashioned hotel, the sort that has big verandas edged with iron lace-work where women in pale flowing gowns rested on hot afternoons. A cricket game played in the foreground. If Didi gazed long enough she could hear the crack of ball meeting bat, hear the children shout.

This weekend the crowd's off surfing, Helene had written. *The weather's perfect and the waves unreal. Too bad you can't be here.*

11

She reread Helene's letter, then took herself for a solitary walk along Mavis Road. There was a party on at number forty-eight. She sidled past, tried to be inconspicuous, watched people with champagne glasses calling cheerful nonsense.

'Why's that girl on her own? Can't anyone hack her?' 'Wonder what's wrong with her?' No one looked her way. Only the music followed her, to part company when she turned into the next street.

She continued walking. Cars jammed the entrance of the football stadium. Didi ignored them. Instead she sent her legs instructions, tried to pretend a coach was running alongside encouraging her pace. Without breaking into an actual sprint she worked at taking longer, fewer strides, stretching every step to its utter limit, letting fluid movement destroy her pain.

When Didi first realised how much she hated St Anne's she thought she would burst; that her terrible rage must engulf everyone. A casual comment by a Phys. Ed. teacher tempted her to walk off her anger. When she returned after a long hike, she was too tired to do anything but eat, read a little, then drop into a dreamless sleep. Providing she was home before dark, no one questioned where she went. Last week after a spectacular fight with Kate, she fled into the streets, tried to exhaust herself before the light faded. If you can establish the right rhythm, walking becomes hypnotic: one two, one two, left right, left right... Didi knew soldiers on long marches stopped thinking for themselves. Her only concern was getting the right swing to her hips, placing each foot correctly, keeping up a strict pace.

Didi walked as far as the Shrine before she realised where she was. 'Oh God, how I hate living here,' she whispered to herself. 'Hate Melbourne,' she repeated out loud. 'Hate it, hate it, hate it! Grey, boring old place.'

But when you're fifteen you get no say in the sort of job your father accepts. There was nothing she could do except grit her teeth, turn round and head for home. Anyway, with the rain setting in she was soaked to the skin.

After showering, she made herself a cup of hot chocolate and settled down to watch television. On a Saturday night it was a poor substitute for the fun and friends left behind in Sydney.

He stood there in the drizzling rain for a long moment. Just looking. There was a sign which read, 'Pawnbroker. We Lend Money'. Inside the window there was a steel grille to protect the shop from thieves. The display was of little interest: some chipped plates, a radio, half a dozen books bound in leather, an old black-and-white television set, a few pieces of artificial jewellery, a stand holding worn gold rings and watches. None of these interested Jamie. He was staring at a small metal box in the far corner. Its grid-like mouthpiece faced his way.

Jamie marched inside.

'Yes?' The pawnbroker remained behind his steel cage.

It took Jamie a second to find his tongue. 'How much is it?' He pointed to the harmonica.

The pawnbroker came out from behind the cage, unlocked the window and handed the instrument over. 'Ever played one of those?'

Had he? Holding the harmonica against his lips, Jamie caressed the grid. There was something strangely familiar about this instrument.

'Why don't you have a go?'

The opening bars of 'Maid of the Mountains' floated through the shop. An old man strolling past paused in the doorway to listen.

'You make that instrument sound like it was yours.' There was grudging admiration in the pawnbroker's voice.

Jamie cleared his throat. 'How much do you want for it?'

'We've had that one a long time. It's good. A Larry Adler.' He paused to look Jamie over. 'It was part of the stock when I took over this business. One old fellow had an arrangement with the previous owner to keep the instrument on display. On no account was it ever to be sold. The old man just wanted to know if anyone came nosing around asking questions.'

Jamie smiled politely.

'This old fellow owned masses of property.' Catching sight of a mark on the upper casing, the pawnbroker began shining the instrument with a chamois, polishing it to some exacting inner standard. 'Owned half of Melbourne he did. Had an uncanny instinct where to buy property. And there he was, worried over a toy. You'd think he could afford a thousand harmonicas.' The greying eyebrows danced. 'Tell you what,' he decided, 'I'll give it to you for thirty dollars. It's a steal.'

'I'll take it.' Jamie withdrew the notes from his wallet and placed them on the counter.

The pawnbroker had expected Jamie to barter. He looked slightly disappointed. 'Want it wrapped?'

Jamie shook his head. He slipped the instrument into his hip pocket. It felt just right. He turned to leave and asked, 'How come you're selling? Won't the old man mind?'

'From where?' The pawnbroker laughed. 'From Heaven? The old boy's dead. He died a year ago, his wife six months later. I suppose she was missing him.'

Jamie nodded. When he stepped into the street it had stopped raining, but even the warmth of the sun didn't lessen his inexplicable sense of loss.

2. DIFFERENT DIRECTIONS

DIDI TRIED A last ditch stand. 'I still don't know why I can't go to the local high.'

'St Anne's was highly recommended.' Jane was beginning to sound rather terse. 'Besides, the local high's full of dope-smoking thugs.'

'How do you know?'

Jane shrugged her slim shoulders.

'But St Anne's is just for girls.'

'You're enrolled,' Jane said flatly, 'and the first-term fees are paid. That's final.' She took the girls to buy their uniforms the following day .

If Didi was older, more like Kate, pretty, popular, able to attract men, things might have been easier. If Didi had been younger, say still at primary school, Jane and Tom might have gone out of their way to get her settled.

Instead, on day one, sent to find her own form room, she stood outside the half-closed door for what seemed the longest minute of her life. The noises coming from the other side were terrifying, yet recognisable as any classroom when a teacher was absent. When she slipped inside, the room was filled with tall, pretty girls, all talking at once. Didi sidled into a desk near the windows. She needn't have troubled. No one paid her the slightest attention.

'Boy, did we get written off last night.'

'Andrew's taking me to the tennis on Tuesday.'

'Peter took his father's Merc for a spin, and you should have seen the old man hit the ceiling when he found out.'

'I just refused to go unless I got some new gear, so Nan took me to Esprit.'

A tall, blonde girl, pretty like the rest, disengaged herself from a group. 'Hi, I'm Emma. You're new, aren't you? What's your name?'

'Didi, Didi Falconer,' she said, determined to be known this way.

'Didi? That's unusual.' Emma looked Didi up and down. 'Where are you from?'

'Sydney, we've just come down from Sydney.'

An eyebrow lifted imperceptibly, just enough to make Didi feel there was something vaguely ill-bred about that city. 'Yeah? Sydney! Who do you know at St Anne's?'

'Well, nobody. We've just arrived.' Emma was no longer listening. A piece of gossip too good to miss caught her attention and Didi was left alone to stare through the windows until their teacher appeared.

This was the way things went that first week at St Anne's. There was no way Didi would be accepted. Different if she had wealthy parents. Or brothers at the right school.

'Oh, you've only a big sister...' and the smallest of the three Caitlins drifted off to the canteen.

Nor did Didi help her own cause.

One morning in the first week, their history teacher turned up holding a stack of textbooks even more battered-looking than herself. 'We're doing the lead-up to the Second World War, girls,' Mrs Hubert announced. 'Please turn to page one hundred and thirty-four.'

'Although recovery commenced in nineteen thirty-three,' she read, 'the Depression was not completely over until the start of the Pacific War. However, monopoly capitalism had been strengthened, for the Depression got rid of inefficient firms. BHP for example, absorbed the Wollongong plant of Australian Iron and Steel.

'Scullin's Labor government in Australia was followed by five years of stable conservative rule. In Europe and Asia, dictatorship and war were growing. Japan attacked China, Italy moved into Abyssinia, Spain fought a bloody internal war against Fascism, and Germany walked into Central Europe. Many of the intelligentsia of the time looked towards socialism as their only hope for a more peaceful world. Others migrated to America, Canada and Australia.'

Mrs Hubert looked up. 'Now girls,' she asked, 'can anyone explain monopoly capitalism to the class?'

Silence. Then a stage whisper, 'Go directly to jail. Do not pass Go. Do not collect two hundred.'

Mrs Hubert's piercing eye wandered slowly over the class and came to rest on Didi. 'Well Eurydice, I hear your father works for a private bank. Perhaps you can explain monopoly capitalism to this class?'

Someone at the back cried, 'Eurydice,' and the class took it up as a body, chanting, 'Eurydice, Eurydice, Eurydice.'

'That's a wog name, isn't it?

'Didn't tell us Didi's a wog.' Screams of laughter.

'How on earth do you spell it?'

All Didi could think was, 'Who told her?' And instead of smiling good-naturedly, admitting she had a pathetic name and saying she preferred to be called Didi, she fled to the lavatories. There, chewing on her nails, she cursed sister Kate. Of course it was Kate. How else would Mrs Hubert have known her real name or about her father's work? Crouched on the white plastic seat, the door firmly bolted, she wept and wept with self pity.

Brooding, vengeful, she considered hiding Kate's perfume, ruining her tapes, ripping into a new shirt. What

17

was the point, though? Jane and Tom would never understand. More predictable was Didi being punished and Kate joking about her pathetic little sister to her brand-new friends.

Five minutes before end of period Didi returned to the classroom, still fuming, but more in control of herself. Mrs Hubert ignored her, but pretty Brooke who belonged to the inner coven called, 'Doesn't take much to upset our Eurydice.'

'Why are things from the North like boxes?'

'Because they're square...' And with this, Didi's reputation became established. At least at St Anne's.

Didi found a haven in the library. There she impressed a kindly librarian with the number of novels she consumed; as if books were Mars Bars or Cherry Ripes and there for enjoyment. Nothing to do with study, or school, or passing.

'How come I never see you do any homework?' Jane asked suspiciously. 'Your grades are going to slip. What's wrong with you?'

'It's not my fault. It's all soooo boring,' Didi muttered. That her parents chose to ignore her unhappiness was their lookout, wasn't it?

But Tom's job kept him away long hours. Most nights he didn't get home until well after eight. With the sort of salary he was drawing it was silly of Didi to expect more attention. As for Jane? No question she was run off her feet. Her job carried as much responsibility as Tom's. Admittedly, wonderful Mrs Patou came in three times a week for cleaning and ironing, but there was shopping and cooking, the general running of a house plus Kate needing coaching in Accountancy and Economics. Didi decided nothing could be more boring than studying Commerce. Her family got so excited at the rise and fall of the dollar, ecstatic over changes in gold values. Didi was the exception. *I'll bet I was adopted,* she despaired, yet with a nose so like Tom's it was unlikely. *I probably have an ancestor who was peculiar like me,* she wrote Helene. *Maybe my great, great-grandmother loved reading novels.*

Meanwhile, a state of permanent warfare existed at home. For Kate was an instant success at St Anne's. So much so, she already had three invitations for the coming weekend, including one for Sunday lunch.

After returning from her walk, Didi had settled down to watch TV, when Kate marched into Didi's room. 'What's happened to my parrot earrings?' she yelled. 'Honestly Didi, if I find them in here, I'll kill you.' With this she began pulling open Didi's drawers, throwing contents everywhere.

Didi flew in from the family-room to rescue her belongings, and found Kate holding the jewellery. 'You little sneak! Who said you could borrow these without asking? I'll bet you've broken the catch.' She hit Didi, hard.

Didi ducked, but Kate was not yet finished. 'Honestly, if I catch you going through my things again, I'll tell Mum and you'll be for it.'

'So tell her,' Didi cried. 'Serves you right for dobbing me in. Who said you could tell those twits my name? Anyway,' she shrieked, for having intended to borrow, not keep the earrings, her sense of justice was outraged, 'who wanted your precious things? I was just trying 'em on.'

But Kate was already disappearing towards her own room. Didi flew into the passage shouting after her.

At this precise moment the doorbell rang. Jane called from the kitchen, 'Get that, will you?'

When Didi opened the front door a young man she had never seen before was standing on the mat.

Didi flushed, her heart gave a peculiar jolt. Later on she

described it as similar to running into a valued friend she hadn't seen in ages. Odd. She had never laid eyes on him before.

'Hmmmn,' he said, blinking as if he was expecting someone else, 'I'm Jamie Major.' Meeting her blank stare he added, 'I'm here for Kate.'

'Kate's not ready,' Jane called from the kitchen. 'Take Jamie into the front room.'

'I'm Didi, Kate's sister.'

'Funny name, Didi. Is it for real?'

The warm feeling vanished. She showed him into the front sitting-room where she scowled. It was her permanent expression these days. Hoping to embarrass him, she asked, 'How do you know Kate?'

'Met her at a rage.' His smile was infuriatingly calm. He dug into his back pocket and produced a rectangular object, about fifteen centimetres long, shiny, with metal teeth on one side. Holding it up to his mouth he played a scale, up and down, up and down. For something so small its tone was astonishingly rich.

Didi forgot to be annoyed. 'Hey! That's great. Is that a harmonica?'

He polished the instrument with a large and very clean handkerchief. 'Sometimes they're called mouth-organs. They're not so popular these days.'

'I don't think I've heard one before. At least, not on its own. Go on, play a tune.' Maybe this new boyfriend was OK. Until now they had been jerks.

The plaintive wail of 'Danny Boy' filled the room. And the strange feeling returned, only this time connected to the music, as if it magically mirrored her feelings. It travelled down the hall to the kitchen where, Pied Piper-like, it brought Jane and Tom to the sitting-room.

'As a kid I once heard Larry Adler play.' Tom looked

puzzled. 'But with all the electronic stuff around I didn't think you kids would be interested.'

Jamie held out the harmonica and laughed. 'It's portable, and called a Larry Adler. Here's something else he played.' With that he broke into 'Flight of the Bumble Bee'. Head cocked to the left, mouth going from side to side, Jamie transported the Falconers to a garden where insects flew in four-four time.

Didi examined Jamie intently, from the thrumming fingers, to his unusual height. Had she met Jamie in the street Didi might have thought him a footballer. No. Too thin. Body out of proportion. Torso too short. Legs like a spider. But his well-cut, brown hair was the same colour as Didi's, if not as curly, his eyes deepset, blue, like the sea on a balmy day. There was an attractive calmness there, yet the tilt of his nose was determined. I'll bet he's full of himself, she thought, deciding to dislike him. Yet, as the music busied itself, she forgot he was too good-looking. Instead the buzzing sound held her attention.

When Jamie came to the end Jane clapped loudly. 'Larry Adler played that, all right,' Tom said gruffly, 'but he took it a lot slower.'

Jamie grinned. He's no big talker but he's probably OK. Keeping score, notching points, she watched every move. Saw sweat beading his forehead. Noted he might have been alone when he played, so absorbed was he in the music. Observed that he cleaned the harmonica the moment he stopped.

Then Kate appeared. Lipglossed, perfumed, her hair gelled and wet-looking. Didi asked, trying not to sound envious, 'Where are you going?' Kate didn't answer. Instead, she tucked her arm into Jamie's, and smiled up at him.

'Private rage,' Jamie said at last. And Didi, watching

from under her eyelashes, decided that his calm manner hid an over-supply of confidence.

'Don't get home late, darling.' Jane was, as usual, worrying over Kate. 'Don't forget you've got assignments to complete this weekend.'

Didi stalked from the room, slamming the door accidentally-on-purpose. She heard Jamie saying, 'Your little sister seems to have lots of character.'

There was a burst of laughter, then Kate's voice, 'That's not the way we see it.'

Wanting to call, 'Hope you have an awful time', Didi started to her room, changed her mind and went to the fridge. She opened the door and stared inside. No one here would notice if she got fatter. It served everybody right. If only she was still in Sydney...

In Sydney there was Helene. Didi pictured her friend's pert features and dark face (Helene was part Sri Lankan) as she mimicked Kate's, 'Is that call for me?' Didi smiled faintly. Helene was ace at sending Kate up. A wave of self pity engulfing her, she stuffed a cold sausage into her mouth, then chewed savagely.

'Get away from that fridge. Dinner will be ready in five minutes.' Jane's voice followed her into the kitchen. 'Go and tell your father.'

Back in the cellar, Tom was perched on a pile of boxes with a newspaper in his hands. 'Listen to this,' he called. *The Governor of NSW, Sir Phillip Game, stunned the nation and rocked the Labor Party when he dramatically dismissed the Premier, Mr John Thomas Lang, from office.* The date's May thirteenth, nineteen thirty-two.'

'Unreal.' Her misery forgotten, Didi searched through other papers. She scanned a page, now fragile and yellow with age, and called, 'How about this? A new women's magazine is being published called *Women's Weekly*. It

22

contains a serial called 'Falling Star' written especially by Vicki Baum for the first edition.' Didi beamed at her father. 'Guess the date?' But before Tom had time, she cried, 'October eleventh, nineteen thirty-three.'

'Unreal...' Her gaze flickered over the crumbling pages. 'Look. There's ads for Gillette razors, Rosella jams. Maybe we should be careful and hang on to these? They could be worth a fortune to a library.'

Tom nodded vaguely and Didi's eye came to rest on the clothes she unpacked that very afternoon. She wondered about their owner. Why had they been left mouldering in this trunk? If not for the smell, that overpowering mixture of musk and naphthalene, they could be worn right now. Interesting how the previous owner had been the same size as her. Short and plump. The wrong shape for tall, skinny Kate. Didi held up the dress. The beaded flowers sprawled gracefully over the bodice, the drape of the skirt successfully camouflaged plump hips.

'Is it OK to take these upstairs?' she asked tentatively.

Tom was engrossed in a copy of the *Sun* with the headline, 'Cricket Gets a Body Blow'. He didn't answer.

Then Jane called down the stairwell, 'Tea's on the table.'

Before they returned upstairs, Didi replaced the clothes in the metal trunk. 'Hey, trying to hide our ghosts?' She glanced up, looking for the trap, but Tom's question was good-humoured.

'I'll check them again tomorrow.' She smiled at him. He smiled back and her spirits rose accordingly.

Before they left Tom added a dollop of machine oil to the trunk's rusty hinges. Then Didi remembered she hadn't set the table for tea. She flew upstairs ahead of Tom, and managed to lay out the knives and forks before Jane got mad with her.

Kate didn't come home until well after midnight. In

spite of this, Jamie was there to take her out again at the crack of dawn.

'He really is a nice lad,' Jane declared, as the door closed behind them. 'His music's good, but we don't want him round full-time. Kate needs to keep up her work. He seems very keen...' Didi interpreted the nuance as over-concern for Kate.

Tom grinned. 'You'd forgive an embezzler if he played well enough.'

Didi laughed. 'Dad, you're being silly.' Turning to Jane she asked, 'What does Jamie do?'

'Year Twelve at our local high. But he's planning to study music full-time.'

'With the harmonica?' Jamie hadn't struck her as having an artistic future. Not that she personally knew anyone who had. Should he be wearing glasses, look weedy? She pictured Jamie's football-hero appearance and nodded. One thing was certain; he would look great on stage.

'He plays piano, flute and clarinet,' Jane told them.

'Well, he must be keen on our Kate,' Tom moaned. 'He was here at sparrows' fart. What else do you know about him?'

'Come to think of it,' Jane wore her typical half-funny, half-worried look, 'only what Kate's told me. He's a country lad. The parents have split up and now he lives with his mother.'

'No worse than Vic,' Tom commented sardonically, 'and certainly an improvement on Tim.' Recalling Kate's previous boyfriends, the family, for once united, frowned with disapproval.

Tom stared at Didi. 'When will you start bringing fellows home?' he asked in the 'let's pretend to be serious voice' he sometimes used.

How insensitive. If they'd stayed in Sydney wouldn't

24

Andrew Fogarty be taking her out right now? 'Never,' she scowled as Andrew sped into the irretrievable past. 'Never. I'm planning to be a nun.' She darted a quick look Jane's way and her mother wore such a look of sympathy and understanding it made her feel angrier than ever.

The rest of the morning passed as slowly as only a dull Sunday can. Didi had brought home two novels recommended by the librarian, the only person she had 'on side' at St Anne's. Neither succeeded in capturing her interest. Tom and Jane were planning a walk. 'Come with us this afternoon, darling,' Jane suggested. 'It'll do you good to get some fresh air and exercise. The Botanic Gardens are beautiful and Tom's friends are very nice.'

'Melbourne's gardens are world famous.' Tom sounded as if he was personally responsible for the best lawns in town.

Didi scowled. If you've nothing better to do than go out with your parents... 'Rain's forecast for later on,' she said dourly. Her father glanced up. 'Thanks, anyway. I've got stacks of homework to do.' Tom's expression changed to one of approval.

After they left she wandered through the house and into the garden. Next-door's cat rubbed itself against her legs. I'll get them to buy me a kitten, she decided. Her spirits rose as she tickled its ears and it arched its back with pleasure. Then the ecstasy became too much, for it hopped over a low fence and disappeared. Even the cat doesn't like me, she sighed. Frankly, she didn't blame it.

Back in the house she raided the biscuit jar and looked about. There must be a way to fill in the long vacant day. She remembered the cellar. Overcoming her stupid fears about gloom and spiders and cockroaches, she opened the stairwell door and stared thoughtfully into the dark. With no one else in the house, it seemed spookier than ever. Tom had pushed the trunk into the centre of the room and it stood alongside other cartons and crates. In the dim light it formed an amorphous and rather frightening shape; like a giant bear or a Norwegian Troll. Giving herself a little shake to rid herself of her imagination, Didi turned on the light, looked from right to left, then descended. Pausing at the bottom of the stairs, she pictured herself tripping over rats, touching spiderwebs, then shrugged, annoyed with her morbidity.

She crossed the room and stood before the trunk. It seemed older and shabbier than before. The lid was jammed shut and she had to fiddle for ages before it opened. She took the blankets out one by one and shook them free. She was only half-surprised when something metallic clattered on to the floor.

Crouched on her hands and knees she probed with careful hands along the floorboards, investigated the inside of each crack, felt along each side of the trunk. At long last her fingers closed on something small, something smooth and round, and she slid it into her pocket. She remembered to close the lid, then hurried upstairs to the family-room and settled herself under the light of a strong lamp.

It took only seconds to realise that the find was valuable. The ring had a large stone, probably a sapphire, which was surrounded by tiny diamonds set in smooth, burnished gold. The claws which held the brilliant blue stone were bigger than any she had seen before. It was obviously handmade. The thick gold band was too uneven. Something in the design told Didi it was possibly older than this house. She slipped it on to the third finger of her right hand and found it fitted perfectly. Interesting, she thought, interesting how, like the clothes in the trunk, it could have been made for her.

She was heading towards the study for Tom's magnifying glass when the front door opened. In came Kate and Jamie.

26

Didi blinked in surprise. 'What are you doing here? I thought you were going to be out all day?'

Kate's cheeks were flushed, her eyes seemed huge, but dithery. Not her usual self-contained sister with everything under control. Not at all. 'I was cold, we came back for my jacket. You know, the one with the hood. It's really windy out there.' She flew into her bedroom as if she was being pursued by the devil himself, Jamie mutely following. If Didi didn't know better, she would have sworn her sister was embarrassed. Almost as if she had been caught doing something wrong.

Shrugging them off, Didi collected the magnifying glass and returned to the family-room. She held the ring up under the light. Too late, her pleasant mood had been spoilt. Thinking about Kate made her angry. These days lots of things made her angry. For the thousandth time she wished she was an only child. An only child living with another, nicer family.

She switched on the television set and settled down to watch the midday movie.

'...all you Australian movie buffs will enjoy *On Our Selection*,' an earnest voice was saying. 'This film was adapted by Ken Hall as a talkie from a short silent movie made by Raymond Longford. Filmed in 'thirty-two, it contains broad farce, romance, a black-hearted villain, murder and a last minute confession...'

The announcer rambled on, but Didi's attention was on her new ring. She glanced up when the opening credits began, then scowled. The film was so scratched and old, everything was in a rainstorm. It didn't help that Tom, with his flair for electronics, had hooked the speakers through the stereo as a way of improving reception. The sound-track of the film was so poor that the amplified songs of the bushland birds sounded reedy and scratched.

Didi watched for a while, but was mildly disappointed. *On Our Selection* made early life in Australia seem crude and grotesque. At the same time she found something vaguely appealing about the characters of Dad and Dave.

The rain had started pouring down outside and suddenly, a very loud peal of thunder echoed through the house. Didi jumped, and glanced nervously at the window. The picture, probably altered by the electrical disturbance, began rolling forward slowly, then faster and faster.

Didi pushed the ring on to her finger. She fiddled with the television controls. As her right hand passed over the screen, the greyish light caught the centre stone and held it in a kind of curious grasp. She looked down and gasped. A faint glow was coming from the ring. A thin beam of light, like a laser, was reaching out and linking the sapphire with the screen. It reminded her of an umbilical cord. Her mouth half-open in astonishment, Didi watched the glow intensify, until it was blinding.

Wincing in disbelief, she sat back on her heels, rubbed her astonished eyes, then glared at the set. She was too close to the screen, she told herself. A case of 'imaginitis'.

She blinked, wriggled her shoulders, told herself to be sensible. Yet for an instant, she would have sworn that something alien in there was looking out at her.

Fortunately Jamie, by choosing that exact moment to come out of Kate's bedroom and head towards the bathroom, broke her sudden panic.

'Hey,' she called after he emerged from the bathroom. 'Hey, could you do me a favour? This tellie's gone peculiar.'

'What's wrong with it?'

Giving him what she hoped was an appealing smile, she waved her hand at the rolling picture, then added plaintively. 'It probably just needs an adjustment. It won't work for me.'

'OK, I'll give it a try.' He tinkered with the controls, waited until the screen readjusted itself, then sprawled out on the couch beside her.

'What's the movie about?'

Now the set was fixed, she wished he would disappear, yet it seemed boorish not to answer. 'It's an old Oz movie called *On Our Selection*,' she said. 'It's not very good.'

'Yeah?' Leaning forward a little he stared at the film and she noted the way his eyes were set deeply in his head, the shape of his nose, his neat hands which seemed too small for someone his height.

Now the mood of the film was changing. The family had fallen on hard times, were stony broke, couldn't even afford to buy the flour for the parson's scones. For a few seconds the speakers cleared themselves of crackle and an unpretentious background tune came through clearly. It reminded Jamie of some country and western music he knew. There was a wonderful feeling of pathos and joy in the tune's mimicry of the bush. He reached into his back pocket, took out the harmonica, held it to his mouth and filled the room with the same catchy notes. A peal of thunder echoed in the distance. In answer, a standing lamp blinked imperceptibly, then its light suddenly faded. The screen flickered once, twice, three times.

Suddenly, it grew larger.

Only then did Didi realise they were no longer in the family-room. Nor at home. Jamie was still there, still sprawled next to her. But for some inexplicable reason they were in a hall filled with total strangers, all seated facing in the same direction. Directly in front was a large screen where, rolling on in front of their shocked eyes, was a swollen, giant-sized *On Our Selection*.

And, making it even worse, everyone around them was clapping and laughing like crazy.

3. WHAT HAPPENED?

IT TOOK JAMIE a second or two to realise something was wrong. He instinctively pushed the harmonica into his rear pocket, and gasped.

No wonder. Fed up with Kate's demands, he had lingered on in the family-room. One minute he was in front of the Falconer's television set watching some old movie, the next he found himself seated between some of the oddest-looking people he had ever seen in his life.

His heart was beating wildly as he saw he was in the middle of a huge hall, facing a large screen. The tune from *On Our Selection* still lingered in the air as the film rolled on before his startled gaze. For a split second he wondered if he was dead. He had the impression he was newly arrived in Hell; that the rows of strangely dressed people stretching as far as his eye could see were condemned souls packed into some sort of eternal waiting room. Only after what seemed like hours, after twisting his body around as far as it would go, did he realise he was seated in a large, filled-to-capacity auditorium. And everyone was watching a film.

A burst of adrenalin forced the blood to his head. Jamie flushed. He took a couple of deep breaths to stop the pounding in his ears. A strange choking sound to his right made him look down. There was Didi, Kate's little sister, still seated by his side. In the flickering half-light, he saw her face was ashen, her mouth open with shock.

His first thought was to blame Kate. Admittedly there wasn't much point, but if there hadn't been that argument he might have been readier to cope. As it was, all he did was scream a silent 'Help!'. His tongue seemed frozen to the roof of his mouth and he stared at the people seated in front. His gaze intercepted a young couple enveloped in a fierce embrace. The youth, misinterpreting Jamie's distraught expression, blushed beetroot, sat bolt upright and pushed his girlfriend away. Forced to lean forward, the girl glanced over, caught sight of Jamie's shocked face and glared back ferociously.

Of course, he was dreaming. Only Didi croaking, 'Wh...what's happening...' clutching him, pinching his arm so fiercely that he thought her fingers would leave bruises lasting for weeks, made him understand that this was real.

'*Come on, Dave...*' The audience was howling with laughter. Jamie gripped the sides of his chair, as if he was careering down a steep incline in an out-of-control roller coaster, and was nearly overwhelmed by panic. Never before had he seen anything like this. These people were alien, foreign.

As this hit him, Jamie's breath started coming in shallow little gasps, as if he was climbing a mountain peak and running out of oxygen. A pulse beat loudly in his head. At the same time, he was aware of a tremor on his right. Didi was quivering like a jelly. 'What's going on? Jamie, where are we?' Her voice came out as a high-pitched squeal.

'Sshhh...' 'Be quiet!' 'We'll have you chucked out,' shot from every direction.

An elbow dug into his ribs. Jamie turned and stared. His mouth fell open at the sight of a very fat man dressed in a shabby grey suit, a high-crowned felt hat on his knees. The man's hair was cut brutally short, his tiny features lost in folds of shiny flesh.

31

The man snarled, 'Hey, what are y' lookin' at, hey?' His female companion, dressed in a brown overcoat and hat with a button-eyed fox face peeping over her shoulder, leaned forward to inspect Jamie and Didi. Disliking what she saw, she frowned, and whispered furiously in her companion's ear. The couple turned and glowered.

There was something very menacing in the alert set of the woman's body and the stony look in the man's little eyes. For a second Jamie closed his own and prayed for the nightmare to end. Bile rose to his throat as the theatre's overpowering stench of cigarette smoke, old sweat and damp wool threatened to engulf him. He croaked, 'Let's get out of here,' and staggered to his feet.

A white-bearded character on the screen was saying, '*For years I faced and fought the fires, the floods and the droughts of this country...*' as Jamie and Didi stumbled over legs, bags and baskets. People glared and swore at them, 'watchit mate... What d'ya think you're doing...' Pretending not to hear, Jamie reached the aisle, and with Didi close behind, scrambled towards a door marked EXIT.

They were forced to close their eyes at the sudden glare in the empty theatre foyer. Empty that is, apart from a lad dressed in grubby white pants and a short jacket. Dumbfounded and gaping, they took in the ticket box with its sliding window, the flight of stairs with its ornately carved balustrades, the high ceilings painted in myriad colours and a gigantic chandelier where small electric globes glistened and shimmered like coruscations set in delicate crystal prisms. On the wall furthest from where they were standing was a pair of glassed double-doors which, Jamie assumed, opened out on to the street.

Catching sight of potential customers, the white-suited lad headed their way. 'Ice-cream, lollies, cigarettes?' He pointed to the tray strapped around his shoulders.

32

Didi stared helplessly. 'Where are we?' Her voice came out in a whisper.

The boy was checking his change, but he looked up when she spoke. 'Whatcha?'

Didi cleared her throat. 'Where are we?' This time she was more distinct.

The boy thought she was mad. His pale eyes bulged at the sight of her small plump figure dressed in stone-washed jeans, sloppy T-shirt and joggers. Switching to Jamie, examining his unusual height, jeans and jacket, the lad shrugged his narrow shoulders and dismissed them both as cranks. 'King's Theatre,' he said, 'of course.'

'King's Theatre?' Didi's stomach plummeted.

The boy stopped counting his change. 'Sure, King's Theatre in Russell Street. First feature, *On Our Selection*. After interval you get to see *Road House* starring Dorothy Brunton.' The lad, not much older than Didi herself, stopped checking his change long enough to ask, 'Hey, you two half-rinsed or something?'

What on earth was he talking about? They stared dumbly at his mocking face. Suddenly Jamie became very angry. What the hell was going on, anyway? He strode over, grabbed the boy by the shoulders and demanded, 'Russell Street? Russell Street where, man? Where are we?'

'Melbourne, Australia, where d'ya think?' He was a head shorter than Jamie, yet the lad pulled fiercely away. Once free of Jamie's grip, he headed towards a door marked MANAGER'S OFFICE. Calling, 'Mr O'Carroll, you in there?' He disappeared inside.

Silence. 'Come on, let's get out of here,' Didi murmured. They made their way through the double doors and out to the street. As soon as they stood outside it struck them how different everything was.

Neither said anything. What could they say? Each knew

they were lost. Each separately recognised they were still in Melbourne. But a Melbourne that was barely familiar. And if they weren't so distressed, they might have agreed then and there to stop and plot a more sensible strategy.

'We shouldn't stop here,' Jamie muttered, and started briskly down the street.

Didi hurried after him. If only, she told herself as she tried to keep up with his giant steps, if only she didn't feel so odd. The shivering, which had started in the theatre, was now an uncontrollable tremor. The further they walked, the worse it got.

Instead of slowing down, Jamie's stride was, if anything, becoming more rapid. 'J-j-jamie...' Her call was thin and quavery. He stopped for an instant, turned, looked at her, then set off at an even faster pace. For Jamie, trying to handle this situation in his own way, was in a dilemma. Instead of marching on, shouldn't he admit how he felt? The only thing preventing him from breaking down was to keep on moving.

He glanced back at Didi. One thing was sure. Handling a hysterical female, particularly one he barely knew, was bad news. But it could be worse. This wasn't as drastic as the time Uncle Greg was caught in a bushfire. Hadn't he heard at least a hundred times how the old fellow saved himself by jumping into a neighbour's dam? And what about the tractor turning over? That was a drought year when, hoping for some late autumn rain, Bill Major was building an extra dam on their property. Jamie had been driving when the tractor skidded, lurching to one side. Thinking in milliseconds, he changed gears, eased the machine into the mud and survived.

But those were life and death decisions. Nothing in Jamie's life had prepared him for this.

'Panicking is the worst thing you can do.' His father's

words echoed in his ears as Jamie strode down Bourke Street and turned into Swanston. He made a gigantic effort to keep the contents of his stomach from rising.

Didi followed blindly. And, as she walked, the trembling began to lessen and she started looking about.

Essentially, the city wasn't that different. There were still many imposing buildings, decorated a little differently to be sure. And the streets had the same wide pavements, the same broad roads. Even the traffic seemed almost as busy as ever. But the cars driving past were different. Mostly they were dark, squarish, with rounded back ends, the mudguards separate from the body. The engine bonnets had grilles like a fish's gills. Some had very noisy engines. A dusty truck chugging past backfired. Didi nearly fainted with fright. Trucks travelling the other way, their wooden rears open to the elements, belched great clouds of black fumes into the air. The people they passed were dressed as if attending a fancy dress party where the invitation read, 'Come dressed as your favourite old movie character.' It was hard not to stand and gape.

They reached the centre of the city, where the traffic was denser. At least, Didi told herself, one or two of the trams rattling past didn't look too different from those she caught each day. The knowledge was curiously comforting.

At the same time Jamie searched for someone to blame. But who? He glanced over his shoulder to see if Didi was still there. He saw her struggling to keep up with his giant steps and slowed down fractionally. His nausea waning, his thoughts becoming clearer, he muttered as she drew up alongside, 'Some film.' They were the first words he had spoken for at least thirty minutes and she was astonished to hear the sound of his voice. It seemed a lifetime since she'd last heard it. Anyway, what sort of answer could she give? She was rapidly becoming defensive, suspecting he might

35

think that she had arranged all this. To tell the truth, she wasn't sure how responsible she was. To kids reared on old videos of *Doctor Who* and *Star Trek* it was glaringly obvious what had happened. All she could do was hope this was a dream, and that eventually she would wake up.

People drifted past. Mostly, the men were dressed in sombre suits and high-brimmed felt hats. Much the same as the people they'd seen in the theatre. Didi noticed they were softly spoken, that they avoided looking at each other, or at them, too closely. She had the impression this action would be considered impolite, even aggressive. She and Jamie must appear different. Their clothes, hair, even the way they walked, a looser, freer kind of style, must be attracting attention. At one point Jamie saw two women staring openly. Embarrassed at catching his eye, the women turned away. One said, 'They must be from the circus.'

'What a pity they don't maintain some respectability. Just look, they're dressed like gypsies.' This woman's own black and white hat, dress and gloves spoke volumes about being properly turned out.

Jamie paused, and Didi realised they were opposite the station. Apparently arriving at some sort of internal decision, Jamie said, 'Come on, we need a newspaper.'

'Whatever for?'

Jamie didn't bother to explain. He ran across the road to a crippled news vendor. Didi followed. In their rush they almost mowed down two pedestrians stepping down from under the clocks. Pausing long enough to mutter an apology, Didi peered at them in sympathy. Those poor women must be stifling in all those clothes. Fancy wearing heavy jackets, hats with little nets over the eyes, gloves, thick cotton stockings, on such a warm day.

'*Herraaald...*' The little fellow waved a newspaper in their direction.

'How much?' Jamie reached into the back pocket of his jeans.

The vendor growled, 'Give us a penny.' Handing over a coin, Jamie grabbed a copy and scanned it for a date.

'My God. It's nineteen thirty-three. Look... It does say Tuesday, October seventeenth, nineteen thirty-three, doesn't it?'

Before Jamie could take in the implications of the date, the little vendor had grabbed his arm and was shouting, 'What's this rubbish you've given me?' He held out a fifty-cent coin. 'That's not proper money! I'll get the police on to you. Give me back me paper.' He grabbed the *Herald* out of Didi's hands, almost ripping it in his annoyance.

There was just time to read something about bodyline bowling before Jamie, breaking into a cold sweat, shouted, 'Come on Didi. Let's get out of here.' They tore along, nearly knocking over several waif-like figures emerging from doorways selling flowers, sweets and tobacco, and fled to where the river flowed sluggishly towards the sea.

Only when they reached the other side did they slow down and stare around in disbelief. The Arts Centre wasn't there. On a grassy paddock, churned to mud by the rain, stood three ramshackle buildings. The wooden one flanking the river was big enough to house just about anything. Over the door was written one word: HIPPODROME.

A sign in front read: WIRTH'S CIRCUS. COMING SOON. GRAND OPENING - SATURDAY 21 OCTOBER.

Jamie studied the notice. The building facing him said it was 'Wirth's Skating Palace' while the one to the left was 'The Olympia Jazz Pavilion'. He paused. To get there you had to skirt a small moat. A miniature Dutch windmill stood in front, its arms whirling protectively in the breeze. Wondering why it was there and what it was meant to do, he glanced over at Didi and saw her shoulders sag. It seemed more sensible to push on.

By now Didi was too exhausted to care where they were. Worried she would cry, scared to disgrace herself before this comparative stranger, she pleaded, 'What are we doing now? I'm stuffed, Jamie. I've just got to sit down.'

Jamie turned and peered into her tired face. Seeing she meant it, he stopped by a low brick fence. Didi perched uncomfortably on it. 'What do we do now?' she asked.

He shrugged. 'You got any suggestions?'

'Maybe the house is still there? Jamie, maybe we should go home? Let's try and find Mavis Road.'

He considered the idea, then shook his head. 'We're closer to my place. I reckon we should try there first.'

Blending into the background, forcing themselves to be as quiet as possible, they headed further south. Twenty minutes later they were in the narrow street where Jamie and his mother lived. But the street was empty. Quiet houses presented blank faces to the world.

At the front fence, they stopped and looked around. Jamie fingered the number nailed to the letterbox. Yes, this was it. Nine George Road. Nevertheless, he suspected they were stupid to have come. No one would be here. The garden was unrecognisable and, although the basic outline of the house was the same, the broken and rusty iron lace-work and a general air of poverty about the chipped paint and drawn curtains confirmed this wasn't home.

Didi looked up into his grim face. 'Still want to go inside?' she asked warily.

He nodded. The gate squealed when he pushed it open, then fell drunkenly to one side. Jamie followed the dusty concrete path to the front door and looked for a bell or a knocker. There being none, he banged the discoloured paint with his fist.

Silence.

'Let's try the back,' he murmured, walking round to the side. When they got there, he frowned and looked about in dismay. 'Those weren't there this morning.' A cluster of lean-tos covered the back fence three-quarters of the way along. To the right was a vegetable patch containing lettuce, carrots and parsley. The small area to the left was partly fenced in. Behind the wire, three hens pecked desultorily at some cabbage leaves.

Jamie walked over to where some chooks were scratching up the dust. He rested his hands on the wire. 'I've never seen any of this before,' he said. 'There's no point staying here. Come on, let's go!'

Didi rubbed her forehead in dismay.

At that moment there was an explosion of angry barking. A monster from one's worst nightmares, a cross between a German Shepherd and a Doberman, a black and tan mongrel almost as big as Didi, dashed out from behind a shed and stood uncomfortably close, its stance one of outrage. With its teeth bared and menacing, ears tuned their way like microphones, there was no question it was poised to charge.

They froze. Didi's heart hammered fit to burst. The only thing stopping the dog from attacking was the thick chain attached to its collar, which could snap in seconds.

A man appeared at the rear door. 'What are you doing here?' His voice and manner were distinctly unfriendly. 'Get off my property, do y'hear? You're trespassing,' It was obvious he needed only the slightest provocation to set the dog on them. 'Get out of here,' he snarled, 'or I'll call the police. Do y' hear?'

'We're lost,' Didi called, backing towards the rear fence. She waved her arms about to show she was helpless. 'We really are lost. We've been trying to find our way home.'

39

The dog growled. Its open mouth displayed yellow fangs, a blackened tongue, glistening saliva. 'How'd you get in?' the owner scowled. It was clear he didn't believe a word, was convinced they were invading his yard and were up to no good. 'Get off my property. We're not buying anything, and we don't want any of you Fuller Brush salesmen here.' He pulled at the dog's collar and there was a menacing growl. Teeth glinting in the sun, it was straining against its owner. It was hard to tell who controlled whom.

Didi shivered with fear. Convinced the chain was ready to give, she stood as close as possible to Jamie and waited for the dog to attack. Jamie whispered, 'Come on, let's get out of here.' Skirting the animal, who snapped threateningly at their heels, they scuttled up the concrete path, past the wooden sheds and around the side of the house until they were, once again, standing on the pavement outside.

'What now?' she asked, once they had caught their breath. 'Do we try my place?'

'What for? You reckon they'll be any nicer there?' There being no obvious answer, they silently made their way to the end of George Street and headed slowly back towards the city. When they reached the river Jamie walked to a seat marked, 'Ferry passengers only'.

No one else was about. Didi flopped on to the wooden bench beside him. 'What time is it?'

Jamie looked up and inspected the sun's position. 'Late afternoon.'

'What does your watch say?'

Jamie checked his digital watch. 'Five thirty-five.'

'So it's the same time. Late in the day.'

'Just over a half-century too early.'

They took some time to digest this. 'Maybe we're dreaming. Or having a bad trip?'

He leant over and pinched the fleshy part of her arm.

'Ouch! Why did you do that?'

He couldn't help grinning, she was so indignant. 'Well, now you know it's real.'

She sniffed, then a smile broke through. 'Want me to check you out?'

'No thanks. I know I'm here.'

'What do we do now?'

'I'm thinking.'

For twenty minutes they sat watching the boats float slowly down the river, the water flickering with its own opalescent light. He inspected the old buildings on the opposite bank, finally deciding they must be warehouses. She counted the barges floating past; six, seven, nine, eleven, laden with goods she could barely begin to imagine. Then her self-control broke down, and she started sobbing.

Five minutes of this was enough. Particularly as Jamie didn't show, not by the smallest gesture, a scrap of understanding. Nor did a single kind word pass his lips. Wiping her eyes and nose she asked, 'I still think we should try my place.'

Silence.

She demanded more loudly, 'What about we go back to that cinema?'

Maybe he was asleep? Typical, she decided, as if he'd found a novel way to leave her. What a jerk. A musician, was he? Musicians were supposed to be sensitive, more sensitive than other people. She remembered the sound of the harmonica, the look of intense pleasure on his face when he played. Well, she'd bet right now he didn't feel like playing. 'I'm hungry,' she complained.

'We haven't the right sort of money to buy food.' Jamie kept his voice expressionless.

41

'I think we should go back to the theatre,' she cried, knowing she was being hysterical, not caring what he thought. He was nothing to her. Nothing. Merely Kate's silly boyfriend, but she wished he'd do something, anything.

He turned. She was astonished at the blankness of his face. Just looking at him dried up her tears like blotting paper.

'And what do you think you'll find?'

'Well...' she hesitated. Forced to be logical, she simmered instead with barely suppressed fury. Why hadn't he warned her he was feeling this way? None of this was her fault. She wished she was absolutely sure.

'Well, because,' she said firmly, 'because that's how we got here, isn't it? If we go inside and wait, maybe we'll find a way to get home.'

He nodded. Expecting him to get up and start walking, she was half-way up the embankment before she realised he wasn't following. 'Changed your mind?' she called, waiting for him to move.

'Let's leave it until dark.'

'Why?'

'We'll probably have to break in.'

'What's the problem?'

'How do we buy tickets? You got any money?' His tone was very sarcastic.

'So what do we do now?'

He shrugged. 'Haven't a clue.'

'Can't you think of something?' She wanted to hit him, this overgrown boyfriend of Kate's. Fancy being stuck with him. She could have guessed he'd be a pain. Gritting her teeth, she folded her arms and waited to see what he would do.

Meanwhile, the sun began to go down, the clouds

changed shape, the sky took on a soft orange and pink glow. Then the wind turned and it became chilly. Didi wished she was wearing a coat, had something to eat, a cup of hot coffee to drink, anything... Gradually, she let her mind empty. For the next ten minutes they sat in silence.

Suddenly Jamie shook himself, turned to her and said, 'It's not everybody who gets a chance to time travel. Let's go and have a look round.'

4. Meeting The Natives

WHEN NIGHT FINALLY closed in, Didi and Jamie were still wandering aimlessly. And as they plodded on, each worried, but separately. What if food and shelter were too hard to find? What would they do? What on earth could they do?

Using shop windows as mirrors, they watched people wend their way home. Probably to hot dinners and warm beds, Didi thought enviously. The further she and Jamie walked, the more the city became lifeless, apart from the queues in front of the cinemas.

Topping things off, and much to their embarrassment, beggars harrassed them. Enveloped in thick layers of clothing to protect them from the cold night air, sexless figures hid away in dark corners, darting out when someone came past to peddle matches or bunches of drooping flowers. Jamie quickly learnt to act as if they were invisible. If the beggars became too persistent, he turned and glared into their gaunt faces. Then, even the bravest amongst them disappeared.

Meanwhile, Didi marched several paces to his rear. Like a Mid-Eastern chick, she thought crossly, hating every moment of having to keep up with his huge strides. But she kept her mouth closed. Jamie might infuriate her, she might wish for the courage to leave, yet the last thing she really wanted was to be left alone. Even thinking about it made her insides squirm with fear.

Determined to jolt him into speaking, she ran a few steps to catch up. 'This place is dead as a doornail,' she cried. 'What do you reckon they do at night?'

His gaze remained fixed on the road. 'Maybe they sit home and watch tellie.'

'You reckon? I thought we didn't get tellie until 'fifty-six. What do you know about nineteen thirty-three, anyway?'

'Not much,' he admitted. 'I hate history. We always acted up in history.'

She eyed him doubtfully. 'Can't you remember anything?'

'There was the Depression. And the Second World War.'

'Don't you know any important dates?'

He nodded, but the length of his stride didn't alter. 'In 'thirty-nine Hitler marched into Czechoslovakia!'

She ran a few metres to keep up. 'This *is* the Depression! That's why those people were selling things. They need money to buy food...'

'A pity we haven't anything to sell,' he moaned suddenly. 'I'm starving.'

They were in Bourke Street, walking towards the post office. Compared to their own decade the lighting was poor, the atmosphere dull, but passing some well-lit shop windows Didi was told to 'Look Smart for Cup Day'.

'These clothes don't look like people are on the dole,' she said thoughtfully. 'They're ace.' Indeed, the clothes were elaborate and very well made. Long figure-hugging dresses of light fabrics were topped by matching open-weave straw hats. 'I reckon it's definitely after the Depression. Things must be looking up.'

Jamie hadn't bothered to wait. Forced to run to catch

up, she called, 'Now I remember where we are, and it's over the worst of the Depression.'

His answer, when it came, was razor sharp. 'Doesn't matter when it is. I'm stuck here and so are you, and I'm buggered if I know how we're going to get home.'

'There's no point getting mad with me.'

Jamie scowled but said nothing. Ignoring the turned-down corners of his mouth, she demanded, 'Anyway, how do you reckon it happened?'

'What do you mean?'

'How do you reckon we got here, of course?'

'How should I know?' His tone was irritable. 'I'm no physicist.'

'But you must have some idea,' she persisted. 'I mean, there was obviously something weird about that film. What do you think it was?'

'Even if I had an idea, what good would it do?'

'It might help us get back. Besides,' she added darkly, 'you weren't supposed to be there. You and Kate were supposed to be out. Why on earth did you come home?'

A slight embarrassment gave him away. As they picked a path over freshly laid pavement, she considered it. 'I'll bet you were coming home because Kate thought we'd all be out and you'd have the house to yourselves. Now you're stuck with me. Well, I don't want to be stuck with you, either. I didn't arrange for this to happen.' And all her efforts to be sensible vanished in floods of tears.

They strode on. Listening to her little hiccups and snuffles, he felt dangerously closed in; as if here was yet another web to entangle him. No more complications, he promised himself. Definitely no more complications. Life was too difficult if you involved yourself in other people's emotions. Even your own parents...

'Stupid bitch! You're enough to drive a saint away!'

'Why don't you stay in town? Go on, go to that woman...'

And the slam of the back door was followed by the noise of the truck's engine revving up.

Jamie's parents fought often. While his father's reaction was to spend his days in the paddocks and sheds, or disappear into town, headaches attacked Liz. Then she went to bed. Sometimes stayed there for days. From being an active woman who ran the house, helped on the property and lent a hand to neighbours, she virtually became a cripple. Jamie guessed guilt drove Bill away, but it didn't make life easier for him. Jamie's older sister, Linda, lived hundreds of kilometres away and someone had to look after Liz, make sure she ate, keep the house quiet.

After the marriage broke up, after they moved to Melbourne, Liz's headaches subsided. He was never sure how long the peace would last. Sure he loved his mother, but secretly he was sick of feeling responsible for her.

Kate putting the hard word on him had been the final straw. So, he told himself, to hell with Kate.

He wished he meant it...

Waiting for Didi to stop sobbing, he said, 'You didn't arrange this to happen. But I could have done without it.'

Having delivered this he strode on ahead, absolutely furious. It was bad enough feeling hungry and tired, unable to work out their next step. Who needed to be lumbered with someone else's kid sister? With no food or beds, the night getting chillier by the minute, neither was equipped to stay out. If all she could do was complain and snivel, he

47

wished she'd piss off and leave him alone. Different if she was a bloke. Two guys could have handled this, no worries. They'd have thrashed out the next move. Girls were OK, but not here. Not in this sort of fix. A pity you couldn't hit them. Anyway, if he did she'd probably scream like a stuck pig.

All this walking. Her legs ached like mad. Why was he so hell-bent on rushing ahead? They were travelling in circles. Didn't he realise they should be looking for food and beds. What a fool he was. She wished she could hit him, knock some sense into his macho-piggy head. Falling back once again, ostentatiously keeping several paces behind, she watched him stride ahead, not caring whether she kept up or not. She hated his long legs, his self-opinionated maleness. He was nothing but an overgrown ocker. One day, she promised herself, she'd show him.

For the next hour they roamed through empty city streets. Passing a block of vacant houses, or houses where no lights showed, reminded Jamie of the George Street cottage. After the work he and his mother had done, it was heart-breaking to see it in such a condition. They had slaved to make the place habitable; sanded the floors, sugar-soaped grimy walls then painted them, cleared the garden of weeds and rubbish. Nor, he suddenly realised, did Liz suffer a single migraine in all of that time.

Like those first few months in Melbourne. Boy, were they grim. He'd hated the noise, the traffic, the kids in his Year Twelve class. City-wise, suspicious, hard to befriend, frequenting pubs and discos as if there was no tomorrow. What with the divorce and buying the cottage, Liz never had enough money. Anyway, he wouldn't have taken it even if she had. But he needed his own wheels. Even though he turned eighteen last September. Even though, like most country boys, he had driven cars and trucks long

48

before that, he just wasn't managing. For six months he had pined for the country, seriously considered rejoining his father, throwing in the music and the music lessons. Only after joining a footie club, becoming the lead player with the 'Window Displays' and earning some bulk brass, did he begin settling down.

Last night, my God, was it only last night? he remembered Kate talking about Didi. 'Ever since we moved to Melbourne she's been such a pain in the bum.'

And here he was, Jamie the sucker. Left to cope alone. If Didi's family found her so irritating, what was he, a comparative stranger, supposed to do? Peeved and resentful, almost in spite of himself, he felt a faint twinge of pity. Kate's tone reminded him of Linda's high-pitched whine. 'Jamie's a rotten little nuisance. He wrecks my room, then gets everything just 'cause he's a boy.'

Different to the sweetness and light she showed when her guy was about. He'd got his own back. Variously. Turned off the hot water when she was in the bathroom. A few Chinese burns. What a bossy bitch she was. And later, when Liz and Bill were nearly killing each other, when Liz needed all the support she could get, a fat lot of help she was. Christ, how families stank! Particularly his.

A sneaking sympathy for Didi was growing by the minute. Glancing back, he became conscious of her smallness. That short frame, those plump little legs. Perhaps he *was* being unfair. Purposefully taking shorter strides, he slowed down until they walked abreast. Maybe, he thought, maybe things would be easier if they could talk some more.

'I've got this theory,' he said, as if there'd been no previous tension between them, 'I've got a theory about what's happening to us. Do you want to hear?'

Didi nodded furiously.

49

'Well, it's pretty simple. I figure we've fallen into some sort of time warp.'

This was so patently obvious, all she could say was, 'We're in a warp, that's for sure.' Then, in case he thought her glib or disinterested, instead of grateful that he was talking and making her forget how frightened she was, she asked, 'What exactly do you mean?'

'I mean, we've travelled through another dimension.'

'Hmmmn?' she enquired.

'There's the three dimensions around us. Right?' She nodded. 'And there's another dimension. Only we don't know anything about it.'

'You mean the dimension of time?'

'Yeah. The fourth dimension.'

'Isn't that a rock group?'

He smiled at her joke before continuing, 'I reckon we probably fell through a crack. Got caught in a time trap.'

'I guess you might be right,' she said doubtfully.

'Watching that film at that particular hour. And me playing that tune. Suppose that created a change in time, like a shift in molecules. That's why we fell through.'

'Well,' she agreed hastily, 'there was certainly some sort of change.'

'Exactly. It probably happens heaps of times, only we don't get to hear about it.'

'Yes, I see.' she said, thinking she didn't. 'What I don't understand is, why did it happen just then?'

'Well, think of the house. It's very old.'

She nodded furiously. 'Dad and me... Yesterday we found all this stuff in the cellar. Most of it dates back to the 'thirties. Hey,' she cried, considering the implications for the first time, 'hey, that's now!'

He had to laugh. She was so amazed. 'What did you find?'

'Oh, blankets, clothes and stuff.' Didi muttered. For some reason, obscure even to herself, she didn't mention the ring which she still wore on the third finger of her right hand, nor the strange beam of light, nor the sensation there was something wrong with the tellie. She didn't want him to think her totally mad.

'There you are.' Jamie looked triumphant. 'I'm sure it has something to do with that house and its vibes. How much do you know about the place?'

'It's an eighteen-eighty Boom-style terrace,' she explained, for hadn't Tom, in his methodical way, checked out the architectural details?

He blinked. 'How can you tell?'

'It's the combination of elaborate iron lace-work and the front bay window.'

'It's much nicer than our cottage. I think it's a very pretty house. I wouldn't mind living there myself.'

To his surprise, Didi's face fell. 'I'd rather be living in Sydney. Anyway, you haven't explained. How do you reckon that got us here?'

'Oh, I figure that was probably a mistake,' he said cheerfully.

'A mistake?'

'Hmmm. A sort of cosmic mistake.'

'I don't see how that works. Wouldn't travelling through another dimension take us to another galaxy or universe? I don't understand how it took us back more than fifty years, and I don't remember going into space.'

'If it took a millionth of a second you wouldn't, would you,' he pointed out.

'Anyway...' She shook her head. 'It can't have been just the film.'

'Why not?'

'Because... if it was just the film everyone else watching

51

would be here with us. There are probably hundreds and hundreds of people watching that movie. They didn't end up here, did they? I reckon it had something to do with that storm.'

And she would have continued with this line, maybe even told him about the ring, but for Jamie interrupting with, 'There's so many things we don't know. What if it's a special combination, like showing a particular film in a particular house at a particular moment, say when there's a thunderstorm, and that's what brought us here?'

'You reckon we've been to the Milky Way and back? Hell, it sure feels like it.'

'Well, I don't know about that...' he began, then joined in her laughter.

The next kilometre was easier. 'So how are we going to get back?' she asked at last. 'Can you work that out? How do we get out of this time warp?'

His grin was rueful. 'It's just a theory. I haven't a clue. Honestly, I just don't know.'

On this pessimistic note they strode past the post office, which looked suprisingly new, and turned right.

'You got any tissues?' she asked. 'Mine's all grotty.'

He searched through the pockets of his jeans. 'Here, have this.' He pulled out a crumpled handkerchief.

'Listen,' he said awkwardly. 'We're stuck in this mess together. There's not much we can do. I'm not blaming you, honest. You couldn't have arranged this, no matter how hard you tried.'

Accepting this in the spirit it was intended, Didi smiled wanly. She wished her face didn't hurt. The crying, plus a cold wind, was chapping her skin. She wiped her face with Jamie's handkerchief, wished she had brought a moisturiser, warmer clothes, wanted a sandwich, prayed for a cup of coffee.

'...we'll have to find food very soon,' he was saying. 'I'm starving.'

'Me too. I like my meals regular. Three times a day. We've missed both lunch and dinner. I could eat a horse.' She blew her nose and handed back the handkerchief.

'Keep it,' he said gallantly. 'You might need it again.'

By the next block Didi was feeling more optimistic and a little positive about their predicament. 'Aren't you curious to find out how people lived?'

'All I know is, I'm ravenous. I'd give anything for a hamburger.'

'What about some chicken or a pizza?'

He groaned. 'Don't, please don't. It hurts.' She grinned at his pained expression. At the very next corner he stopped, made a decision and turned left.

'Why are we going this way?'

'Why not?'

'I think we should go to Mavis Road,' she said decisively. 'Or back to the theatre. What if the time warp, or whatever it is, disappears? We'll never get back.'

'Maybe.' He was beginning to sound irritable. 'I can't think any more, not without food in me.'

'Are you sure we can't use your money? Maybe we should try again. Didn't they use pounds and shillings? Maybe they'd take dollars and cents too.' Having to run to catch up, she decided his stride was a barometer. The more anxious he got, the faster he walked. 'It's dark and spooky,' she called. 'Why are we going along this street?'

'We might find food near the markets.'

They were now in a poorer part of the city. The buildings were shabbier, needed repairs and paint. For the first time they saw people less carefully dressed, heard languages spoken other than English. Two young men leaning against a hotel wall eyed them off.

53

One called out something unintelligible. Both laughed. Jamie recognised the tone as derogatory. He glared back, aware how strange Didi's jeans looked. They were too figure-hugging, showed too many curves. The women he had seen were more modestly covered. Clenching his fists he whispered, 'Stay cool,' and, anxious to avoid a confrontation, she clung to his side. The men watched every step they took. The shorter of the two said something in an undertone to the other, then slipped away.

Jamie decided the young man must be foreign. His head was held too high, his posture was far more erect than the local slouch.

Trying to look confident, which he didn't feel, and speaking slowly in case the man knew little English, Jamie said, 'We're new in town. We need food,' He mimed eating. 'But we've no money. We're flat broke,' He emptied his pockets in a universal gesture.

The young man grinned disarmingly. He was about twenty, of average height, yet thickset enough to suggest strength. Very short pitch-black hair parted high on one side, brilliant dark eyes and olive skin would have resulted in good looks, but for the slightly too-square head. And the nose. Once badly broken it gave him the look of a fighter. 'Where are you from?' he asked in good but heavily accented English.

'We're from the States,' said Jamie, hoping this covering story was good enough. 'We're from New York. We've been robbed and now we've no money for food or a bed. This is what's left,' and he held out a one-dollar coin.

The young man took the coin, examined it, then slipped it into his own pocket. He studied their faces. Liking what he saw, he said brusquely, 'There's the Susso shelter in Richmond. It's meant for people with no money.' He paused, considered Didi's woebegone expression for a second, then suggested, 'But it's late. And there's never enough beds. Tell you what,' a smile lit up his olive features, 'you'd better come home with me. I've a decent landlady who'll feed you, give you a room for the night.'

What if we're kidnapped or murdered? flickered through Didi's head. Then, looking into the young man's liquid eyes, she rejected the idea as quickly as it had come.

Disarmed by the young man's generosity, not quite sure of the correct behaviour for such a situation, Jamie held out his hand rather awkwardly. 'I'm Jamie. This is Didi.'

The young man shook Jamie's hand very politely, took off his cloth cap and swept Didi an elaborate bow. 'Pleased to meet you. I'm Sam. Sam Cohen at your service. Now, if you don't mind following me...'

He began half-walking, half-running at a pace Didi considered more suitable for fun runs. 'Where's he taking us?' she muttered, for Sam was leading them through the dark streets to the north of the city.

Breathless, Jamie gasped, 'Where do you live?'

'I've lodgings in Carlton.' Sam could talk at the top of his voice without changing pace. 'I know my landlady has a spare room. If I tell her you're my friends she'll let you stay.' Stopping so abruptly that they almost collided with him, he added, 'My landlady's very respectable. It's none of my business, but to Mrs Finkelstein it will be very important to know you are married,' then hurried them on.

They walked along streets where nothing moved. Not even a stray cat prowled. Past a cemetery they went, up two alleys, round a park and over Lygon Street. A little further on, two mouths gaped in astonishment. Sam was leading them into a familiar area, into a street where time had wrought some change.

'I knew it,' Didi cried. 'I just knew we would be coming back here.' Jamie, pinching her arm, turned her cry into a

55

shriek of pain, but Sam, travelling several paces ahead, didn't turn round. He continued down the road and they, trying to behave as if nothing strange was happening, followed obediently. By the time Sam stopped in front of a large terrace, both saw what was happening as curiously inevitable.

'Here we are!' Sam opened the gate. 'These are my lodgings. This is the Finkelstein's house. Fifty-four Mavis Road. You'd better remember the address.'

If previously told she would never see this house again, Didi would have shrugged and pointed out that it was never her idea to shift to Melbourne in the first place. But looking at the terrace, she nearly burst into tears. Like a friend fallen on ill times, it was tired and run down. The elegant dusty aqua paintwork, with its details picked out in a darker shade, was instead, dirty white paint, peeling away to reveal chipped bricks. The iron lace on the balcony was damaged and rusty, and the elegant garden was just a square of couch grass flanked by concrete paths.

She turned to Sam. He was asking Jamie, 'What's your last name? Mrs Finkelstein will want to know. And she had better be wearing a ring, or Mrs Finkelstein will smell a mouse.'

Perplexed, Jamie asked, 'Don't you mean a rat?'

Sam grinned, his teeth gleaming in his swarthy, rather Spanish-looking features. 'Oh, generally speaking I'm the rat around here.'

Wondering what he meant, praying Didi would remember to shut up, Jamie forced himself to smile back. 'I'm Jamie Major, and this is Didi Falconer. Didi, are you wearing a ring?'

Didi nodded and transferred the ring from the third finger of her right hand to the third finger of her left hand. Under the light thrown by a street lamp the old-fashioned setting was as lovely as it had been that very morning. A sapphire surrounded by tiny diamonds set in burnished gold.

Sam tapped his head knowingly. 'You've no luggage, and no money. Sam's no fool. No fool at all. You've jumped ship, eh?'

Didi replied with a hiccup and Jamie studied his feet as if he had never seen them before. Sam's smile grew broader. He nodded his square head. 'I thought so. You're running away. Together, right?'

Silence. Sam put his arm around Jamie's shoulder. 'Your secret's safe with me,' he promised. 'I'll tell no one. I swear it. I know what it's like when there are difficult parents.' His expression became suddenly so forbidding, Didi gave an involuntary shudder. 'But you're cold and hungry so let's go inside.' And, as mercurial as they would always find him, he was beaming with pleasure by the time the wooden front door opened.

The hallway was barely recognisable, but with the delicious smell of home cooking rising to meet them, Didi and Jamie were almost too famished to notice. They crossed the polished lino, passed by the staircase which led upstairs, and stepped down the short flight to the kitchen. Didi halted, incredulous. She could scarcely believe this was the same room she had breakfasted in that very morning.

A plump woman pushed herself away from the table. Middle-aged, dressed in a pink cotton cover-all, no make-up and hair in a bun. There was little glamour here. Instead, her eyes were laughter-lined and her cheeks soft and ruddy. Seated at the table, blinking at the newcomers, was her husband, Ben. Sparse hair struggled to cover a pink head and the rims of his glasses glittered under the bare light bulb strung overhead. Caught literally in his shirt sleeves, he was struggling to put on a jacket. Cards were laid out. A game was in progress.

Didi returned the woman's friendly beam with a smile of her own. 'Such a handsome couple you bring us, Sam. Perhaps they wish to stay?' His landlady stared with unabashed curiosity at Jamie and Didi.

'Here are my very good friends, Jamie and Didi Major,' Sam announced, as if Didi and Jamie were about to perform an act on stage. 'They've just arrived in Melbourne and they're hungry and need a bed for the night.'

'Tch, tch, poor little things,' cried Mrs Finkelstein. 'They look exhausted. Come sit down, sit down. I have soup in the ice chest. It's not much, but if you are hungry, everything tastes good. Come. My soup will give you strength.'

But Didi was desperate for more immediate comforts. 'Please, may I use your loo?' And forgetting it could not be there, she started in the direction of the powder room.

It was Mrs Finkelstein, shaking her head and pointing towards a rear door, who brought Didi, aghast at her own stupidity, to an abrupt halt. Of course the powder room was not there. This house was totally different. As Mrs Finkelstein ordered Mr Finkelstein to, 'Give the young lady a candle, and show her where to go,' Didi instructed herself to behave like the stranger she was.

With his trousers worn low enough to be almost hidden by his pendulous stomach, Ben Finkelstein led Didi out into the back garden. There, where in fifty-seven years time a glass-walled family-room would lead on to a paved courtyard filled with pot plants, hanging baskets and a small swimming pool, was a small wooden lean-to. A bundle of neatly cut-up newspapers tied together with string was hung on a nail behind the door. After Didi finished using the lavatory she jumped off the wooden seat

58

and looked for something to press or pull. Nothing. Only a dreadful smell rising up from the murky depths. Shuddering, she scuttled back to the kitchen.

Mrs Finkelstein was stirring a saucepan on a stove built into a high recess. 'My brand-new gas cooker,' was introduced. 'You wouldn't believe how much wood we chopped before this arrived,' she cried, polishing the gleaming top with proud strokes.

Didi hoped she looked properly admiring. It seemed ridiculous to compare this pleasant but frugally furnished room with the stark white kitchen fitted with the latest in dishwashers, freezer-fridges, microwave and convection ovens she knew.

Sam was filling the Finkelsteins in on his friends' arrival in Melbourne from America. Only to be robbed. Yes, a miracle they'd found him. Jamie's grandfather was from the village of his father's cousin, Moshe. In the Old Country they'd been like brothers so, while Jamie was in Australia, Jamie was his, Sam Cohen's responsibility. He played the story to the limit of credibility and Jamie, listening silently, smiled at how skilfully Sam fielded embarrassing questions.

'So this boy's father is from Lodz?' Mr Finkelstein's head shook with wonder. 'So few of our people have such blue eyes, or are so tall. The air in America must be special.'

Although Mrs and Mr Finklestein were dying to quiz the young couple, one look at their exhausted faces and Mrs Finkelstein shooed everyone from the kitchen. 'Just a little to eat and straight to bed.' She clucked about Didi like a mother hen, looked long and searchingly into Jamie's face. 'How young you are to be married,' she declared.

Because they were ravenous, Mrs Finkelstein's soup was the tastiest they had ever eaten. Each managed two large servings and when she produced home-made apple strudel, light as swansdown, spiced with cinnamon and served with long glasses of hot, weak, black tea, Didi sighed, 'That was terrific.'

Sure they could eat no more, Mrs Finklestein took them upstairs. Their room at the back was tiny, tucked away where, when the house was grander, a maid would have lived.

It took Didi a moment to adjust. Yes, here was part of the ensuite dressing and bathroom leading off Tom and Jane's room. At present the tiny room contained a narrow wooden bed, a thin mattress, a couple of orange and brown blankets in a vaguely familiar pattern. The other furniture consisted of a small table with a basin and jug on top, and a small wardrobe with an ill-fitting door where, one day Tom would shower and shave. That was all.

Didi looked about for Sam. He had vanished, gone to bed, she guessed.

Jamie collapsed on to the bed and stared bemusedly at the walls.

Didi inspected the bed carefully. 'How on earth are we going to fit on that?'

'More to the point, how do we pay for it? I don't like conning these nice people.'

Didi shrugged. More concerned with the immediate arrangements, she offered, 'How about you lie one way, and I'll sleep the other...'

Jamie looked at her incredulously. 'You're sacred, I promise,' he cried. Taking off his jeans and jacket, he crawled under the bedclothes and closed his eyes.

Didi watched him in silence. Shortly after, she did the same.

5. Morning

IN SPITE OF the tiny bed they slept well.

After a nightmare which involved getting lost in nineteen thirty-three and not knowing how to get back, Didi woke with a jolt. She lay back with closed eyes, hoping that when they reopened all this would be gone, that she would be back in her own space, her familiar posters looking down at her instead of these cream-kalsomined walls. Having strangers living in her bedroom further down the hall made her feel peculiar. Yet knowing that her own room must be as unrecognisable as the rest of the house, made her snuggle down further under the bedclothes.

She was forced to open one eye when the first few bars of 'Ain't Misbehavin'' drifted around the room. Jamie was peering out at the back garden. Things were certainly different. He remembered this area as laid out with expensive terracotta tiles and a small pool, hidden from view by a jasmine and ivy-covered trellis.

He was staring out at a large square of sparse grass. Chickens were scratching up the dust by the back fence. The only concession to horticultural beauty was a straggly rose bush. A lemon tree drooped next to a carefully tended bed filled with parsley, cabbages, carrots, lettuce and silver beet. At the end of a phrase Jamie stopped playing long enough to say, 'Sam's already left for work. He left you a pressie.' He picked up a tiny brush and tossed it at her.

Didi sat up and caught it. 'Unreal. A toothbrush.'

'Naturally. Natural bristles.' He had the grace to grin at his corny joke. 'Hope you've got nothing nasty in your mouth 'cos we have to share.'

'Just my tongue.'

'Be that as it may.' His tone was equally sardonic. 'I reckon I can handle just about anything. Look at this!' And producing a cut-throat razor, he waved it terrifyingly in her direction.

'Sure you know how to use it?'

'Course,' he said confidently. 'I just did.'

She peered up at him. 'You've cut your chin.'

'I may need more practice,' he said loftily, before beginning a rather jazzy version of Beethoven's Fifth Symphony. Music so early, no matter how good, was enough to make her burrow back under the blankets. 'By the way, if you want breakfast you'd better get up. And I think you've missed the last of the hot water.'

'Terrific.' Her body was stiff from sleeping in such a confined space. She stood up and slowly stretched. 'Is the bathroom still in the same place?'

He nodded. 'Just down the passage.'

Two bathrooms and a powder room had been added when the terrace was renovated. When the Falconers first saw the main bathroom even Didi was impressed. Kate, who openly loved luxury, had gone overboard about the glossy tiles and high tech fittings.

Dad should see this room now, Didi thought ruefully. It would please his sarcastic sense of humour. All the luxuries had vanished; the spa, toilet, bidet, dressing table, mirrors, all the things Kate had gone ape about. Also gone were the marvellous glossy black and white Italian marble tiles. The current fixtures consisted of a free-standing sink and an enormous rust-spotted bath standing on torn linoleum.

In a way she was sorry. It was the mirrors she missed most. Didi liked watching herself in the glass, enjoyed pretending she was split in two and a part of her was a peeping Tom. Whenever she considered it, which was probably too often, it seemed unfair that a short girl who looked squat and bulky in clothes, should look great stripped. Back in Sydney, Helene used to joke that Didi should go to nudist beaches, stay permanently naked. Whenever she caught sight of herself in the bathroom's dressing-table lights, whenever she examined her high breasts and pale pink nipples, the small waist which curved into full hips and her strong legs, it seemed unfair that she couldn't walk round like that all the time and show the world how good she looked.

As far back as she could remember, people had always commented on Kate's looks. Not that the two sisters' features were too dissimilar. You could certainly see the relationship, but Kate was half a metre taller than Didi and very slim.

A shame that. Being plump, like the women in the paintings they studied in art class, was bad news these days. Thinking about art classes reminded her of Andrew Fogarty, seated two tables away. Did Andrew ever picture what she looked like stripped? Something in the way his eyelids lowered when they smiled at each other, something sexy about the shape of his mouth, had made her think he might. For a moment she imagined them alone and close, and all that might follow. Was this the way Kate felt about Jamie? With him being such a prickly pear it was hard to imagine. Didi sighed enviously. Kate was lucky to have someone keen on her. Without actually being told, Didi knew Jamie was keen. There was something about the way he had looked at Kate, a softening in his eyes.

When they first moved to Melbourne, Jane tried to

console her by pointing out that Tom's job finished in just eighteen months. Didi found this cold comfort. Someone else would be bound to snap Andrew up. It was all Tom's fault, she thought morosely. Tom's new job was destroying her life. Attending an all girls' school didn't help. When they got back to their own decade she would have to find other ways of meeting men.

If they ever got back to their own decade.

This idea being too terrifying to pursue, she hurriedly turned on the outsized tap over the sink. It ran cold clear liquid. Didi tried the water. It tasted great, better than any she had tasted before. She ran the hot tap over the bath. Icy water gushed out, so she turned it off. Today, even the thought of a cold shower made her shiver. Compromising, she splashed her face, under her arms, and wondered if Jamie had a comb.

He had. Once she shook out her jeans, T-shirt and joggers, and put them back on, she felt ready to face the downstairs world.

When they entered the kitchen Mrs Finkelstein beamed. Although this was her usual way of greeting the world, Didi felt Mrs Finkelstein was really pleased to see them. A very pretty girl was seated at the table eating breakfast. Probably no more than seventeen or eighteen, she had dark, almond-shaped eyes, a long, oval face, a finely sculptured nose and pale, ivory-coloured skin. Her dark-brown wavy hair was cut short and parted on one side. When she smiled her mouth curled up deliciously at the corners. The girl examined Jamie and Didi quite openly, it was clear Mrs Finklestein had been discussing her new guests. Then, 'My daughter, Selma,' was introduced and Mrs Finkelstein placed bowls of steaming porridge on the table.

Selma was almost finished. 'Her boss won't pay her for half a day if she's even a minute late,' her mother explained as Selma rose to leave. She urged, 'Have an egg, you still have time.'

Selma shook her head. She stood up and Didi saw she was short, as short as Didi herself. But slim, very slim. Fine boned like Kate, Didi thought enviously. Picking up a hat, gloves and bag from the dresser, Selma said, 'I'll see you at six. Mamma, don't work too hard.'

'If I don't, who will do it for me?' Mrs Finkelstein asked imperiously.

Selma, smiling vaguely in the general direction of the room, disappeared towards the front door. Mrs Finklestein placed platters piled high with fried tomatoes and toast in front of her new boarders. 'Selma's boss is a terrible man. But what can she do? It's a job. Such a world where young girls are taken advantage of and men, breadwinners, can't find jobs!'

She sighed loudly, checked to see that they were eating everything set in front of them, then added, 'Sam left you a message. He says to go where he works. Maybe there's a job.'

Jamie's face lightened. Mrs Finklestein nodded. 'No matter,' she cried, 'you will pay me when you find work. You I trust. You are like my own children.' And midway through cleaning up after her other lodgers' breakfasts, Mrs Finkelstein settled herself comfortably, a cup of tea cooling in front of her, to tell Didi and Jamie a long and involved story about other people newly arrived in Melbourne whom she was helping get settled.

Jamie, nodding politely at regular intervals, kept right on eating. Mrs Finkelstein smiled with approval and reloaded his plate. 'A good appetite is wonderful. I love to see a man properly fed.'

Didi couldn't help grinning at this convenient alliance.

Mrs Finkelstein finished her story with much side

tracking and homespun philosophy. Didi waited politely, then chimed in with, 'Would there be work for me?'

'In those clothes?' Mrs Finkelstein's eyebrows rose. 'Perhaps Selma has something you can wear.' Her voice dubious, 'Do all young girls wear such, such...' pausing as she searched for the right word, 'unusual dress in America?'

Didi's green eyes glinted in amusement. Pointing to her stone-washed jeans she asked, 'Don't women ever wear pants?'

Mrs Finkelstein shook her head. 'Sometimes society women wear slacks,' she said, 'but those are not clothes for respectable women.'

'Mrs Finkelstein,' Jamie interrupted, 'could you lend Didi a skirt?'

She could and did. Then insisted Didi borrow a brown gaberdine jacket, hat and gloves, claiming no decent girl was seen in the street without them. Didi thought her white joggers and socks would attract even more attention, but didn't dare voice her objections. There was something rather overpowering about Mrs Finkelstein.

Thus properly equipped, they set off for the day.

Didi asked, 'Are we going back to the theatre?'

'I think we'd better go see Sam first,' Jamie countered. 'These people have been so nice. I hate the idea of running out on them.'

Embarrassed that she hadn't thought of this herself, Didi murmured. 'You're right. If we go back home, they will think we've run out on them. We'll have eaten their food, slept in their bed and I'm wearing their clothes. There's only one thing for it. We'll have to tell Sam what really happened. Where does he work?'

'He's grooming horses at the circus.'

'Reckon he'll believe us?'

'We could try. But maybe we should wait for the right moment,' he said doubtfully.

'Why not tell him now?'

'It's going to take stacks of information to convince him, right?'

'What do you mean?'

'Well, what's the best way to make someone believe you're from the future?'

'By telling them what's going to happen, of course.' A smile illuminated her face.

He studied her thoughtfully before continuing, 'Yes. So they can try to stop all the bad things from happening.'

'Well, what's wrong with that?'

'I'm thinking it over,' was all he would say as they continued to walk through Carlton and the city to Wirth's Park to find Sam.

6. GETTING SETTLED

WHEN THEY REACHED Wirth's Park, Sam was nowhere to be seen. A shortish man wearing faded trousers and a checked shirt, his face tough and weather-beaten, was sweeping the inside of the Hippodrome, that huge wooden barn used for circus performances. Jamie went over to ask him where they might find Sam. The reply was unexpected.

'What d'youse want with that kike?'

It seemed to Jamie that even the dust held its breath.

'Sam's my friend,' he said softly. Not wanting to appear cowed, yet determined to avoid a brawl, he looked the fellow straight in the eye and they measured relative sizes. Stretching, so that he towered well above the sweeper's head, Jamie repeated, 'Now, are you going to tell me where Sam is?'

The sweeper backed down immediately. 'You'll find him over at the railway. Those Yid bastards steal jobs from dinkum Aussies like me.' Ill-fitting teeth bulged his cheeks downwards in waves.

Didi's eyes snapped. 'Isn't Sam an Aussie?' Longing to hit the fellow, she turned expectantly towards Jamie, and was horrified to see him walking away.

'...Twenty, nineteen, eighteen.' Jamie was counting. 'Stay cool. Seventeen. Breathe slowly...' Why was Didi provoking this guy? She'd complain loudly enough if they got bashed up.

Sneering openly at their cowardice, the sweeper went back to his work. 'Who the hell do you think you're calling a kike?' Didi was asking when Jamie grabbed her by the shoulders and whisked her outside.

'You larrikins and your sheilas better watch it. We don't need any Bolshies in this town. There's a reckoning coming...' The sweeper's cry followed them outside.

Didi turned on Jamie. 'Why did you do that? Why did you let him talk like that about Sam?' Too late. Jamie was already galloping towards Flinders Street Station, his long legs consuming the pavement in giant strides. But then, how could Didi have guessed what was common knowledge around Kyneton: that anyone silly enough to antagonise Jamie on a football oval was likely to come off second best? An ex-member of the only successful school Aussie Rules team to beat the Intermediates, Jamie knew he needed to learn greater self-control. His previous coach, Bob Gilligan's comment, 'Watch out for Major when he's having a major,' still rankled.

Didi called, 'Why didn't you say something?' The wind swept her words away. 'Why didn't you thump that fellow? How could you let him say those things?'

Jamie was disappearing into the distance. She sprinted to catch up, and was shocked to see his face distorted by rage. 'Someone ought to teach that fellow a lesson.'

'So why didn't you?' Her voice dripped acid.

'Don't be so bloody stupid. All we need is the Fuzz. What if the cops start asking questions?' And his anger propelled him far ahead.

A quick spurt, and she caught up to him. 'Maybe you're right,' she admitted. 'All the same, it's weird being so close to the Depression.'

'What's that got to do with it?'

'I reckon being out of work makes people screwy,' she said, neatly completing her point.

'Just the same, it makes me mad listening to that stuff.'

'Don't we carry on the same way about dole-bludgers?' she asked doubtfully.

Jamie scowled. 'Some people!'

Keeping up with him was exhausting. 'Hey,' she cried, breathing heavily. 'Do you reckon you could go slower?'

He glanced down. 'Sorry. Lost my temper.'

'I know,' she said magnanimously. 'I know just how you feel. But we should be tolerant, even if they aren't.'

He laughed tiredly. 'You make coming to the past sound like we're touring a foreign country.'

'Foreign city is more like it,' she contradicted. They were, by this time, nearing the station. 'Anyway, isn't it? Some of their attitudes are the same, others real different. Same city, other times. It's like we're visiting a new city.'

'Yeah?' he said discouragingly. 'Seems to me this is still Melbourne, Australia.'

'Isn't it just the same as taking a trip? Doing a tour of Singapore, London or New York?'

'What on earth are you talking about?'

She perched on the broad steps leading up to the station. He towered above her, scowling. For a moment she thought he was about to take off. Then he sat down, waving away an insistent newspaper vendor.

'Well,' she began cautiously, 'for a start, the people we've met are more generous than those at home. I don't know anybody who would have treated us like Sam and Mrs Finkelstein. Do you?'

'Maybe in the country. People are pretty good to each other in the country.' Slipping the harmonica out of his pocket he played a scale, then broke into a tune.

70

'What's that?'

He stopped in mid phrase. 'It's called 'Lilli Marlene'. They used to sing it during the Second World War. *'Underneath the lamplight, by the city square....'*

'You sure that's been written already?' she asked worriedly. 'Maybe you should watch what you play. Stick to things they know.'

'Haven't you noticed? I keep to really old songs.' He began fooling around with the melody. Listening to the musical web; crotchets and minims spilling into the air like clear drops of crystal, she knew he was good. Very, very good. She waited for the next pause in the music before asking, 'Do you miss not being in the country? Being with your dad?'

He considered this. 'Not as much as I thought. It's easier living with Mum. Particularly when no one's arguing, or expecting me to take sides. Anyway, I came here to study music. I can't do that properly in the country.'

'What are you going to do with it?'

'Be a world-famous musician, of course.'

'I thought you might want to be a footballer.'

Lowering the harmonica, he stared at her in surprise. 'Who told you that?'

She looked slightly embarrassed. 'Oh, I don't know. Well, aren't you?'

'Hell, no,' he said emphatically. 'You have to be brilliant.'

'As good as you are at music?'

He grinned. 'Probably better. Besides, I'd spend all my time in the sin bin. I lose my cool too often.'

'You're so lucky,' she said plaintively. 'Fancy having two things you're good at. I don't seem to have anything.'

'What about music?'

She laughed and confided, 'You know, when I was little,

Mum and Dad sent me to learn music. You know, at Yamaha?' He was playing soft arpeggios, but nodded to show he was listening. 'I must have been the worst drop-out they ever had. I reckon I'm tone deaf. I just couldn't do a thing right.'

He shook his head. 'You like listening to music. And you recognise songs. You'd have to have some sort of ear. Sure you haven't?'

'No.' Pleased to find something good about herself, for a change, she beamed at some people strolling past. They stared through her, then turned to face the opposite direction. Embarrassed by their reaction, Didi reddened. Jamie noticed none of this. Sliding the harmonica into his pocket, he said, 'We ought to get going.'

She glanced up at the clocks above their heads. One set of hands pointed to nine forty-five, another to ten, one even to ten thirty. The largest said it was nine forty-three. Rising from the steps, where they were attracting unfriendly stares, they brushed themselves off and walked inside.

A porter watched suspiciously as they clattered past. 'They don't seem to like people being themselves,' Jamie noted. 'They're awful proper.' He looked down at her from his great height. 'Yesterday, your jeans nearly made 'em burst a blood vessel.'

'It'd take me forever to get used to wearing all this gear,' she admitted.

Inside the station they saw everything was covered in a layer of black cinders. 'Where's the circus train?' Jamie asked a porter.

He waved them on. They came to two large green and black steam engines pulling carriages, with 'Wirth Bros.' Ltd. Circus' written on the sides, and knew they were there.

They stood behind a barrier separating the platform from the station and watched the unloading taking place. A porter in a navy, peaked hat and jacket guarded the gate. The sign above his head read 'NO ADMITTANCE WITHOUT PLATFORM TICKET'. Beyond, judging by the iron bars on their sides, were the cages carrying wild animals. Transfixed by the sight of two elephants picking up a heavy cage then lifting it on to a truck, they didn't hear Sam come up from behind until he spoke. 'Quite something, isn't it?'

They nodded, too overcome to answer.

'In the old days Wirth's used to travel with ten elephants, fourteen cages of wild animals and fifty-two horses and ponies. Apart from the artistes, it would take a hundred and forty people to help run things efficiently.' Sam announced these statistics as if they were his.

'What about now?'

'Mr Philip Wirth had to cut the numbers or go broke. The Depression...' Sam left his sentence incomplete. It not being part of his ebullient character to remain sad, he cried, 'Jamie, I've found you a job. We need another man to help with the horses while the circus is in Melbourne. How about it?'

'That'd be great. Only, we think there's something we should tell you first...'

Jamie stopped, uncertain how to proceed, and Didi stepped in. 'We ought to get some of our things. You know. From the boat.' Perhaps they should tell Sam the truth. Soon. But only if their next move failed.

'Hey, Cohen, what are you doing? We don't pay you for standing around talking.'

Sam took Jamie to meet his boss. 'This is my friend Jamie Major. Remember, you said you had a job for him?'

The boss was fiftyish, burly. The top of his short-back-and-sides grey hair stood up like a parrot's crest. Looking

Jamie over, noting his height and wiry frame, he asked brusquely, 'Ever had anything to do with horses?'

'I grew up on a farm.'

'Good. Be here tomorrow at seven thirty.' As he walked away he noticed a cage being incorrectly unloaded and stopped to chastise the workmen. Sam smiled wryly. 'He's got a rough tongue. But a great heart I can promise you.'

'More than you can say for Rambo back there,' said Jamie. Sam's eyebrows shot up.

'He means one of the fellows at the Hippodrome,' Didi explained. 'The one sweeping the floor.'

'Oh, you mean George?' Sam chuckled. 'You're right. He isn't too keen on foreigners. He says they're bloody reffos and un-Australian to boot.' Remembering he was meant to be working, he ambled off, tossing a coin in the air and crying, 'See you later.'

As they emerged from the dark station they blinked a little at the sudden rush of light before heading towards King's Theatre. Providing they kept to a decorous pace, neither walking too fast nor too slow, no one took any notice of them. Carefully avoiding eye contact with passers-by, Didi felt successfully camouflaged. I'm a sparrow, she thought, looking down at her dull brown jacket and dark plaid skirt. A city sparrow. Like the other office girls. She watched two women hailing a tram. How uncomfortable they looked. They wore high-heeled shoes with matching handbags which they clutched with one gloved hand, while the other clung to large hats with tiny veils. But men could wear what they liked. It struck her as unfair that Jamie wore jeans and no one took the least bit of notice.

She turned to study the traffic. It would take a long time to get used to engines which hiccuped instead of purred. Every so often a car backfiring made her jump. Even so, living with fewer vehicles was pleasant, pedestrians having rights, delightful. In daylight the shops seemed drabber than ever, their display windows a jumble. Tough if you were looking for something special, she thought, nearly walking into Jamie. He had stopped under a sign reading, 'King's Theatre'.

'What,' she demanded, looking at him sideways, 'exactly do you intend doing?'

Jamie shrugged uncertainly. 'Haven't a clue. Get inside and look round, I suppose.'

'What makes you think *On Our Selection* will get us back?'

'You got any better ideas?' His voice was surly.

'But we haven't any money. We'll have to break in. What happens if we get caught?'

Jamie's laugh was mirthless. 'Then I guess we'll soon find out.'

They walked inside and looked around. The unlit chandelier was dusty, the carpet worn, the ticket box closed. 'Guess they don't show films this early in the day,' Jamie whispered. A boy emerged from a door marked 'Private'. The same boy as yesterday. Today he was wearing paint-covered overalls and carrying a wooden crate filled with rubbish. Before either Didi or Jamie spoke he called, 'The box office's closed. Come back tonight at seven.'

Jamie cleared his throat. 'We... uh... we wanted to see *On Our Selection*. What time does it start?'

'*On Our Selection*'s off.' The boy looked faintly triumphant. 'Last performance was yesterday. This week we've got *Night After Night* with Mae West. She's a grouse sheila.' He winked knowingly. Then something about Jamie; maybe his height or his unusual clothes, reminded him of being manhandled. 'Hey, weren't you two here yesterday?'

75

Jamie shook his head, but the boy's eyebrows rose in disbelief. He edged towards the door marked 'Private' and disappeared inside.

'My God, Jamie, what do we do?' Didi cried in despair. 'Without the film we'll never get back. What do we do now?'

Instead of answering, Jamie headed for the door leading into the theatre. Didi followed demanding, 'What do you expect to find in there?'

Lit by a bigger chandelier than the one in the foyer, the auditorium seemed very large, very empty. Seen close up, the velvet curtains pulled across the stage were worn and dirty, the seats shabby and neglected. Jamie studied a small window set into the rear wall. Suddenly yanking Didi by the arm, he dragged her back into the foyer and through a doorway marked 'Private'. Inside was a door marked 'Manager's Office', and a winding flight of stairs.

'Shhh,' he warned. They tiptoed up to the next floor, opened another door and found themselves inside the projectionist's booth.

Thankfully it was empty. Didi didn't have a clue as to what they would have said if someone was there. Three bulky, old-fashioned projectors aimed their lenses at the screen. Two sides of the room were lined with shelves. *On Our Selection* was somewhere up there, she thought despairingly. But where? The walls were stacked high with film. There were literally hundreds of metal canisters on the shelves. In the centre of the room was a table littered with papers. The remains of morning tea, a sandwich and a half-empty cup of tea, testified someone could walk in at any moment.

'We'll search those shelves,' Jamie whispered. 'I'll do this side. You take the other.'

Didi did as she was told. Some of the titles were

interesting; *The Miracle Man, Mammy, A Farewell To Arms,* but there was no sign of *On Our Selection.*

Suddenly they heard a bang, the sound of a door closing, footsteps running up the stairs. Her arms filled with canisters, Didi froze with fright. The door flew open. A man appeared. There was just time to see he was short and fair, that he wore his shirt sleeves rolled.

Taking in what was happening he lunged towards Didi. 'Hey, what's going on? The public isn't allowed in here. I'll get the police on to you.'

Only Jamie's shout of, 'Run, Didi run,' galvanised her into action. The canisters clattered on to the floor and she fled, ran faster than she had ever done before in her life. They were down the stairs, through the door marked 'Private', along the foyer, out the doors and at the next city block before they even started slowing down.

'Damn! Not a thing,' Didi sobbed, bending over to ease the stitch in her side. 'Now we'll never get home. Just our luck they had to take that film off yesterday. We'll never get home.'

'Come on. Let's sit down.' Jamie's hair was wet through. They leaned against a shop window, their breath emerging in little sighs and gasps, their hearts pounding.

Didi whimpered, 'Now we'll never get home. I just know we'll stay in stupid 'thirty-three for ever. We'll never get home. Can't you do something?'

'Oh, shut up, Didi,' Jamie cried, equally frustrated. 'Stop bawling, will you? I'm trying to get us back. Don't be such a pain in the bum. You're carrying on as if I've nothing better to do than be stuck here with you.'

'I suppose it'd be OK if it was Kate instead of me,' she hit back. 'You wouldn't get mad if you were sharing the bed with Kate.'

He glared at her. 'You know something, Didi? Sometimes

you're a real little bitch!' And he jumped up and headed into the distance.

'Why don't you just piss off and leave me,' she screamed. But they couldn't afford to lose each other. She scrambled to her feet and they strode silently side by side down the city streets.

It was Jamie, feeling sorry for himself, walking unhappily towards the river, who was the first to break down. He felt badly, about himself it was true, but also about her. They were in this mess together. He was older. This meant a certain, if unwelcome, responsibility. Perhaps he was expecting too much. Thinking it over, he didn't know too many people who'd stay sane in these circumstances. Sometimes he wished it was OK to cry. Like her. Rid himself of the tightness in his chest. 'We'll get home. Don't get yourself into knots,' he said, showing a confidence he didn't feel. 'But we need help.'

Didi muttered, 'Who'd help us?'

Depressed, despondent, they headed south.

Didi remembered she hadn't mentioned the ring. Hesitatingly, the story coming out in dribs and drabs, Didi told him the basic details. He was interested, questioned her again and again. Where had she found the ring? What sort of beam did she think it was? When she mentioned her odd feeling that there was someone strange, perhaps an alien presence watching from inside the television set, she half expected him to scoff, but all he said was, 'What we need is someone's help. I reckon we should try combining the film with the ring.'

'Where are you going to get hold of a projector?'

He wasn't listening. '...We'll need to combine the film, the ring and the house. Then maybe we'd have some sort of answer.'

'Like what?'

'Well, getting all those things together might affect the passage of time as we know it.'

'Maybe you're right,' she shrugged tiredly. 'But who'd be idiot enough to help us break in?'

They had travelled half a block before she remembered Sam. 'We're so stupid. We'll get Sam to help. I can't think why we didn't think of it before.'

Jamie relaxed fractionally. 'But not yet. We shouldn't say anything. Not yet. That projectionist must be wondering what we were doing in there. Maybe he's waiting for us to return. I mean, it's not as if we were starving or anything. If we go back too soon, we might fail.' Didi shivered at the thought. 'Let's wait before we say something. It'll be a battle getting Sam to believe us. And even if he does, we need to watch what we say. We need to be careful we don't change things too much.'

'How can we do that?'

He wouldn't explain. Instead, he said, 'We could change the future irrevocably,' and stared pensively into the distance.

They spent much of the day wandering about the suburbs and walking along the beach. They passed boarding houses getting ready for summer visitors, small kiosks selling oysters, prawns, a crayfish for threepence. Closer to the ports they saw there were pubs on every corner. The air stank of stale hops. Didi's nose wrinkled. 'Want to watch the drunks?'

'We're too early for six o'clock closing.'

They turned and before long were back in South Melbourne. A short cut through a side street brought them upon a disturbing scene. A family's few pitiful possessions were exposed to everybody's view–a pile of clothes, a battered kitchen table, three scratched chairs, some old mattresses, the makings of some iron bedsteads. A small child carrying a baby almost as big as herself watched her parents arguing with three tough-looking men. Neighbours were surveying the action from nearby windows and yards. The silence was oppressive. No one moved or spoke.

'I thought the worst of the Depression was over,' Didi whispered loudly. 'No one's helping those poor people. Can't we do something?'

'You got any money?'

She shook her head.

He shrugged. He's so offhand, she thought crossly. Can't we do something? Then, after thirty minutes of hanging about she realised that, apart from moral support, they were in no position to help. Walking further, they talked about the look of savage despair on the father's face, the hopelessness on the mother's. 'Poor bastards,' Jamie muttered. 'Fancy being chucked out just 'cos they can't pay the rent.'

Knowing he felt strongly, in fact as strongly as she, made her feel fractionally less lonely.

Inside the Botanic Gardens they wandered down leafy paths flanked by exotic flowers. 'At least this hasn't changed too much.' Jamie didn't bother hiding his relief.

She looked away. 'Honestly, I don't know. This is my first visit here. I was supposed to come yesterday. Instead, all this happened.'

'It's one of my favourite places.' He stopped to admire a spectacular bed of roses. 'Since we came to the city, I spend heaps of time at the Botanics. The gardens in Melbourne are great.'

However unintentional, this remark reopened an old sore, reminding her as it did of Tom. Recalling her father brought back that old empty feeling. Distracting herself she grumped, 'Anyway, I don't like Melbourne. It's always cold and grey and there's never anything to do.' Annoyed with her outburst, irritated that she displayed her feelings so openly, she turned to sniff at a flower. It was good to be away, great to have a break from the family.

But what if she never got back? A throb, maybe of fear, went through her. She ran down the slope to where half a dozen workmen were dredging the swampy marsh. While seagulls and small brown ducks burrowed their beaks in the mud, other stagnant pools reflected the clouds high above.

Didi hid her hands in the pockets of her borrowed skirt. Staring at the ducks, she wished she'd brought some bread.

Jamie caught up. 'When we get back,' he suggested. 'You'll have to come here with your oldies.' He flung himself under an oak and looked up at the fresh foliage. 'Wonder if this tree will still be here.' He took out his harmonica. 'I'm getting tired. It's after two and I could use some lunch.'

'So could I,' she replied, amazed she was hungry after such a huge breakfast.

'What'll I play?'

'Anything. I like most music.'

He broke into some Rick Astley songs. An audience quickly gathered. 'What strange music,' cried a lady in a large black hat. 'Where's it from?'

'The future.'

'Is that a musical?' her companion sniffed. 'Strange I've not heard of it. I attend all the musicals at the Theatre Royale. I've tickets for *Maid Of The Mountains*.' And but for the others hushing her she would have chattered right through Jamie's performance.

When he had finished, Jamie bowed gracefully, marking the end of the concert. 'Thank you. Thank you very much.' There was applause, coins thrown in their direction which Didi retrieved by scrambling about on her knees.

'Well, at least we'll never starve. What now?'

81

'Don't you want lunch?'

Walking back to the city, they looked high and low for a 'take-away'. They finally found a small fish shop where they bought two pieces of whiting covered in a thick batter and a bag of chips.

'We've got ninepence left,' he calculated. 'I'll leave it with you for tomorrow's lunch.'

'What about you?'

'Sam'll lend me more.'

'Thanks.' For travellers, polite distances are hard to maintain. His generosity embarrassed her. How was she expected to behave? If instincts were reducible, like an essence or perfume, her gut feeling was that she'd rather be lost with anyone, anybody, but sister Kate's boyfriend. Above all she didn't want to start liking Jamie. An inkling of the complications that could ensue horrified her. In the end she decided it easiest to stay bad-tempered. Not another word was said all the way to the Finkelsteins'.

Everyone was home from work. Hearing them arrive, Sam poked his head out the door to his room next to theirs and called, 'Tea's ready in half an hour.' He seemed unaccountably pleased to see them.

They seated themselves at the long wooden table where Selma, as fresh and pretty as she had been that morning, introduced them round. Useless. The Jewish names reeling off her tongue were too foreign to remember.

Mrs Finkelstein's lodgers were mostly in their twenties; mostly recent arrivals from Russia and Poland. Loving a forbidden romance, they smiled with more than normal friendliness at this young couple. But Didi remembered to behave as if she and Jamie were close and Jamie's calm manner could be interpreted any way one chose. Nobody questioned their story. Yet, knowing Sam, they suspected it had been lavishly embellished.

Seated near them was an older woman who spoke no English. A layer of white powder, like icing sugar, covered her face. There was a daughter roughly Didi's age. When Selma introduced Jamie and Didi as Mr and Mrs Major from New York, the woman whispered something scathing, for the girl blushed and refused to meet their eyes.

The food Mrs Finkelstein served was hot, plentiful and tasty. At mealtimes, as well as enjoying her excellent cooking, Mrs Finkelstein's boarders liked to exchange gossip, ideas and political notions. As they downed a rich beef stew filled with floury dumplings, talk flew around the table. These people spoke other languages as naturally as eating. Didi thought they were speaking merely one, but Jamie's musical ear picked up two, even three. Bemused, too confused to even guess what was under discussion, their tired heads reeled. These people questioned in one language, answered in another, eavesdropped in a third. Fortunately, someone called out in English, 'We want to know all about America. Tell us how you live?'

Jamie cleared his throat, but no one was listening. A young man named Yankel called, 'In America you don't have royalty. Here, Australians are expected to call England "Home", no matter where they're from.'

'And George the Fifth is so conservative,' Sam cried. 'Last year he tried to prevent Australia from getting their own governor-general. I'm a convinced republican...' his voice was loud enough to be heard over the din. 'In America anyone can be president. There's opportunity for all.' He banged his glass on the table. 'I ask you, could I ever become king?"

'But we've got an Australian governor-general now. We've Sir Isaac Isaacs,' Yankel protested. Brown curly hair topped a face as round as a button. 'You can become governor-general, or prime minister like Joseph Lyons.'

Sam's look was disparaging. 'It's not the same thing, not the same thing at all.'

A young woman, fiercely dark, like a Spanish flamenco dancer, whispered, 'I'm sorry for Edward. Such a good-looking man. It must be hard knowing one day you'll be king. So many girlfriends...' Her tone was shocked but her eyes sparkled with interest.

'Do you know my brother in New York?' a small chap asked Jamie. 'He looks like me.' He pointed to a head as bare as a billiard ball.

Jamie murmured politely, 'I didn't catch your name,' when the conversation changed, spun to telling stories about lucky folk who had migrated in an earlier wave and were doing well. The bald man, whose name turned out to be Joe, joined in with alacrity.

'Now you are in Australia, you must work hard,' said Mr Finkelstein. 'Exert yourself, and there are opportunities for everybody.' Anyone in the know would have seen Sam and Selma grin, for, as Didi was later to learn, Mr Finkelstein always avoided work whenever he could manage it.

'I came here in time for the Depression,' Yankel said gloomily, his curly hair bobbing up and down on his round head like the springs of a clock. 'What chance do I have of making a fortune?'

'How would you know?' Sam called derisively. 'For anyone from your little village, a depression in Australia looks like milk and honey in Grodno.'

This comment, instead of settling opinions, opened up a hornet's nest. One side maintained that all that migrants needed was a little bit of luck, while the other claimed hard work was everything. Didi noticed city people, such as Mr Finkelstein and Sam, sided in favour of luck, while folk immigrating from villages presented an argument in favour of hard work.

Finally, Mrs Finkelstein settled the argument. 'Success,' she cried, 'depends on both.' For weren't there opportunities galore in this new land? Wasn't the Depression over its worst? Rising from the table to wash the dishes she summed up her philosophy with, 'Those lucky ones born in this country don't know the meaning of hard work.'

'Tomorrow,' Sam warned Jamie, 'it's an early rising. We leave at seven. Make sure you're up on time.'

Selma, who had been collecting the plates, stopped to call, 'Didi?' Didi halted half-way up the stairs. 'Are you interested in a job?'

'Am I?' Didi gave Selma one of her special smiles. 'You betcha!'

Selma giggled. 'The way you Americans talk... Seriously, there's a vacancy where I work. They need a junior to run messages, write invoices and give change. Are you interested?'

'I can try.' Didi managed to sound keen. 'I mean, it can't be too hard, can it?'

Selma smiled at this. 'I've told them about you. If you come with me tomorrow, I'll introduce you to my boss. But I'd better warn you, he's a terrible slave-driver.'

Didi nodded. 'I know. Your mother told me. By the way, thanks for the gear. I'll return your things as soon as I can.'

'You need some clothes for tomorrow. You can give them back to me when you earn some money and buy your own.' With that, Selma dashed back to the sink, calling, 'Breakfast at six-thirty.'

In order to be fresh the next day they went to bed early, but the mattress was so small, they kept each other awake half the night trying to get comfortable.

7. AND OFF TO WORK WE GO

THAT NIGHT JAMIE dreamt there was a fire at his mother's cottage. For some inexplicable reason both his parents were sleeping in the same room. Woken by the crackling and smoke, Jamie fought to get them outside before all three perished in the flames.

Startled awake, he sat up and stared round. The tiny room was still pitch black. Only a faint touch of indigo at the window told him dawn was approaching.

He rolled over on to his side and went back to sleep.

Tossed and turned as if she was at sea, Didi sat up in bed with a jolt. All she could hear was the sound of Jamie's even breathing. Wide awake, she began worrying about the next day, only drifting back to sleep just before it was time to get up.

At breakfast, still tired and crotchety, Didi peered out at the world through half-closed eyes. Mrs Finkelstein was stirring porridge, cutting bread, sausage and tomato for lunches. 'Today I make much sandviches. Enough for everyvone,' she announced, handing out packages wrapped in newspaper.

At this hour Mrs Finkelstein's strange accent seemed more marked than ever. When she noticed the dark circles under Didi's eyes, she said disapprovingly, 'To be married is vone thing, but you must also sleep.'

Didi went scarlet. Sam tittered loudly. The more Didi blushed the more Sam laughed. And as for Jamie... His smile was like a cat finding a hole in the canary's cage. Which, Didi thought angrily, he had, in a way. What a suck. But at the same time she saw the good sense of keeping the Finkelsteins on side.

Starting a new job, taking any job, produced a sinking feeling in her stomach. Too churned-up to eat, she spooned her porridge into Jamie's plate, then watched him bolt it down. How pathetic to be ruled by one's stomach, she thought disdainfully, forgetting how often Jane had scolded her for raiding the fridge.

Once breakfast was over, Selma hurried Didi upstairs. 'I don't want to give Mr Bent time to interview someone else,' she patiently explained. 'Like I told you last night, it's cashier work. There's a new vacancy for a junior. One of the girls left last week.'

This gave Didi a fresh worry. Was the girl sacked and if so, why? She ran to fetch her jacket, and peered with dismay into the mirror. At this rate she would be an old hag in months. Smoothing her unruly hair, which stuck up more than ever after a bad night, Didi knew she was bound to slip up and say something idiotic, wished she was more experienced, wished this wasn't her first job.

Having ducked upstairs to get his jacket, Jamie caught sight of her distraught face. 'Reckon you can work with pounds and shillings?' he asked offhandedly.

'I've enough trouble handling dollars and cents.'

'Well,' he said, 'keep your gob shut, then you mightn't give anything away. Maybe you'll pick things up as you go along?' His expression belied his words.

They stepped out briskly, walking up several lanes, past the cemetery to the tram-stop. A cable-tram rattled noisily to a stop. 'One day all our streets will have electric trams,'

Sam boasted, showing his city off to foreigners. Meanwhile, as she was forced to sit next to an open door, Didi's hands were numb with cold. All four got off at the same stop.

They stood shivering in the wind. Sam asked Jamie, 'Aren't you going to kiss your wife goodbye?'

Jamie bent to peck Didi's frozen cheek then headed off with Sam to Wirth's Park. Selma led Didi to Foy and Gibson's department store. She halted before the staff door. 'Didi, what sort of work have you done before?'

'It's my first job,' she admitted. 'Can you tell me exactly what a cashier does?'

'Lots of things.'

'Like what?'

Selma wouldn't answer this directly. 'If you haven't worked before this is excellent training.' Didi hoped she was right. They climbed stairs covered in torn grey lino, to a tiny cloakroom. Selma smoothed her own hair, then checked Didi's. Selma is so methodical, Didi thought. So neat and precise. She wished she was the same. Life with Didi tended to be messier. Only after Selma was convinced Didi would pass inspection, did she say, 'I work in the central register where they send the money. We have a junior to run messages and generally help out. In return, you'll be trained to handle the machine.' She added very seriously, 'You must pretend you're only fifteen. And don't on any account admit you're married.'

'Won't be hard,' Didi promised weakly.

'It's lucky you look younger.' Selma's frown was a faint blemish on her perfect skin. 'They like employing young people...' Clearing her throat Didi lost the rest of Selma's sentence. 'They pay so little. But it's a job. I suppose we should be grateful.' Not knowing what to say, Didi nodded obediently. 'With this sort of experience,' said Selma, 'you'll be able to go on to something better.'

Didi was led into the cashier's office. Here the walls were covered with a multitude of painted pipes which flowed into a machine resembling the keyboard of a giant organ. 'These are our vacuum tubes,' Selma explained. 'When a customer buys something downstairs, the assistant places the docket and the money in one of these.' She held up a brass container twenty centimetres long, and six centimetres wide, with felt padding at both ends. 'These tubes come and go to every department.' She showed how some tubes sucked up, others sent back. 'I know you have the latest inventions in America.' Was Selma actually apologising? To her? 'I'm sure you've seen all this before.'

'Well, not exactly,' Didi muttered. Bewildered, she stared at these organ pipes dedicated to the process of making money. This machine needed a mechanical genius, at the very least. She thought about Kate. Kate could handle this. She was good with machinery and great at maths, whereas Didi still had problems with long division...

For the first time since leaving home Didi wished Kate was here, even if Kate had the knack of making her own interests seem adult and important, and Didi's trivial and infantile.

At that moment a gentleman with the most upright stance Didi had ever seen came into the office and settled in at the centre desk. Selma whispered, 'This is Mr Bent. Be careful how you talk to him. He was caught in the trenches in France and gassed. You know, mustard gas. It's made him a little strange.'

Didi blinked nervously. 'How?'

'I think... well, he really dislikes people.'

'So why does he work with them?'

But all Selma would say was, 'Try and handle him carefully,' and nip Didi's arm in warning.

Mr Bent forced the girls to wait, as he shuffled papers

from one side of the desk to the other. Then, peering at them through metal-framed eyeglasses, his eyes obscured by smoke from one of the sixty cigarettes he smoked each day, he dared Selma to speak.

'Mr Bent, this is my young cousin, Didi Major.' Selma pushed Didi to the front of his desk. 'You said you might have a job for a junior.'

Squinting at Didi, Mr Bent demanded, 'What I want to know young lady is, will it be worth employing you? Will the time and trouble I take in training you be repaid?' Her reply was lost in his, 'Can you add, subtract, multiply, or do I have to teach you everything?' He glared at her, as if she was found out already, and she looked into a mouthful of broken, tobacco-stained teeth.

'I-I-I think so...'

'Well, you don't look too intelligent to me. However your cousin has put in a good word for you, so we'll try you out. You can start today. We pay fifty shillings a week and our hours are eight thirty to five forty-five precisely. You'll get three-quarters of an hour for lunch, like our other girls. Mind you're on time. I won't tolerate lateness. If you can remember that you'll get on.'

Didi stared at the top of his head, examined his wispy grey hair, and nodded. She was shaking, trembling nearly as much as when they'd first arrived. Only this time with fury. As far as she was concerned he could take his rotten job and stuff it up his jumper. But then, there was the money... Don't show your feelings had been Selma's advice, so she swallowed her pride and stayed quiet.

He got up to check the machine and left her standing, as if on guard duty, shifting from one leg to the other. Twenty minutes later she was still on her feet. Today's lesson: That she was an insignificant cog in a well-oiled machine.

Already settled at the long console, Selma was working

on yesterday's invoices. Other cashiers drifted in, greeting each other. By eight forty-eight it was a normal working day.

Mr Bent was chief cashier and general dictator. As six girls worked at packing and unpacking the vacuum pipes and brass containers, sorting receipts and handling change, he sat at a desk on a platform in the centre of the room. Didi, employed to make his life more comfortable, spent her morning brewing cups of tea.

That was the best part. At least it got her away from his prying gaze and out into the corridor where she boiled water on a small paraffin stove. She found the other girls friendly and good-humoured, in spite of working under Mr Bent's finicky, sarcastic eye. There was Molly, Betty, Prue and Madge who was, 'Called the same as my mother and grandmother before me.' Aged between seventeen and twenty-five, the girls were unmarried and living at home. Madge and Betty were the only people in their families with proper jobs. As Madge said, 'The money isn't much, but we do get to eat.'

All this was learnt in a quiet spell while Mr Bent was away.

'How's that fellow of yours, Selma?' Betty asked. 'How's Sam?'

Selma smiled. 'Sam's fine.'

'When are you two getting married?'

Selma continued smiling, but shrugged her pretty shoulders.

'Who needs marriage?' Madge called. 'I've enough on me hands with Mum, Dad and me little brothers.'

'Everybody wants to get married,' Betty cried. 'Who wants to be an old maid,' and peering mischievously at Mr Bent who had just returned to the office, 'or a bachelor?'

'I see Miss Anderson has run out of invoices.' Mr Bent so

91

disliked the girls gossiping, that if he caught them at it he searched for punishments. 'If there's nothing left for you to do, I've plenty more here.' The office was run like a reformatory, Didi thought. Did he threaten the girls with the strap? It was hard to see how they managed to remain so good-humoured. Working conditions were gloomy, rewards meagre, yet Betty produced fresh lamingtons to share round and Madge promised to loan Molly a special dress for the opening night of the new Forty Club. 'Same building as the Green Mill, you know, Wirth's Park,' Betty explained in answer to Didi's questioning look. 'They've done the old place up proud. We'll be dancing to Joe Aronson's band. He's called the Rajah of Jazz.'

'Australia's answer to Paul Whiteman,' Prue snorted. 'Thought he'd had his day. Didn't his band play at the Green Mill years ago when it first opened? You'll be shaking to 'Black Bottom' and 'Messin' Around.''

Betty looked horrified. 'Course we won't. Who'd do those old-fashioned dances? We'll be tangoing, doing the foxtrot.' Mr Bent was out of the room, so Betty pulled Prue into the centre and between desks they gave a brief but vigorous demonstration.

'Bet you can't get old Herbie to move like that,' called Madge. 'He's so skinny he'd snap in two if he bent over.' Comments made about the girls' long-standing boyfriends told Didi there was little they didn't know about each other's lives. As Betty and Prue swooped, swayed and tangoed dramatically around the office, everybody clapped and roared with laughter. Didi joined in happily. After all, this was little different to any school when a teacher was absent. Only the vacuum tubes' demanding whistle settled them down before Mr Bent returned.

Selma introduced Didi as her cousin from New York. After their initial curiosity faded, the girls treated her well, offered her boiled sweets, demonstrated the workings of the vacuum tubes with alacrity, were even proud of them. As far as Didi could see, no one minded the job being repetitive, boring and poorly paid.

'What's Didi short for?' asked Betty of the thick red hair and freckles.

'Is it American?' Madge wanted to know. Her family had moved to the city at the height of the Depression, 'For there wasn't a job for love or money to be found near our farm.' Her eyes were the blue of limitless skies and her pink cheeks hinted at coming from generations of farmers. For Didi's benefit Madge described the yellow wheat fields of the Mallee. When times were better they would return. Didi believed her. Madge had a very determined chin.

Molly was the eldest, and what with helping raise six younger brothers and sisters, the most worn. A little shrewder than the others she said, 'You don't sound American. Not like anyone I've heard in the movies.'

Selma flew to Didi's rescue. 'How would you know? You're too busy cuddling Dave in the back row to listen.'

As the girls roared with laughter, Molly reddened, the vacuum tubes whistled, the bronze containers demanded attention. They weren't the sort of girls to question too closely. Simply, Didi was accepted because she was Selma's cousin and because she was there.

Although Didi spent her morning making tea for Mr Bent, she wasn't offered a cup, nor were the other girls given a break. In between keeping the kettle boiled Didi was told to stand behind the cashiers' chairs to watch and learn how it all worked. By the middle of the morning her legs ached so much she wondered if she would last the day out.

In spite of the girls' friendliness the atmosphere was oppressive. If she was back home talking to Helene, always on her wavelength, she would have found it hard to explain exactly why. There was a greyness about the building, the people, the dirty cream-kalsomined walls which, acting like a camera filter, distorted ordinary articles, making them dross. Didi felt desperate for her own times, even prepared to flee without Jamie. For when she remembered him, which was rare, it was to see him as someone to whom she was inadvertently tied.

As for now, she needed an escape from this overwhelming dourness. She reminded herself of the brilliant plastics, exploding colours, technological wizardry of her generation. Even with their ever present fear of nuclear weapons and ecological disasters, at least she told herself, her generation was alive. Here was grey, stagnant, boring. If she'd ever thought Melbourne a dull miserable place she now knew how far it had come.

With a minimum of three girls needed to operate the tubes, breaks were taken in shifts. At twelve forty-five, Selma and Didi marched up the street to eat lunch on the lawns at the State Library. 'I could learn to hate old Bent and his bloody vacuum tubes,' Didi said. Ravenous, she uwrapped a sausage and tomato sandwich and took a huge bite.

Selma giggled and asked, 'Do all girls in America use bad language?' Didi only laughed. With the sun warming her, grass prickling her legs and the sparrows' cheerful chirp, she munched on her sandwich and felt better. Maybe this wasn't so bad. If one imagined the cashier's office as an unpleasant school, Mr Bent a dreary headmaster, the work no different from any boring lesson, one might just survive. Besides, there was the joy of knowing anything to do with St Anne's was half a century away. This thought made her sit up straight, all the better to admire Selma's peach-like skin, thick eyelashes and lustrous almond eyes.

She found herself comparing Selma to Kate. Kate, being taller, looked more athletic even though she probably wasn't. Kate's appearance was twenty-first century, she supposed, suppressing her usual envious twinge. Personally, she found Selma's fragile beauty more appealing. Probably because Selma's much nicer, she decided. It was a shock to realise Selma and Kate were exactly the same age. What a pity she couldn't swap them about. It would be much nicer to have Selma as her sister.

'Didi, you mustn't show Mr Bent how you feel,' Selma was saying very seriously.

'Why not? The old bugger deserves what he gets.'

To her surprise Selma became quite upset. 'Didi, you're very brave, but we can't afford to be so open. Women have a hard time finding work.'

'So why do you put up with old Bent?' Didi's brow creased belligerently. 'I caught him timing how long we spend in the loo. Why do you let him get away with it?'

Selma shrugged. 'What else can we do? It's a job, isn't it? It's too hard finding others. Two years ago, department stores like Foys sacked dozens of people, managed with two cashiers instead of ten. Things are better now than they've been for ages.'

Didi knew she had gone too far. If she carried on like this there'd be some hard questions to answer. 'I'm real grateful you found this for me,' she said awkwardly. 'Don't think I'm not. It's just that you work in such awful conditions. No tea break, and having old man Bent breathing down your neck.'

It had taken only a morning for Didi to realise Selma's importance to Foy's. She was head girl, knew where any receipt or docket could be found at a moment's notice, yet they paid her exactly the same as when she first started. 'When I finish my Bookkeeping Certificate they've promised me a raise. Then maybe Sam and I can save enough to get married,' Selma said hopefully.

Didi reached out and stroked Selma's arm. 'Gee, I sure hope it happens soon.'

'Tell me,' Selma whispered, 'is it wonderful being married?'

Didi jumped. 'Mmm,' she spluttered, 'course. Unreal.' Quickly changing the subject, and curious about these people who'd befriended them, she asked, 'How come you're the only one who speaks English without an accent?'

'We came here from Poland when I was still a little girl. So I guess it was easier for me.' Selma smiled, her mouth tilting deliciously.

'Is that why Mrs Finkelstein doesn't like Sam?'

Selma started. 'How did you know?' Then she added, 'Is it so obvious? No. It's because Sam used to be a socialist and she doesn't approve.'

'Why not?'

'She thinks he'll get involved in politics again and get us into trouble.'

Didi's knowledge was vague. Was socialism the same as communism? Not wanting to display her ignorance she changed the subject, 'How did he get a job with the circus?'

'He went to Wirth's and told them he knew about horses. He said when he was a small boy he used to be around them a lot.'

'Did he? Lucky thing,' Didi said enviously.

Selma giggled. 'Course not. Sam's a town boy. Most of us come from the cities.'

Didi frowned. 'How did he get away with it? I mean, don't you have to know something about horses to work with them?'

Selma shrugged. 'When you need a job you learn anything. He picked things up as he went along.'

This was interesting. More so than politics. But Selma, looking down at her pendant watch, exclaimed they would be late, and they were back in the dingy office before Didi found time to draw breath.

Didi's afternoon was spent searching for various departments. She carried messages from Mr Bent. It was better than making cups of tea, yet, walking past racks of dresses and suits, shelves packed tight with materials, she wished there was time to check them out. Prices were low. A wax mannequin draped in a red-sequined dress triggered the memory of a navy dress with beaded hibiscus flowers. The red dress cost twenty pounds. Twenty pounds is only forty dollars. But this was her wage for thirteen weeks! What a rip-off, she decided.

Told to seek out specific people, becoming lost around the store, shop assistants frowning like cross crows, feeling more and more uncomfortable, she wondered what she had done to merit such unfriendliness. 'You'll have to dress in something more suitable if you're to be seen out front,' one wizened-faced floor manager said disapprovingly as he brushed a speck of dust off his jacket. 'We can't have you wandering around looking like that.'

Didi fingered her borrowed plaid skirt. 'Won't this do?'

'Our assistants are instructed to appear in black.' His gaze went straight through her. 'If you wish to be employed at Foy's you will have to wear something more appropriate.'

Muttering under her breath how stupid they were, Didi passed a woman clothed in an expensive coat and hat, fox fur flung over her shoulders, coaxing a girl about the same age as Didi into a new dress. 'It looks divine on you, darling,' the mother was saying.

'Oh Mummykins, the clothes here are so dull.' The daughter barely stifled a yawn as two shop assistants fawned and bobbed before them.

97

Mum would never tolerate Kate or me being so rude, Didi thought and felt a pang, a 'missing mother' tremor pass through her. Yet it seemed almost natural not having Jane about. She was always so busy. Didi once calculated that Jane's working day began at seven and didn't finish until midnight. First thing each morning, Jane flew round tidying up from the night before. Then, while the rest of the family drifted into the kitchen, Jane headed towards her bathroom. It took a long time, but she emerged looking as if she came out of *Vogue*. Didi often wondered how Jane could stand always looking right, but Jane claimed that women in executive positions had to dress the part. Watching Jane use up every moment of her day completing what Didi perceived as boring tasks for work or home, Didi felt exhausted for her and determined not to do the same. Tom was always telling Jane she would wear herself out. But no, he didn't have time to help. Nor, Didi suspected, did he have the inclination.

Once, after scrutinising Jane's tired face, Didi asked her why she worked so hard. 'Doesn't Daddy make enough money to support us?'

'Oh darling...' Jane looked at her with the familiar half-laughing, half-worried expression which always made Didi's heart ache. 'The money's good, but that's not the only reason I work. We women have spent too many years at home raising kids, working awful jobs.'

At the same time Jane was busy sorting the ironing into four different piles. This was only preparatory to the real night's work which was finishing off some accounts. Folding a sheet into four, she added, 'Women owe it to themselves to find good jobs. Then to treat them as seriously as men always have.'

Even when there's not a moment for me? Didi wanted to say. She stopped herself in time. What was the point? The net result would be Jane making a conscientious effort to give Didi more attention for the next few days, then everything drifting back to exactly as before...

At the end of the day she and Selma caught the cable-tram home. Didi demanded to know how they could expect her to buy clothes before her first pay.

'We could dye what you're wearing!'

'And ruin your good skirt?'

'Maybe one of the other girls has something you could use,' Selma suggested, but Didi merely grunted exhaustedly. It was hard to be grateful. For reasons she couldn't explain to herself she was mad with everyone. Maybe it was the way Selma and the other girls accepted their lot, the way they hadn't, as yet, stormed the Bastille or held a Boston Tea-party.

So it was Jamie, already home half an hour and looking calmer and more cheerful than she could ever be again, who caught the worst of her tongue.

He was looking through the window and playing something new. He raised an eyebrow at the sight of her tired angry face and stopped to say, 'Not much fun?'

A few bars of *'Tote that barge, lift that bale...'* forced a smile.

'Yeah,' she admitted. 'A bit like that. How was your day?'

He grinned. 'Interesting.'

'How did you make out?'

'Mucked out the stables, groomed, brushed and fed the horses. They wanted a general dogsbody about the place and looks like I'm it.'

'What'll they pay you?'

'I should get about three pounds fifteen shillings.'

'I'm only getting two pounds ten!' Didi exploded. 'How

bloody unfair.' She pulled off her shoes and sank on the bed. 'How much do we owe the Finkelsteins?'

'They want two pounds a week from each of us. Together with what you're bringing in, that leaves two pounds for travelling and clothes.'

'Two pounds five shillings,' she corrected glumly. 'Not much, is it?'

He refused to be rattled. 'We'll manage. Stop panicking and let's get some grub. I'm starving.'

8. What A Way To Earn A Living

IN THEIR ROOM after dinner Jamie said, 'Sam sure knows his way round.'

It was icy cold. Wrapped in a blanket with only her face showing, Didi smiled knowingly. 'He's just learnt. Particularly about horses.'

'What do you mean?'

'Sam's a city person,' she explained. 'Selma sort of hinted he bluffed his way into Wirth's.'

'Well, he knows plenty, so he must've spent his holidays in the country. Listening to him talk, you'd have sworn he was born in the saddle.'

'Does he know more than you?'

Jamie's laugh was disdainful. 'Course not. But he knows enough to get by. Maybe my dad would have picked him up. He's ace with horses. He works with thoroughbreds, trains racers.'

'Oh, is that what he does?' She glanced sideways. 'Do you still miss the farm?'

'Yeah, well, shows you get used to anything.' Changing the subject, the opening of 'Ain't Misbehavin' ' sounded faintly into the night. 'Anyway,' he continued when he stopped playing, 'it was best for everybody when Mum and Dad split. They fought like mad, made each other dead

101

miserable, then had the cheek to say they stayed together for my sake.'

'Sometimes I wish my parents would split.'

Jamie blinked at the envy in her voice. 'You'd want them divorced? I thought your oldies got on OK.'

'They get on fine,' she scowled at the ceiling. 'But if we didn't live together, my dad would have to find time for me on weekends.'

He stared disbelievingly. 'But you've got your dad all week!'

'He'd have to take me out. Maybe just the two of us...'

'But you're together all week,' he repeated.

'Sure,' she snapped. 'Sure we share the same house. But we don't do anything together. He's too busy with his job, and... all sorts of other things.'

'Like what?'

'Oh, collecting wine, working out at a gym. Mostly, he stays back late at the bank.'

'What about your mum?' he asked more warily.

'Yeah, she's OK. But she's got a lot to do. Besides, she helps Kate with her exams. Anyway, I need Dad. I'm more like him. Kate's like Mum.'

Four more bars of 'Ain't Misbehavin' ' as he thought this through. Life with Bill and Liz, he supposed, would sound equally strange if stated out loud. 'It's hell raising parents,' he said at last. 'Now look at my mum. I just wish she'd ignore me. Since she and Dad split, she's always on about where I'm going, what I'm thinking, why I'm not practising...'

'One man's meat,' she groaned. 'Crazy isn't it?' Then, wanting to change the discussion to something which made her less miserable, she said, 'You have to admire Sam's cheek, don't you?'

'Hell, I understand. Work is hard to get.'

'I know, I know! If one more person tells me there's a depression, I'll scream.'

'I guess we should feel lucky we found jobs,' he said doubtfully. 'Being dumped here, not knowing anybody. Sam says there's a long queue for any advertised work. Pay's half what it should be.'

She grimaced, so he left off to begin describing his day. 'Sam nearly caught me out. I thought I'd spill the beans.'

'So what? I'll bet we could tell them a thing or two. Maybe we should.' She thumped her pillow decisively. A few feathers drifted out. He watched them float about before landing on the torn lino.

'You reckon they'd believe us? We'd be giving heaps away.'

She refused to answer. Perched precariously on the end of their small, wobbly dressing-table, he stared moodily out at the night sky. She glared at the back of his head, climbed under the blankets, closed her eyes, and pretended to fall asleep.

Outside, a three-quarter moon was colouring the garden silver, black and indigo. A branch tapping against the glass sought his attention, but Jamie was too busy watching Didi's reflection in the glass. She was stubborn, he decided. Too much like himself. He remembered himself at fifteen. For him that had been a year of change, at least musically speaking. Until then his mother had driven him twice weekly to piano lessons sixty kilometres away.

It was Mr Higgins' habit to sit close enough for Jamie to count the hairs on his chin, smell his musty odour. He was a human metronome beating time and crying, 'tempo, tempo' until Jamie got it right. The old man would drop his lower lip into a U when Jamie played badly. If Jamie played well, he was rewarded with a brief half-smile, a rare occurrence, for Mr Higgins' standards were exacting.

They had gone on that way quite amicably until Jamie rebelled against Mr Higgins' strict discipline. The old man argued that if Jamie had enough guts and talent to succeed on the concert platform he could get him there. But only if the boy practised every spare moment and gave up playing with the local rock group.

Bill Major was the only person pleased with the outcome. But then, he had never understood his son wanting to be a musician. He thought it something to be grown out of, like mucking around with Lego, or toy trains. As far as Bill was concerned, music was a fine hobby, but one day Jamie would inherit the property, and with this came certain adult responsibilities. Yet when the lessons with Higgins ceased, Jamie picked up the clarinet and flute, found the harmonica...

Looking back, Jamie was sorry. The old man had been good. A better teacher than anyone else he was likely to come across. He wished he'd worked things through at the time. He thought of telling Didi the story, then changed his mind. Later. But what would she make of it? For Jamie, half a century away in time, but three years ahead in wisdom, the whole thing was painful to recall. Eyes half-closed, letting arpeggios ripple, he watched Didi wriggle further down the bed. From the calm way she'd threatened to 'tell them a thing or two', he recognised her blind spot. Fancy believing you could tell people you were from the future and not expect some amazing repercussions. They'd be considered bonkers, locked up, the key thrown away.

As if she knew what was passing through his mind, she opened her eyes. 'I think,' she said determinedly, 'we'd do a lot of good. We could warn them about things. Like the Second World War.' She couldn't believe him. Here was an opportunity to remake the world and he was worried whether they should.

'We'd end up changing the future. Imagine what'd happen then? I think it's a stupid idea.' It was getting colder by the minute. He crawled into the tiny bed and pulled the quilt over his legs.

'Maybe we'd stop some of the worst things happening. How could that be wrong?'

'Have you considered we could change things so much, we mightn't get born? Then we'd really be stuck. Anyway, everyone knows you shouldn't try changing history.'

'Who says?' Arguing with Jamie was like moving in quicksand. One wrong step and you were lost.

'I read it somewhere.'

'No one's ever tried. Anyway,' she pointed out, 'if they have, how would you know?'

Both knew this to be unprovable. 'All the same,' he murmured, 'if we change things now, we won't know the end result.'

'How could things get worse? Have you forgotten Vietnam? Or, or...' she thought rapidly, 'or the Middle East?'

'What happens if Hitler wins the war?'

She rubbed her tired legs despondently. 'Maybe you're right. I can't see how us getting home will help Hitler win the war, but maybe you're right. How come you're so sure we'll get back?'

'Cos that's where we started,' he cried triumphantly. 'In the future. That's why we mustn't change anything here. If we leave the past exactly as it is we'll get back, for sure.'

'You don't know if we had a future in our own times! Haven't you heard of people disappearing, never being seen again? What if we're stuck here forever?' She shuddered. It was one thing having a well-deserved break from Tom, Jane and Kate, quite another to never see them again.

'Don't be silly. You're tired and depressed, not thinking

clearly. You'll feel different tomorrow, I promise.' And he added, trying to be helpful, 'Sometimes, after we played footy against a rambo team and lost, I used to feel that way. Like I'd never play again. What's the point of getting battered and bruised for a piece of pigskin?'

She smiled bleakly. 'What made you go back?'

'I don't know...' he shrugged. 'I can't stand giving up half-way.'

'Yeah?' She bit her lip thoughtfully.

'Still want to hear about my day?' he asked, settling down as comfortably as the awkward little bed would allow.

When Jamie and Sam arrived at the far side of Princes Bridge the circus was setting up around the Hippodrome. While the actual performance took place in the huge warehouse, tents were being erected to house performers and sideshows. Two men were nailing up a board which read: 'This Way to Madame Zara. Come and Hear your Future for sixpence.'

Other signs promised:

THIS WAY TO THE FATTEST LADY ON EARTH.

COME AND LOOK AT THE FIVE-LEGGED COW.

SEE THE SHEEP WITH TWO HEADS AND FIVE LEGS.

Jamie wanted to stop and look but Sam hurried him on. The horses were stabled in large tents at the back of the building and work began early. Sam said, 'Jamie, could you find the boss yourself? He's somewhere in the main building. I'd better get started.'

'No worries.' Jamie crossed the muddy track which led to the Hippodrome, passing the sweeper coming in the opposite direction.

'What do y'do with your money, Shylock?' George called. 'We don't need no more kikes round here!'

Jamie pretended not to understand. Yet meeting George acted as a dampener on a promising day. It took several minutes for him to cool down before he eventually located the boss's rooms.

He knocked at a door with 'Main Office' written on it in flaking gold paint. A squeaky-wheelbarrow sort of voice called, 'Come in.' Seated by a desk, feet high on a stack of newspapers was a very small man. No taller than a four-year-old, he had the large head of a mature man and a face which had weathered many seasons.

Jamie cleared his throat. 'I'm looking for the boss.'

Pale blue eyes stared blankly. 'What's your name, young man?'

'I'm Jamie, Jamie Major. The boss told me to report here before starting work.'

'You mean old Ferguson? What's he hired you to do?' White teeth too good to be real gleamed frostily.

Jamie grinned back. 'Clean stables and groom horses.'

The little man rocked with mirth. 'We're getting a better class of chappie to clean horse manure.' When he swung down from the table he came up to Jamie's thighs. The room was filled with his personality; the way he cocked his head, the way he strode about on his short legs. 'What else can you do apart from looking after horses, young Major?'

'I play this.' Jamie took out his harmonica and the first four bars of 'Basin Street Blues' rang out, the sound bright and challenging.

The little man nodded his oversized head . 'Not bad, not bad at all. My name's Smithers. Donald Smithers. Clown Extraordinaire, at your service.' And he held out his hand to Jamie who bent down to shake it.

Just then Ferguson appeared. 'Oh, there you are,' he growled. 'You're late. We've got over thirty horses and

107

ponies in this circus and I want each one looked after like it's going to win the Cup. Understand?' Jamie nodded. 'Sam's a good man. He'll show you what I want. You can get started by raking the stables and laying fresh straw.'

As Jamie turned to leave, Donald Smithers gave a funny little bow and they grinned at one another; one artist intuitively liking another. 'Come and visit me and play the rest of those blues.' He grinned and winked broadly.

Back in the stables Sam was polishing harnesses, but he offered to show Jamie around. A dozen men kept the horses comfortable and well-groomed. Sam pointed out horses with speciality training, like six handsome geldings billed as Gladys Wirth's Australian Brumbies. They knew there were carrots in Sam's pockets and nuzzled with soft noses. Jamie chuckled. 'They're not much like bush horses.'

'Believe me, these horses aren't wild.' Sam said. 'They do a drill like you'd see in a fancy military academy. They're steady, very well disciplined. They have to be. Miss Gladys stands on their backs as they gallop around.'

Sam's other responsiblities included caring for the Shetland ponies. Monkeys dressed as jockeys somersaulted on their backs as they careered round the ring. Sam dutifully doled out pieces of carrot. The ponies crunched noisily. 'They can be bad-tempered little fellows,' he warned. 'Watch they don't have a mouthful of you.'

By far the most impressive animal in the stable was Queenie, the big white mare Miss Doris Wirth rode. 'She's my favourite!' Sam declared. 'I think she's more intelligent than most people I know.' He patted the smooth flanks and she whinnied softly. 'Queenie is The White Statue Act. Isn't she beautiful? Most times Miss Gladys rides her, but it makes no difference who's on her back, that horse has a heart of gold.' Sam traced his hand over Queenie, who pricked up her ears and searched in his pocket for carrots.

'Wirth's must be quite a family,' Jamie said thoughtfully.

'They've been circus people for over fifty years.'

'Have they ever offered you a permanent job?'

'Of course.' Sam's voice rose a little. 'Naturally. Every time they're in town they offer to take me on tour.'

'So why don't you go?'

'And leave Selma?' Sam shook his head. 'In an entire year the circus spends less than a month in Melbourne. What sort of life is that?'

'Wouldn't she go with you?'

'Think what it means,' Sam said despondently. 'We'd be out on the roads in the heat and dust, having to set up house every week. Sometimes the circus stays no more than a couple of nights in the towns they play. It's no life for us. Selma and I intend renting a new flat when we settle down. In a nice suburb. Maybe St Kilda. How could we do that on the road? Anyway,' he added briskly, 'I won't always be a worker. I intend to start my own business. I'm building up a little capital.'

'What do you do when the circus is out of town?'

Sam grinned mischievously. 'A bit of this, a bit of that. Selling, mostly.'

Jamie was very curious. 'Selling what?'

'Junk. Stuff other people throw away. There's quite a market for that sort of thing. Particularly in a depression,' and he would have continued outlining his business plans except for Ferguson poking his head through the doorway. 'What's the time?' Sam muttered. 'We'd better get back to work.'

Jamie glanced at his digital watch. 'Eight fifty-three.'

Sam's hand snaked out and held him. 'Where'd you get that?' It took a split second for Jamie to realise his mistake and he muttered something about the watch belonging to an uncle in Brooklyn, a crazy inventor.

Later, Sam took Jamie to meet the artistes, which is what the performers called themselves. How to best describe the excitement, the pandemonium he had come across?

During the First World War the Hippodrome's huge expanse had been used to store bales of wool. Now it was abuzz with a different kind of activity. Wooden seats rising in tiers around the sides of the building were being set into place by a gang of workmen. In the centre of the vast room, men were marking out the ring. 'It has to be precise. Forty-two feet and seventeen inches in diameter, the international measurement for all circuses,' Sam, who loved statistics, told Jamie. In the very middle was a steel cage where the dangerous animals, lions, tiger and bears, did their acts. And in the middle of this mellee of animals, clowns, acrobats, riders and workmen, the artistes rehearsed their Melbourne season.

Sam took Jamie to the dressing-rooms to meet the artistes who were sitting around having a smoko. There were a couple of young kids working as acrobats. Jamie asked one of them how he came to be working there.

The acrobat had been very shy. 'I joined up last year after my mum died.'

'What about your dad?'

'He lost his job and went on the grog. I'm on my own, but,' he added defiantly, 'I'm real proud of being here.'

'Jim turns somersaults high in the air.' Sam said, his proprietorial attitude showing.

Jamie looked up at the high trapeze wires. 'Don't you get scared?'

'There's nothing to be frightened of.' The boy pointed to a group of huge-chested men sitting quietly in a corner. 'Those big fellows catch me. We're the Seven Nelson Troupe.'

110

'They must be game,' Jamie whispered to Sam.

Sam nodded. 'Still, they get nervous. Circus people are terribly superstitious. There's sure to be some funny feelings around this afternoon. Five years ago, to this very day, there was a death under this roof.'

Jamie's eyebrows rose. 'How did it happen?'

'A group of high-flying acrobats. From America. Just like you and Didi...' Was there an ironic glint in Sam's eye? 'One of their troupe was forty feet up, halfway through a flying act.' Sam pointed to the high ceiling.

Jamie gestured at the safety nets. 'Weren't they using those?'

'It was a freak accident. Before my time.' Sam was ready to launch into the story but was stopped by a cry.

'Hey there, young Major, come and play some music for us,' and there was Donald Smithers, half-dressed in clown's costume, bare legs like a child's dangling from the chair. He was darning a costume and complaining in his high-pitched voice. 'I could do with someone to fix this. Miss Violet's hopeless.'

He stopped to introduce Jamie to the other small clowns. One was a raggedy doll, the other a sad-eyed harlequin. Their only woman, Miss Violet, a perfect china .figurine, had dark curly hair parted on the side and the pert features, the small nose, cupid-bow mouth, the arched plucked eyebrows of a silent-movie actress. To emphasise this resemblance she wore a velvet dressing-gown and feather boa. Miss Violet smoked Turkish cigarettes from a long ivory holder and seemed to be always enveloped in a cloud of smoke. Jamie guessed they'd walked in on an argument for she had a fixed look on her face and was blowing rings into the distance.

'Sam was telling me about an accident which happened here a few years back...' Jamie said. Donald immediately concentrated on threading his needle and the rest of the troupe looked away.

Realising his mistake, Jamie blushed, 'Sorry.'

Donald looked up and smiled. 'You must try and understand...' His squeaky voice filled the large room. 'We love the circus. For some of us it's the only life we know, but if you're careless it's a dangerous place to work.' Sighing loudly, he offered Sam and Jamie a cigarette. Sam lit up, but Jamie shook his head. 'That matinee will be stamped on my mind forever.'

Perched on a high stool he continued, 'We were playing to a full house. The five acrobats called themselves The Flying Lamars. Two couples, plus an extra girl they'd picked up in New Zealand. To this day I think it was her fault.'

'Why was that?'

'You must realise there's no room for jealousy in an acrobat's life, no room for private feelings to get in the way of safety. You see...' Donald paused to emphasise his point, 'acrobats, clowns, all circus people have to trust each other absolutely or they get hurt.' His big head nodded violently. Their argument forgotten, Miss Violet tucked her little hand into his. 'The accident happened just before the Final Parade. The cleverest of the acrobats was a girl who called herself Valmai. She handled the trapeze like a ballet dancer and was married to their boss, a fellow called Bill Lamar. It seems he'd taken a shine to the New Zealand lass and Valmai was jealous. Before the matinee opened somebody heard her screaming how she intended leaving both Bill and the show if he didn't stop giving Miss New Zealand the eye. She was too upset to concentrate properly. When it was her turn to throw herself from the trapeze, she misjudged the distance. They caught her by only one hand. Her swing carried her against the far wall and she knocked herself out.'

'What about the safety nets?'

'We don't allow the acrobats to go up without them.'
This was a full-sized clown wearing a shiny, red nose.
'What happened next was a freak accident. After Valmai
hit the wall she fell sideways on to the net, then bounced
on to the wooden forms below.'

There were tears in Miss Violet's eyes. 'In full view of the
audience.'

'They took her to hospital by ambulance.' Donald was
determined no one else should finish his story. 'But it was
too late. She was dead on arrival.'

Didi was silent. It sounded much better than spending
one's day in the cashier's office. 'What did you find out
about Sam's background?' she asked.

'His family have money. They own a big factory, and he's
been in this country three years.'

'Wonder why he left?'

He shook his head, yawned loudly, asked, 'Now, what
happened to you?'

She told him. About the cashier's office, how awful Mr
Bent was, how nice the girls were, and how she needed
proper clothes. He kept dozing off so she kicked him
awake. 'Did you get to play the harmonica for Smithers?'

'Yes I told you.'

'Maybe they'd use you in their band?'

'Circuses don't have live bands. They use this gadget
called a Panatrope.'

'A what?'

'Don't ask me.' He shifted about uncomfortably on the
narrow mattress. 'You know, I reckon we're earning enough
money between us to see if Mrs Finkelstein's got a room
with two beds. This is hopeless.'

113

Didi was huddled into a ball trying to keep warm. 'This bed must've once belonged to a kid,' she groaned. 'Don't suppose there'd be a job for me?' she asked tentatively.

'Where?'

'At the circus of course.'

'Tell you what,' he bartered, 'if you don't wriggle about too much tonight, I'll ask tomorrow.'

Two minutes later she heard a gentle snore. She should do the same. Considering the heavy day, how early she had woken the previous morning, she should collapse with exhaustion...

She drifted off, and found to her surprise that she was back home and standing in front of the television set. Suddenly she felt herself being drawn forward, moving through the screen, parting the glass as easily as if it was butter. At the same time she heard alien voices. They were so peculiarly inhuman it was impossible to have heard them before and not remembered their tone and timbre. And making it worse, they were calling, 'Coooomme, Didi. Didi, coooomme...'

Their frosty notes, like crystal drops of a stalactite petrified by aeons of time, enveloped her in a sort of protective shell. Frozen, unable to twitch a muscle, she felt herself become buoyant, lighter than air, begin moving swiftly up, then out beyond the planets and the stars. Passing through oceans of space in an eyeblink, she witnessed asteroids, unknown planets, other suns. Lights grew, flashed brilliantly before her eyes before fading away to infinitesimal specks, then nothing, blackness, a void.

After a while she began to slow down. There it was. The star looming up in front. Something told her this was her destination. Blue fires millions of kilometres high leapt into space in a fanfare of welcome. The star grew bigger and bigger.

114

She started to spin, falling, plummeting in ever-decreasing circles. She was heading towards the centre of the ball of blue fire.

Thoroughly terrified, she jolted herself awake.

After that she was too frightened to close her eyes. Staring wide-eyed into the dark, she trembled. For a moment she would have sworn black and blue, even on a Bible, that the nightmare was real. And she wondered, if she hadn't woken at that precise moment, what would have happened? Would she have survived the plunge into those cobalt fires? Would the alien voices have answered her questions, explained why she and Jamie had been brought here? Or if this was just a dream, admittedly more explicit than most, what on earth did it mean?

In the dark and poky little room at the back of number fifty-four she relived it again and again. Some of the details didn't surprise her. Like being back home, and the television set doing weird things. But those icy voices... Even the memory of the frozen tones raised goose bumps on her flesh. Who they were and where they were from she couldn't imagine. Desperately frightened, she considered waking Jamie, then didn't dare. She had promised to let him sleep. It was a nightmare, she told herself, but her body stayed rigid, her eyes remained open. As she listened to the sound of Jamie's even breathing, she was very, very scared.

She remembered the ring sending out its strange beam of light. The horrid sensation that someone was exploring the inside of her head. Lying possum-quiet, she twisted the ring around and around her finger and prayed that Jamie would wake.

Eventually, she began to feel calmer. She was terrified but unhurt. Whoever, whatever had induced the nightmare had done little harm. Gradually, gradually, she began thinking of other things, allowed her mind to drift over the last few days.

At that quiet time when only honesty will do, Didi admitted to herself that these last couple of days were the happiest she had known since leaving Sydney. For the first time she had a purpose, even if it was only getting home. But what fun it could be to stay on, she told herself. Not unlike being on vacation.

Grown up, that's what had happened to her. Not because she and Jamie were having the sort of experience that doesn't happen except in fiction, but because everyone treated her as if she was older, maybe seventeen or eighteen. She had a job, a husband, even if he was only a pretend one. Everybody here treated her as if she was an adult. What a change from the family. No one here told her she was juvenile, lumpy and awkward. At the same time she thought it would be nice to visit home, tell Jane and Tom she was fine. But she supposed Tom would make his usual witty comment and she'd feel childish and stupid.

Good she and Jamie were liking each other. She would tell him about the nightmare in the morning, but for now she must get to sleep. Count sheep. One, two, three... ten... twenty-five... forty-six... One hundred and forty-three had a face like old Bent. Yuck! Think of Sam and Selma. 'Once we've got some money together, our only problems will be little ones.' How pathetic. Hope they're right. They deserve all the luck in the world.

She tossed and turned, trying to get comfortable. Jamie cried out, protested, but didn't waken. How long would it take Sam and Selma to save for a home? Sam was saying they wanted her to be their bridesmaid, but as she was married she couldn't. She was reminding Sam she wasn't really, and she supposed she could, when someone was knocking on their door.

9. HOW MANY LANGUAGES CAN YOU SPEAK?

DIDI STAGGERED OUT of bed and opened the door.

'Try these on,' Selma commanded, handing over a pillow-slip filled with clothes. 'They're Rachel's. We think you're about her size.'

Who was Rachel? Didi recalled the mother and daughter who occupied the largest room on their floor, the room that would, one day, be Tom and Jane's. 'Hey, that's awfully nice of you,' she cried, but Selma was already half-way down the stairs.

Didi took out the first article. A petticoat, edged with cotton lace and finished with a white satin ribbon. A chill ran down her spine. Wasn't this the same garment Tom had found in the trunk? A little less crumpled it's true, but still the same. She held it up to her face. The stink of naphthalene wasn't there. Instead there was a faint scent of lavender.

Jamie was in the bathroom, so, with the whole room to herself, Didi emptied the pillow-slip on the bed to examine each piece. The nightdress looked exactly the same, with pink flowers on white background, narrow white ribbon at the neck and wrists. Then the underwear. Three pairs of baggy cotton underpants, one chemise top threaded with pink satin, four thickish flesh-coloured cotton stockings and the cotton laced petticoat.

117

And here was the black jumper and matching skirt which, she knew, flared nicely around her calves.

'Jamie, this is the stuff Dad and I found in the trunk!' Didi exclaimed as Jamie returned. She stared at the clothes. The navy dress with the beaded bodice was missing. A curious bulge made her turn the pillow-slip inside out. A mystery item appeared, something the size of her art folder at school. Made from shiny flesh-coloured satin, with two steel pieces for stiffening. Hooks, eyes and pink cotton laces hung from two sides, and off the third dangled some little rubber eyes with metal clips as fasteners.

'It's a corset,' she explained to Jamie. 'It's meant to make you look skinny and hold up stockings.'

'It looks pretty uncomfortable to me.' He eyed it doubtfully.

'Can you believe it?' She threw the corset on to the bed. 'You reckon they're telling me something?'

'Don't be an idiot. They haven't invented pantyhose as yet. Besides,' he added appeasingly, 'you've got a good body, even if you are a bit on the short side.'

'It's OK for you,' she interrupted. 'Nobody's going around saying you look a mess.'

'Aren't you being a bit rough? I'll bet all the women wear them. Anyway, seeing me in jeans, they probably think every guy in America wears denim. Like in westerns. You know, cowboys and Indians...' He exploded with laughter. After a while she joined in. 'Tell yourself we're wearing fancy dress. Want a gig at Sam's shirt?' He held it out. 'Look, the collar's pure cardboard.'

'But I haven't a clue how to put this on.' She looked up to see if he was listening, and saw him pacing up and down. 'Hey, what's up?'

He wheeled about. 'Don't you think it's weird that this is the same gear?'

'Doesn't it mean,' she spoke slowly. 'Doesn't it mean that we'll get back for sure? I mean, someone must have hidden all this stuff. Later on, after I wore it.'

'How do you know?'

'Because of that awful smell.'

'What if it's exactly the opposite?'

She tilted her head to one side. 'Like what? I don't know what you mean.'

'You're not being very logical.' He sounded very critical.

'OK, OK,' she bristled. 'So you come up with something sensible.'

'Most old things get musty smells. You'd already found those clothes. That's in our past. It doesn't tell us we get back to the future.' And because she still looked puzzled, he added, 'You found this gear *before* we got back, not after. Right?' She nodded. 'So it's all happened already. All this proves is that we come from the future, not that we ever get back. Besides,' he added grimly, 'because we can't explain what happened to us in the first place, there's no way we can work out our next step. I reckon we're stuck. Let's face it, we haven't a clue how to get home.' He looked very tired.

Didi was suddenly reminded of her nightmare and her heart gave a nasty jolt. How could she have forgotten? The clothes. The clothes had banished everything else from her mind.

She would tell him later. When things were calmer. 'I guess,' she said, 'it's no weirder than all the other things that have happened to us. Look, I've got to get into this gear.'

While she struggled with the clothes, he slipped away to the kitchen. By the time she put on the corset, hooked on the flesh-coloured stockings and rushed downstairs, breakfast was almost over. But Mrs Finkelstein complimented her on

119

her appearance and later, hurrying towards Foys, she caught sight in a shop window of a slim, sophisticated lady of at least seventeen or eighteen. Her cat's eyes gleamed with satisfaction.

'You'll have to spend some of your first week's pay on decent shoes,' Selma ordered as they walked up the back stairs of Foys. Peering down at her battered joggers, Didi meekly agreed.

On his arrival, Mr Bent directed her into the same routine as the day before. Didi suspected that working for him, her schedule would remain for ever unchanged. Her morning was spent brewing pots of strong tea, adding three heaped teaspoons of sugar to each cup. 'You'd think it'd sweeten him up,' she whispered fiercely to Selma. Between times, she stood behind the girls at the big desk, watched them writing dockets and counting change. Her legs ached, but she didn't complain. If Mr Bent ordered her to relieve someone and she didn't learn fast, there'd be trouble.

Standing first on one, then the other leg, she learnt there were twelve pence to a shilling, twenty shillings to a pound. A guinea was twenty-one shillings. It was very complex. No wonder decimal currency would one day be introduced. Yet she nodded politely when Madge said, 'Nobody in Australia would ever want to use dollars. Not like you do in America.'

Precisely at twelve forty-five she and Selma marched up to the steps of the public library. It was a perfect spring day. The sun shone from a cloudless sky and a pleasant breeze fanned anyone picnicking on the grass. In the bright light of day her nightmare seemed just that, a bad dream, and better forgotten. Munching their sandwiches, the girls amused themselves by making up stories about the office clerks and typists hurrying by. The forty-five minutes passed in a flash.

In the afternoon Didi carried messages from Mr Bent to the various departments. Clad in black like the other employees, she blended in easily. Yesterday's disapproving looks were forgotten. Even the floor manager with the mouth like a draw-string purse managed a wintry smile. Because the day was less tiring, that evening she took a greater interest in their fellow boarders.

Although Mrs Finkelstein cooked regularly for a dozen people, Friday nights were special. A starched white cloth was laid out on the scrubbed pine table, heavy cutlery brought out by the family from the Old Country gleamed invitingly. A pair of lit candles set in embossed silver candlesticks decorated the centre of the table, together with a bottle of wine and a plaited eggbread. This was the Sabbath. Although, as Selma explained, the Finkelsteins could not by any means be called Orthodox, they liked to maintain this tradition.

Didi's previous religious experiences were limited. Once Tom and Jane had taken her and Kate to a Christmas service at the local Unitarian Church. A young friend of Jane's got engaged and the Falconer family attended the wedding and the subsequent Christening. During Didi's Grade Two year a pastor paid monthly visits to her class. They sang songs and he told them stories from the New Testament. As far as Didi was concerned religion, like Aussie Rules, aerobics or windsurfing, were for other people. She squinted anxiously at Selma. 'Does this mean we eat a special meal?'

This innocent question made Selma pounce. 'Don't you know? I thought Jamie came from a Jewish family? Isn't he related to Sam?'

Didi thought quickly. 'Yes, he is, but I'm not.'

This answer seemed to satisfy. For Didi's benefit Selma listed, 'We'll have soup with home-made noodles, chopped liver, sweet-and-sour fishballs, baked brisket with roast potatoes, carrot pie, fruit compote and almond macaroons.'

'Fine.' Didi kept her face impassive. 'What's for everybody else?' Selma giggled and the awkward moment passed without fuss.

Just after six, the Finkelstein's lodgers began trickling into the kitchen. Mr Finkelstein directed people to their seats and Didi numbered off those present. There was the family of course. This included Sam. She and Jamie made six. Seated directly opposite was Rachel, whose wild, coppery hair drained all colour from her face. And her mother, Mrs Bruns, who blew cigarette smoke at her fellow lodgers if their conversation ever drifted into English.

Didi felt sorry for Rachel. The same age as herself, Rachel never dared backchat or argue. Rather, she sat quiet as a mouse, blended into the background as far as possible, never offered an opinion on anything. Didi wondered what went on in Rachel's head. She couldn't imagine being mothered by someone whose face powder turned brown from the number of cigarettes she smoked. Even in her unhappiest moments Didi loved Jane dearly, and admired her smart appearance.

As for having no father. Didi had to concede that the little she saw of Tom was better than nothing at all. So she made a special point of thanking Rachel for the clothes. Used simple words to get her message across. Gesticulated wildly. At her last school there were Vietnamese, Cambodian, Turkish kids with no English. Thinking she understood what living in a new country was about, Didi went out of her way to get Rachel to talk. In spite of these efforts, Rachel refused to say anything but, 'My pleasure,' and stared shyly at the tablecloth until Didi left her alone.

Didi turned her attention to Sonia. Slicked black hair combed smooth, the parting white and severe, eyebrows

122

plucked to a thin, thin line, Sonia was very 'soignee,' to quote Selma, in matching sky-blue skirt and shirt, an ivory cameo at her neck. Sonia told Didi she 'finished' clothes in a small factory.

'What exactly do you do?'

'I make the coat lining. This we attach under the arms here,' Sonia pointed to her own shirt, 'and I sew up, like so,' she showed Didi the hem of her skirt.

Apart from the more formal apparel Jane insisted she wear whenever the Falconers went out collectively, Didi adored clothes. Wishing for the hundreth time that she had Kate's proportions (Kate managed to look good in a canvas bag) she peered intently at the fine stitching. 'Oh, that's great,' she blurted. 'Neater than anything our Husqvarna can do.' Jamie kicked her under the table. Didi blushed. Too late.

'A machine is invented for this?' Sonia's English deteriorated when she was upset. 'Now I earn pennies. Soon, I'll have no work. What does it cost to keep a machine?' And from that moment she picked disconsolately at her food, refusing to join in any conversation.

Fortunately, Mr Finkelstein called out, 'A bit tastier than cocky's joy, eh, young lady?' They were half-way through the soup.

'Goodness, Ben,' Yankel spluttered, 'you expect these Yanks to know what cocky's joy is?'

Mr Finklestein settled down to explain. 'Cocky's joy is a mixture of boiled wheat and treacle,' he began in a solemn voice. 'It keeps poor farmers and their families alive.'

'Sometimes,' Sam interrupted, 'to give a little flavour, they throw in an underground chicken.'

'Underground chicken?' Jamie chuckled. 'I know what underground chicken is. That's rabbit.'

'Yes, rabbit.' But Sam wasn't laughing. 'Many city folk were forced to the country when they lost their jobs. To survive, all you need is a gun.'

'But this year things are much better,' cried Mrs Finkelstein as she placed heaped bowls of vegetables on the table. 'You know, one summer three years ago, we had so little food Ben borrowed a street barrow. He knocked on people's doors, trying to sell them bananas.'

'But no one else had any money,' her husband continued, 'so I brought them home and we ate them ourselves. They'd gone soft and brown from the heat. For days we ate nothing but those rotten bananas.'

To Didi's astonishment everyone rocked with laughter.

Sam overrode the mirth. 'Yet there are thousands of people on the roads still homeless, still living in squatters' camps, worse than pigs. And our landlords get richer every year.'

Didi was startled. 'I thought everyone suffered equally in a depression?'

'Only the poor,' Sam cried angrily. 'The landlords make a great deal of money buying up cheap property. And our government supports them.'

Mrs Finkelstein was becoming increasingly distressed. 'That's enough of your socialist ideas, Sam Cohen,' she growled. 'Keep politics away from my dinner table. Times are much better. With all your big talk you'll wish it on us again.'

Their fellow diners had heard this before. Everyone began calling out and taking sides, as if a fight between Mrs Finkelstein and Sam was an expected performance. Only the music prevented a general free-for-all.

Apart from Sam, Didi thought Yankel was the most interesting of the male lodgers. The moment the argument looked about to take over, a smile appeared on his benign round face and he began to sing, his strong baritone filling the kitchen with Polish, Russian and Hebrew music. The other lodgers took this so calmly Didi understood it to be a weekly event.

After listening intently for two minutes, Jamie produced his harmonica and began accompanying Yankel, using the instrument to harmonise with the melodies. More voices joined in.

'Sam, you've brought us a fine musician, a very fine musician indeed.' Mr Finkelstein's cry could be heard over the general din of plates, cutlery and loud voices. Something like 'Rojsinkes und Mandlen' was begun, yet Didi couldn't be sure. Yankel was singing, 'Mayim, Mayim'. Selma said this meant 'water, water,' without mentioning in which language, before dashing off to help her mother serve up the next course.

Mrs Finkelstein loaded the table with plates of thickly sliced brisket covered in a rich brown gravy. She began protesting when Yankel, in fine voice, began a new verse.

'What's more important, food for the body or food for the soul?' Yankel demanded. After preventing the last fight, he seemed to hanker for one of his own. As he and Mrs Finkelstein started bickering, the others helped themselves to the main course, piling plates high with beef and vegetables. Yes, times were considerably improved. Even Sam agreed. And Yankel was left to finish his song alone, a chorus of chewing mouths his only accompaniment.

As they sat waiting for the dessert, Sam and Mr Finkelstein began singing an unusual melody. Didi's ears pricked up. 'What's that song?' she asked.

'Otchi chornya, "Dark Eyes". It's a Russian folk song.'

'Yes, a love song,' Sam said looking pointedly at Selma who fluttered her eyelashes in return.

Mrs Finkelstein sniffed. Her face set in disapproving lines. 'My Selma is too young to worry with such nonsense.'

Selma reddened with annoyance. Sam stage whispered, 'The old girl hates me being involved with politics. She wouldn't talk like that if I was wealthy.'

'Poor Selma,' said Jamie voicing Didi's thoughts. 'Can't be much fun for her, stuck between you two.'

Didi watched Sam turn a deaf ear. Interesting how Sam never heard criticism. How would he cope with Tom's sharp tongue? She wondered if Sam could teach her to be less sensitive. As he began humming another song, Mrs Finkelstein looked thunderously around the table and everyone, even the newcomers, held their breath.

It was Mr Finkelstein who averted this new crisis. Soothing his scarlet-faced wife, he promised, 'After a glass of tea, we'll have a singsong around the piano.'

'We're very musical,' said Joe.

Over the resultant catcalls, Yankel cried, 'I could use a few decent musicians to drown out this lot.'

In the next break, Jamie asked Joe what language he was speaking.

'That was Yiddish.'

'Do you always speak Yiddish?'

'Sometimes we talk Polish or Russian.'

'Can everybody here speak four languages?'.

Joe pointed to Mrs Bruns. 'She speaks German and Spanish as well. That makes six.'

'Only the English we don't speak,' Mr Finkelstein interrupted. 'It's impossible for us. The 'th' we cannot say.' He rolled his tongue into a peculiar click. 'But for you,' he bowed in Didi's direction, 'we make the big effort!'

There was a third lodger whose name Didi never did catch. A weedy fellow whose moustache had the old-fashioned waxed ends worn three decades earlier. He fled from the kitchen as soon as they finished eating.

'Last week,' Sam chuckled, 'I offered to introduce him to a nice girl. Since then, he can't get away fast enough.' They were completing their meal with the odd habit of sipping tea through pieces of loaf sugar clenched firmly between the teeth.

Joe asked Sam, 'Any more trouble at work?'

'You mean George?' Sam shook his head. 'Not really. He had a go at Jamie. He's quite a lad. '

'George has some powerful mates,' Joe explained to Jamie and Didi. 'They call themselves the New Guard. They're ex-soldiers, mainly from New South Wales, but we've a few crackpots down here in Victoria.' He watched Sam and Yankel as he talked. 'They're not too different from Hitler's National Socialists in Germany, or Mussolini in Italy and Mosley in England.'

Sam returned Joe's stare with interest. Turning to Jamie, he called, 'Surely you've heard of the Fascists?'

Jamie blinked nervously. He half turned towards Didi before framing a careful reply. 'Well yes, we do have... '

'No, I don't agree,' Joe interrupted. 'They're not the same thing at all. George and his friends are just thugs. The New Guard are Great War veterans who are scared of a communist takeover. They hate the Reds and want law and order.'

'Is that why De Groot beat Lang to the Grand Opening? You call that keeping law and order?'

Didi was finding all this too hard to follow. She whispered in Selma's ear, 'What's Sam talking about?'

'De Groot...'

Didi held up her hand. 'Who's De Groot?'

'De Groot's an army officer,' Joe explained, 'and Lang's the Premier of New South Wales.'

Selma said, 'De Groot doesn't like Lang's politics. He thinks he's a Bolshie. At the ceremony for the opening of the Sydney Harbour Bridge, Lang was supposed to cut a special ribbon before people walked over the bridge. De Groot rode up on his horse and cut the ribbon himself. Last year in Australia it was a very big scandal, but I don't suppose you heard about it in America.'

'Maybe these two can tell us if Roosevelt's New Deal will improve things?' Joe looked expectantly at Jamie.

Jamie gulped. He was saved by Sam crying, 'And what about Germany? There's hardly anything in the newspapers, but the wireless tells me thousands of people come to listen to Herr Hitler. Since he came to power this January, he's been holding huge rallies, hundreds of thousands of people come to hear him speak. Now he's got rid of his opposition and outlawed the other political parties, he tells people the Depression is all we Jews' fault. As we are the World's Bankers we must own all the money, and this, naturally, gives him a right to take it away.' With this he helped himself to a macaroon.

'Well,' said Mrs Finkelstein emphatically, 'we can't have this sort of thing happening here. If he came to Melbourne he'd be very sorry.'

Someone laughed rather raucously. 'Ouch!' Didi rubbed her shin. The kick was an extra reminder from Jamie to shut up. No one heard. Sam, as a peace offering, was congratulating Mrs Finkelstein on the first-class quality of her macaroons, saying he hadn't eaten better anywhere. With such extravagant compliments Mrs Finkelstein found it hard to stay huffy. Nodding her head, she showed some slight forgiveness for his troublesome tongue, and interest in her daughter.

Joe wouldn't stop talking about George. 'Perhaps a few of us ought to get together, warn him off?'

'Thanks for the offer,' Sam said quietly. 'If he or his friends cause any trouble we'll be ready for them, won't we Yankel? Jamie?' They nodded. There was enough menace in the atmosphere to make Didi wriggle uncomfortably.

'Not here.' Behind Sonia's tired voice were centuries of persecution. 'We don't need this here. We ran away from that. My aunt was murdered by the Cossacks. I saw, with my very own eyes, I saw how they terrify a village, try to burn it down.' The light in the room seemed to dim as faces turned apprehensive.

Determined things stay on a happier note, Sam cried, 'Hey Joe! Someone told me about a dead cert cure for baldness.'

Joe's face lit up. 'What is it?'

'You take a cow pat and some blackberries, mix them together...' Even Joe joined in the laughter. The mood lightened, everyone began making puns, telling what Didi considered to be rather wet jokes.

'Do you know what the girl driver said to the constable after her number plate fell off?' Mr Finkelstein asked. He's like a small boy, she thought, but nice. She shook her head.

'She said it didn't matter, 'cos she already knew it.'

Didi giggled. 'That's the worst joke I've ever heard.' From his pleased look she gathered this was a compliment. Collectively they were as pleasant a group as one would meet anywhere, Didi and Jamie later agreed in the privacy of their own room. For the present Mrs Finkelstein and Selma washed the heavy plates, placing them on the jarrah bench for Didi and Rachel to dry. Then everyone flocked into the front room which the Finkelsteins used as a combined office, living-room and bedroom, to crowd around the piano by the bay windows.

Most of what they heard was folk-song. Although she didn't understand the words, Didi hummed along when the melody was easy to follow. Jamie's ability to play anything he heard riveted everyone's attention. With Yankel accompanying, vamping it up on the piano, he interspersed the old melodies with configurations and rhythms of his own, giving the music quite unexpected twists. Mr Finkelstein murmured. 'I've never heard the harmonica played like that. Who'd have thought it possible?'

When people tired of singing, they urged Jamie to play alone. He chose a sixties musical, *Fiddler on the Roof,* and without saying what it was, wove his own intricate harmonies into the melodic line. The tunes modulated from one key to another and the melodies turned themselves inside-out and upside-down. Slow waves of movement contrasted with faster dances and Slavic rhythms fused with Eastern tonalities.

Sam mused, 'Strange. I feel I know this music, yet I've never heard it before.'

'It's based on old Jewish folk-songs,' Jamie told him. To add a little variety to the evening, he sat at the piano and, playing a Bach two-part invention and fugue, wove some jazzy rhythms into the fugue.

'Definitely. He must come to the Kadimah. Sunday night,' Yankel insisted. 'The audience will love him. I predict he will be a great success.'

'What's the Kadimah?' Didi asked.

Joe explained. 'It's a Yiddish theatre in Lygon Street.'

Yankel snorted disdainfully. 'Nonsense. It's much more than a theatre.'

'That's true!' Joe's face and head were glistening with excitement. 'We go there to hear interesting speakers, watch plays, films.'

'Do only Jewish people go?'

Sam shook his head vehemently. 'Heavens, no. Anyone in Melbourne who's interested in the arts comes along. It's the place to go on Sunday nights. You must come. Jamie will play, and the audience will adore him.'

Didi glowed with pleasure for Jamie.

'You sure wowed them,' she told him once they were back in their little room. 'They think you're a mixture of Mozart, Elton John and Sting.'

He grinned wickedly. 'Aren't I?'

'You're not bad,' she conceded. Then, remembering her previous night's experience, she sighed. She had to tell him. Even though she didn't want to, even though telling him would destroy their happy mood.

To her relief, rather than dismissing it as a nightmare, which was what she had really expected, Jamie listened carefully. He had lots of questions. He wanted to know exactly what the voices sounded like. What did it feel like being frozen? Drifting through space? Where might that blue star be? Could she remember exactly what it looked like? He asked so many questions she began to wonder if he suspected her experience was real. She wriggled uncomfortably. Nearly twenty-four hours later, she doubted it herself. 'You know,' she said feebly, 'it only lasted a few seconds. I'm sure it was a nightmare.'

'Well, we got here in a flash. I guess that to whatever brought us here, travelling through space is no big deal.'

'You reckon I really did travel through space?' Didi's eyes opened very wide. As the idea slowly sank in, she muttered, 'Bloody hell.'

Jamie said, 'You must have been terrified.' She dumbly agreed. To make them feel better, he played some of her favourite songs by Stevie Wonder, Rick Astley's 'When Ever You Need Somebody' and Pink Floyd's 'The Dark Side of the Moon'. He leaned against the bedhead as he played and watched her face lose its tenseness and her fears gradually dissipate.

131

She wasn't stunning to look at. Not like Kate. Not with the sort of appearance which compelled one to stop and admire. As he thought about Kate, an ache vibrated through his body. He put the thought away and concentrated hard on Didi. It hadn't taken long to see she was a tabby. Those slanted green eyes set too far apart, the pointy chin, the snub nose. She had, even in the way she moved her sturdy body and strong legs, a curious feline quality. He didn't mind those unsheathed claws. They were Didi. Wanting her different was useless, like expecting a canary not to chirp, a dog not to bark. It was her nature to be prickly and stand-offish one minute, warm and good company the next. Tabbies were like that.

He played some oddly different songs he'd written himself, the melodies using achromatic scales, the rhythms faintly Indian. The evening's combination of good food, wine, company and music lulled him into a sort of content. This, in spite of them being here, the curious coincidence of the clothes, the terror of Didi's dream...

Later, before dozing off, Didi remembered she hadn't asked him about his day. Most people needed hundreds of words to say what they felt, then found them inadequate. Jamie spoke about himself through his music. She knew, from the way he belted out those songs, that in spite of all the strange happenings, he was enjoying this stay.

As for herself, nothing could have altered her as much as this. In addition, she and Jamie were becoming mates, even if there wasn't the same closeness she and Helene shared in Sydney. But, she wistfully remembered, that relationship had taken ten years to solidify. She sighed at the thought. Maturing three years in as many days was plain hard work.

She knew their friendship could never have happened at home. There were obvious restrictions. He was older, Kate's boyfriend, part of Kate's new crowd. Not that it would have crossed her mind, but if Didi had thought of getting to know him as a personal friend, she would have been told to, 'Piss off. Stop being a pest around here. Go find your own friends.' On no account must she forget that she was Kate's little sister. She recalled the premonition when they met, the feeling she was meeting up with an old friend. A sixth sense had known Jamie was important, but who would have dreamt that it would be in such a bizarre way?

In the empty corridor outside the Finkelstein's bedroom a clock sounded midnight. By the fifth chime Didi was fast asleep.

And it was Saturday.

10. It's All A Mistake

THE FOLLOWING EVENING Sam, Jamie, Selma and Didi set off for Wirth's Circus. As neither Didi nor Jamie had any actual cash, Jamie accepted Sam's kind offer of a loan of six shillings to cover their expenses.

They caught the cable-tram to the city and strolled the rest of the way arm in arm. The October night was balmy, almost like summer, and their voices rang out above the clatter of trams and the chugging of cars. Aware of how much Selma liked to gossip, and how much she knew about the other lodgers, Didi asked where everyone worked. Selma was only too happy to fill her in. 'Rachel's apprenticed to a milliner in Collins Street. This fellow is so smart, you wouldn't believe.'

'Smart, smart,' Sam snorted. 'In Australia you don't have to be a genius to get on.'

'So?' Selma glared at him. 'Then how did he manage to keep his workroom intact right through the Depression? What about the others who went broke?'

Sam glared right back. 'No wonder he does well. With an artist like Rachel working for him, he must be making a fortune.' He turned towards Didi. 'Rachel sews exquisitely. All her feelings go into her work.'

Selma nodded enthusiastically. 'Wait. Wait until we get

home. I'll show you her work. It's wonderful. She beaded a dress for me with flowers. They're so beautiful.'

'She really is an artist,' Sam interrupted, 'just like a painter.'

'She should be working in Paris. For a big designer.'

'Her beaded hibiscus look better than the real thing.'

Didi's ears pricked up, but Selma was already on to something new. 'A pity the others weren't as lucky.' At Didi's enquiring glance, she explained, 'Joe and Yankel migrated to Geelong to work in a textile factory. When it went broke they came back to Melbourne.'

'In the long run they've been just as fortunate,' Sam cried impatiently. 'Now Yankel has a stall at the market and Joe helps out. They're building up a good business selling material, buttons and laces to the public.'

With the circus lights beckoning them to come closer, they tracked across the grass to Wirth's Park. Selma and Didi stopped near the ticket box. There, they read a conspicuously displayed billboard,

WIRTH'S CIRCUS - GALA OPENING NIGHT.

'It's far too early for the performance,' said Sam. 'Let's take a look at the sideshows.'

Already the grassed area surrounding the circus was packed tight with people. Men and women in their very best clothes were queuing up in front of the ticket box. Lines began forming in front of the tents of the fat lady and the five-legged, two-headed sheep. One family's children had already bought red, green and blue balloons from a white-faced clown. Others were persuading reluctant parents to buy.

The area outside Madame Zara's cubicle was still empty. Suddenly Didi felt an overpowering urge. It came on her quite abruptly, as if an unknown bystander had leapt from the crowd and was forcing her to the ground. Impossible to

135

ignore, the urge was pushing her towards the fortune-teller's tent. What's more, it refused to let go.

She rushed over to Sam and Selma and pointed to the sign. 'I think I'll try her.'

'You can't believe this fortune-telling rubbish?' Sam was very disapproving. 'It's most unscientific.'

'Actually,' Didi tried to explain, 'I really don't believe in fortune-tellers, but I have this strange feeling.'

Sam's voice was cold. 'I've no time for superstitions! No time at all. There's enough real horror in our world without these impostors creating imaginary ones. The fortune-teller's real name is May Broderick. She's a broken-down acrobat who can't get up on the wires any more. What do you think she's going to tell you?'

His irritation only made Didi more insistent. Whatever, whoever was commanding her wasn't letting go. If anything, the urge was getting stronger. How to explain she had little choice? She said faintly, 'All the same, I'm going to try her out,' and, ignoring Sam's incredulous expression, she tapped at the main pole which served in lieu of a front door.

'Come in.' An everyday kind of voice, and Didi, wondering what else she could have expected, stepped inside. The front of the tent had been partitioned off. She was in a dimly lit cubicle. At the back was a table, on it a glass ball shaped like an inverted fish bowl. Seated at the rear was a figure so heavily wrapped in scarves it was impossible to tell what sex it was. All she could see was the tip of a red nose and a pair of watery eyes.

Madame Zara's opening remark was unexpected. 'Atchoo!'

Didi nearly jumped out of her skin. 'Cross my palm with silver and I'll tell your fortune,' Madame Zara snuffled. Well, that's what Didi thought she said, but the poor

136

woman's nose was so blocked she was difficult to understand.

Didi placed sixpence on Madame Zara's palm. Like feeling the skin of a baked fish, she thought, hot and dry and scaly. Madame Zara sneezed again. Didi felt very sorry for her.

Madame Zara made Didi wait while she wiped her nose on one of the many scarves about her neck. She coughed twice. Only then did she intone: '*I can see you're very lucky... you'll get married to a doctor and have three children and...*'

Stopping in midstream, she paused to examine Didi's palm. Closing her eyes she began to sway; backwards and forwards, forwards and backwards. The movements became stronger and stronger until, before Didi could get up, run away, or call for help, Madame Zara was in a trance. Exactly as if she'd been injected with a powerful, fast-working drug.

Then, in the sort of voice one would describe as perfectly normal, without a trace of cold in it, Madame Zara cried, 'There's the lad as well. I need to see him. Where's the boy? Bring him to me.' Muttering fiercely, swaying so vigorously Didi thought she might fall and hurt herself, she made unintelligible noises which were curious rather than frightening.

How did she know Jamie was outside? Apprehension fluttered down Didi's spine and settled in her stomach. She began to tremble.

Then, in a voice as clear as any CD, Madame Zara cried, 'Warning. Warning. An error has occurred. You are instructed to neutralise error. Return at once to your own time.'

Didi rose from her narrow stool and stood gaping. Then, recollecting where she was, she raced outside to where the others were waiting and grabbed Jamie's arm. 'She knows all about us. That you're with me. She says she's got to see you too.' Shoving his lanky frame past an astonished Selma and Sam, she pulled him into the tent. Once inside the front flap, she whispered, 'She says we've got to go back. Straight away!'

'What on earth are you talking about?' he said irritably. She shushed him quiet.

Madame Zara's eyes remained closed. Huddled uncomfortably on one stool, they waited to hear her out. The minutes drifted slowly by. Didi felt Jamie becoming more and more restless. As he turned to her to whisper he was going, Madame Zara moved imperceptibly. Eyelids fluttered open. Tiny pinpoints of blackness, her pupils bored into their very souls.

'Warning. Warning. An error has been made,' she said. It wasn't so much what she said but the way it was spoken. It was terrifying to listen to such a different sound, to hear the alien tones from Didi's dream emerge from Madame Zara's mouth. The real fortune-teller had disappeared. Her soul or spirit, call it what you like, seemed taken over by something inhuman. They might have been eavesdropping on a clever computer or synthesiser. The sound mimicked something that should be flesh and blood yet wasn't. Listening to the strange utterance, Jamie turned the colour of parchment and Didi, remembering the other, earlier voices, began shivering. Awake, the sound was so much worse. To listen to such vacancy of tone, to such discordance of pitch, was to imagine the void beyond all time and matter, to feel the utter coldness of eternity, to remind them that they were no more than a speckle of dust in time's eye.

The Voice continued talking. Iciness beyond conception. 'It is dangerous to stay. You must return.'

138

'That's all very well...' In spite of the bile rising into his throat, the sour taste in his mouth, Jamie still attempted to explain. 'The thing is, we don't know *how* to get home. We could certainly do with some help.'

Madame Zara's eyelids closed down and cut off Jamie's statement as effectively as a jammed transmitter. When they reopened, her gaze fixed unblinkingly on him. He swallowed and fell silent. 'There has been an error,' Madame Zara continued as if nothing Jamie said had penetrated. 'This time warp is terminal. Return or stay for ever. Our instructions are to neutralise error.'

Her hunched body resembled a bundle of rags, a scarecrow. She repeated softly, 'This time warp is terminal. Return or stay for ever. Cancel error.'

Though they tried their hardest to follow, the effort was useless. They frowned and squinted into the gloom where Madame Zara crouched. It seemed fanciful, though they later agreed it did happen. Madame Zara's body seemed to fade, her outlines became indistinct, transparent. They could see right through her to the torn canvas at her rear.

'Please, do tell us what we should do to get home,' Jamie cried, terrified she would disappear completely before they got the necessary information.

'We don't know how to get back,' Didi cried. 'Please tell us how to go home.'

Madame Zara opened her eyes. Her body grew more substantial. Blank eyes stared through them with such a farseeing gaze they were convinced she saw to the ends of the universe. Gradually, they found themselves drowning in her black pupils, being sucked into an eddy, turning, spinning, whirling... Their bodies were frozen, packaged, moving upwards, then out towards the stars. Like last time, Didi found she was swirling about in limitless space, then heading towards an icy star with raging blue fires. Dizzy almost beyond belief, she held out her arm to stop herself from falling, and banged into the table.

Madame Zara's eyes closed immediately. Didi and Jamie were back in the dimly lit cubicle. 'Return or stay for ever.' The Voice was becoming indistinct. 'Neutralise error. Film. Music. They must sychronise. This warp is terminal. Return or stay for ever. Ring must be left behind to cancel error. Combine film and music.'

Then the oddest thing of all happened.

'Youwillbeverywealthyandhappyandlivealonglife...' Madame Zara's eyes opened. Didi saw they were red and watery. Sitting before them, waiting expectantly for their response, was a middle-aged woman with a very bad cold.

At first, all Didi could say was, 'Are you all right? You sound really sick.' As for herself, she felt as if she was recovering from a bad illness. Twitching all over as when she'd had a bad flu, she looked at Jamie who rarely felt the cold, and saw he was very, very pale and convulsed by a fit of shivering.

'Was it all right, lovey?' Madame Zara pulled her scarf away to expose broken, stained teeth. 'I must have dozed off there a moment.' Sounding a little embarrassed, she asked anxiously, 'Did you like your future? Can't say I remember what I said. That happens to me these days. Sometimes... I'm getting a bit forgetful.' She waited expectantly for them to thank her and leave.

Instead, Jamie grabbed her by the arm. 'What was that all about?' he demanded.

Well and truly frightened, Madame Zara wrenched out of his grasp. 'I don't know what you're talking about,' she cried. 'I never say anything to hurt. It's just a bit of fun,' she insisted. 'What on earth are you on about?'

And that was all they could get out of her.

11. ROLL UP, ROLL UP!

THEY CAME STUMBLING out of the tent, blinking against the harsh light.

'What happened?' Didi cried. 'What was that all about?'

Jamie turned on her. 'For Christ's sake,' he whispered savagely, 'do shut up. Sam'll guess something's up.'

'Yes, but...'

She stopped short as Selma came over and took her arm. 'You've been in there for hours,' she complained. 'What on earth was she saying?'

'She said I'd marry a doctor and have three kids.' Didi tried hard to sound casual. 'And she said that when Jamie's older, he'd be very wealthy.'

Selma snorted in disbelief. 'Then Jamie'd better get a medical degree quick smart.'

'Perhaps she thinks we'll get divorced and I'll marry someone else?'

'Good Lord.' Selma's smile vanished. 'Only wealthy people get divorced. Then the newspapers write them up. You wouldn't like it one bit.'

Sam came over to demand, 'So, what took so long?' When told, he nodded. 'Told you she was a fraud.'

'Don't we get to see the fat lady and the five-legged sheep?' Jamie interrupted. 'I thought you were keen.'

'We've no time for anything else,' Sam complained. 'If you still want a decent view we'd better get moving.'

Scowling irritably, Jamie shrugged his shoulders and walked away. At the same time he prayed Sam hadn't noticed anything odd.

He needn't have worried. It had taken years to acquire the blank expression he used in the theatre-of-war his family called home. He wasn't perturbed about himself, rather his concern was how Didi would cope. The sooner Sam and Selma were inside, distracted by the show, the better off they would be. Besides, he needed time to figure things out.

One thing was obvious. The Voice was the most frightening sensation he'd ever experienced, and that included their arrival here. He didn't question its authenticity. What he had seen in Madame Zara's tent was too chilling, both literally and figuratively, for that to be necessary.

Worrying over who sent the message or the exact location of the blue star was in the end, irrelevant. Either they got home as fast as possible or they could expect heaps of trouble. He shivered. Even Sam's handknit woollen socks didn't stop the cold induced by the Voice biting his toes.

Determined things appear normal, he pulled the harmonica out of his back pocket with his frozen fingers and four shaky bars of 'Ain't Misbehavin'' emerged.

They pushed their way through the crowd gathering around the ticket booth. A sign read, ADMISSION: 2/-. 3/-. 4/-. 5/-.

Didi had time to pull herself together as Sam, never one to stand on ceremony, walked straight to the head of the queue. His brash manner attracted the usual disapproval.

'Some people,' barked a bald-headed man with a large moustache. Rather like a seal missing out on a big fish, Didi thought.

Other voices chastised Sam with, 'Here, what do you think you're doing?'

'Go to the back of the queue!'

'Bugger off, mate!'

Ignoring the comments, Sam bought four two-shilling seats. Then, smiling expansively as if they were the best in the house, led the others inside.

Once they were there, after falling over people's feet, muttering 'sorry' and 'pardon' and 'excuse me', they climbed to the top of the wooden forms. Though starting time was still fifteen minutes away, the Hippodrome was chock-a-block, full as any modern rock concert. In a crowd of over two thousand people, family groups predominated. Men in high-crowned hats and darkish jackets, women in their finest millinery, matching gloves and coats. Those children lucky enough to be seated close to the ring waved Union Jacks. Boys carrying boxes strapped to their shoulders clambered over seats selling sweets and ice-cream. Programmes fluttered expectantly. The combined smells of sawdust, greasepaint, animal and human sweat made a heady perfume that would be hard to forget.

The strong lights above the ring were switched on and the Panatrope produced a contorted version of Paul Whiteman's band playing 'The Merry Widow Waltz'. Jamie winced. But discordant and amateurish as it seemed, it cast some unexpected glamour over the shabby old building.

Sam had hustled for seats with a good view, both of the ring and the trapeze wires. In spite of their splendid position, Didi found it hard to concentrate on her surroundings. Much as she would have liked to dismiss Madame Zara as so much hogwash, the fortune-teller's confusion was real, terrifyingly so. Or she was the most amazing actress Didi had ever come across. And that icy voice, the extraordinary feeling of spinning into space,

143

seeing the cold fires of that blue star. Interesting how she could easily accept that contradiction, a fire that burnt both hot and cold. What she would make of it later on, she didn't know, but for the present the experience felt very real, very scary. *'Cancel error,'* the Voice had said. *'Or stay for ever.'* Not words to easily dismiss.

How unfair it was.

Not as if it had been their decision to come to 'thirty-three. Nor that they weren't trying their hardest to get home. And now this. Anyway, what had the Voice meant by, *'Synchronise the film and the music. The ring must be left behind to cancel error'?* Glancing down at her hand, she saw the sapphire gleam under the strong circus lights.

And if one accepted that Madame Zara was merely the messenger, who or what was talking to them? And where was that icy star with its fierce blue fires? Although she was listening politely to Selma's chatter, Didi struggled to find answers to these questions and noted that Jamie was equally preoccupied.

Selma noticed nothing. She rattled on. About how the women were dressed, what the programme promised, how she was looking forward to the performance. Meanwhile, Didi tried rubbing life into her frozen fingers. Then it struck her that the whole thing might be a piece of trickery, a clever deception. What proof did they have that anything had taken place? She had once read how through suggestion, hypnosis could freeze someone as efficiently as walking through the Antarctic. Then, remembering her dream, the terrible sound of the Voice, once heard never forgotten, she knew it was real. Enough that on an overly warm October night both she and Jamie were chilled to the marrow, neither daring to touch the others for fear of the comments this might bring.

Silent and frozen, as much from fear as anything else, icy

144

fingers digging deep into their pockets, they watched the lights dim. The background music grew loud, took on a martial note. An expectant hush heralded the Grand Parade led by the ringmaster himself, Mr Philip Wirth, clad in black tie, tails and shiny top hat, and cracking a long whip. Right behind stalked the elephants. As they lumbered round and round the ring their trainers, turbanned and jewelled, turned blank faces on the world. The clapping grew. Then came the horses, hung with elaborate harnessing, tails intertwined in long ribbons, their young riders dressed in spangles and tights. Later on they would perform outstanding equestrian feats. For now the audience was captured by the Shetland ponies and their prankish jockeys, the monkeys.

At long last, the acrobats arrived. Clad in brief leotards, performing double and triple somersaults, they ran alongside the ponies, held out spangled cloaks, bowed elaborately.

There was a roar of delight. The applause grew deafening. Finally, gambolling about like naughty puppies, white-faced with red-gashed mouths, turning somersaults, hitting each other in mock savagery, calling out to the children, came the clowns.

Their arrival jolted Jamie from his chilled lassitude. 'Look,' his voice rose above the din. 'Look. There's Donald Smithers and his friends.' Didi made a mighty effort. They waved, cheered and clapped and the show had begun.

The first half of the show was devoted to Captain Eric Flyger. Inside a metal cage placed in the centre of the ring, he set about demonstrating his skill with wild animals. To begin with there was a great deal of noisy whipcracking. Eventually, a huge brown bear was persuaded to pose in certain unlikely positions.

Didi was horrified. 'How degrading for that poor animal,'

she protested. But watching the bear climb to the top of a ladder, then slip smoothly down a slide, quietened her down.

Sam announced, 'One night Flyger was attacked by a bear.'

Selma shrank into her seat.

Jamie grinned, waiting to be amused. 'What happened?'

'It was a polar bear.' Sam was too busy teasing Selma to notice his neighbours' glares. 'This bear escaped from the centre cage and got into the ring. It took Flyger three and three-quarter hours to get him back inside.' Speculating on the difficulties, Sam nodded appreciatively. 'Flyger says he'd rather tame a hundred lions than one bear.' After that, Jamie and Didi watched the rest of the act with far greater respect.

'Clever fellow, isn't he? He learnt about animals working as a keeper in zoos.' Sam shouted.

Wondering if Sam honestly believed their neighbours enjoyed these titbits, Jamie intercepted a ferocious scowl from a lady seated in front. In spite, or perhaps because of the contrast with the earlier part of the evening, he started giggling, and ended up out of control. The more people turned and stared, the more he laughed and spluttered. The sound became so infectious that, in the end, Sam and Didi added their guffaws to his.

Their neighbours became savage. 'Sshh!' and 'Bloody foreigners!' In spite of the loud discordant music the words were surprisingly clear. Selma, who in all this time hadn't twitched a facial muscle, went quite white.

'Silly old cow.' Sam's voice rang out clearly. Didi thought him very brave. The woman in front was fiercer than any animal in the ring.

It took some time for things to calm down.

Because Jamie had described the horses in some detail, Didi was keen to see the equestrian acts. A drill performed

146

by the six Brumbies displayed some clever riding from young Philip Wirth and his sister Gladys. Miss Gladys jumped on to a horse as it cantered round and round the ring. Leaping back to the ground as the horse kept moving, Gladys ran, vaulted, stood bareback and tossed kisses to an ecstatic audience. For Didi, the small figure of Gladys was the first half's most memorable act.

'Just look at that...'

A pretty girl, billed as Freda Elroy, contorting herself on top of a big globe, resembled an upside-down U. 'She looks like she doesn't have a proper bone in her body,' Selma cried. 'She's brilliant. The best act they've got.'

Sam liked to disagree. 'Actually, my favourite act is the elephants. One time, the circus was travelling by ship to Sydney. One of the engineers on board decided to play a joke on an elephant and gave it an orange stuffed with pepper. After he swallowed it the poor chap made so much noise he frightened the other animals and there was a huge row. It took the circus hands ages to settle things down.'

A born story-teller, Sam knew when a pause in the right place helped his audience appreciate a situation.

'Everybody forgot the incident. A few weeks later the circus was returning to Melbourne and the same engineer was on board. He passed by the elephant who picked him up with his trunk and tried to throw him overboard.'

'Serves him right,' Didi cried. 'Fancy being so cruel.'

'All the same, if there'd been no rigging on the side of the ship to catch him, he would've died.' Sam's story finished rather lamely as it was interval break and they were pushing their way through the crowd, heading towards the dressing-rooms.

'Come on, hurry up,' Jamie urged Selma. She had stopped to apologise to a lady for tripping over her feet. 'We've got twenty minutes before the second half starts.'

147

He led the girls to Donald Smithers' room. They found him about to plunge a sewing needle into his costume. He held up a bleeding finger for Jamie to view. Then, catching sight of the girls, he sprang to his feet and clicked his heels together. 'Miss Finkelstein, Mrs Major. Charmed, I'm sure.' Draping a towel around his waist, bowing as if he was at a formal party, he dusted a metal trunk with his costume and invited them to sit down.

Jamie looked around. 'Where's Miss Violet? We didn't see her tonight.'

'She's got the flu.' Donald's big head wobbled sadly. 'She's very sick. Imagine, too sick to get out of bed for tonight's performance.' From his concerned tone Jamie realised Miss Violet must be very ill indeed. As far as circus folk are concerned, the show must always go on.

'When I saw her this morning, she seemed fine,' Jamie murmured, half to himself. 'I really wanted Selma and Didi to meet her.' After a warning of such impending disaster it was a minor disappointment, yet he would have liked Didi to have met the miniscule artiste, felt her flamboyant personality.

Despite his air of confidence, Donald was no less worried. He gave Jamie a shrewd glance, sensed there was something wrong, wondered what it was. 'There's a terrible flu about. Let's hope no one else catches it.'

Jamie's head shook dispiritedly. So preoccupied was he, Donald's comment didn't register. Only when Didi said, 'Madame Zara's pretty sick, isn't she?' did it cross his mind to connect the fortune-teller's weakened state with the Voice's message.

Then, like Didi earlier on, it occurred to him to wonder if they had been fooled. Or had Madame Zara's sick condition, in some peculiar kind of way, triggered off things more easily explained with better information?

148

The thought lifted his spirits. There's a reason for everything, he decided. Even a spooky voice. The important thing was not getting downcast, not letting themselves believe they were caged by an unknown, unpredictable master. Instinctively, he knew that their greatest danger lay in giving in.

'I can turn cartwheels, make children laugh, but darning's got me beat,' Donald was complaining.

As she listened to the high, penetrating sound of his rapid chatter, Didi felt her head begin to spin. Donald picked up a pair of shiny white overalls, part of the clown outfit. Didi noticed that one of the leg seams was torn.

'Give it to me. I'll sew it together in a jiffy,' she said, looking about for needle and thread.

Jamie blinked. 'You never said you could sew.'

'Can't you tell they've been married a short time?' Selma carolled. Forced to join in the laughter, Jamie silently cursed his own slip.

It took Didi less than five minutes to complete the seam with neat strong stitches. But then, how could Jamie know that at her high school in North Sydney, the textiles teacher Ms Holdsworth, had been one of her favourite people? And that Didi and Helene spent many a wet lunch hour helping out in the sewing room?

When she handed back the costume, Donald behaved as if she had made him a new outfit. 'Come and work here the rest of the season. We never get anyone decent for these jobs.'

'A full-time job mending costumes?' Sam said incredulously. 'Surely not.'

'Oh, there's plenty of other jobs about,' Donald laughed. 'Plenty of unfinished work round a circus.'

Didi shook her head. 'How I'd love it. But your season ends on the twenty-second of next month. If I give up the

Foy's job,' she shrugged sadly, 'I'd have trouble finding more work.'

While Selma smiled at her good sense, Jamie just stared. Did she really believe they would be staying on? After tonight, he was convinced more than ever, that they needed to find a way home. Fast.

Disappointed, Donald cried, 'Let me know if you change your mind.' Before they left he made Jamie promise to bring Didi to tea one afternoon, calling, 'Bring that harmonica of yours as well.'

They reached their seats just as the lights began to dim. The second half of the programme featured the Seven Nelson Troupe. Sam was pointing out the young acrobat, Jim, to the girls as the loudspeaker announced, 'The Seven Nelsons will now perform without their safety nets.' The music came to an abrupt stop. Drums rolled imperiously. A slight figure in blue-spangled tights shinnied up the rope to catch the trapeze where he somersaulted three times through the air and was caught on the farthest wall by two partners.

The worst effects of the evening having worn off, exhausted yet absorbed by the performance, Didi was impressed enough to forget where she was.

'Shit,' she cried, 'that was terrific!' And, in one of those dreadful silences which can happen even in the densest of crowds, the words wafted clearly across the seats. Some of the audience, those previously glaring at Sam, stared even more disapprovingly. Selma went scarlet and peered down at her hands.

Jamie looked at Selma and chuckled, embarrassing her even further. Hadn't she heard that word before? Jamie found he liked shocking these folk. They were all so proper. Except for Sam, everyone tried so hard to be dignified. Now Didi had broken their rules. He wished she'd break more. As transients, blow-ins on 'thirty-three, he was fed up with minding all he said and did.

'Give 'em hell,' he whispered to Didi, wondering how come he'd let some silly fortune-teller with a scary voice frighten him half to death.

12. REVELATIONS

AFTER THE FINALE, while the audience was still clapping furiously, they left via a door which took them past the Garrick Theatre where Coral Browne was performing in *Children in Uniform*.

'Let's go there next Saturday,' Sam suggested casually, as if their going out together was an established event. 'I enjoy a good play.'

'What's it about?' Jamie asked.

'The Fascists. You know, the death of democracy in Germany.'

Sensing a political discussion, Selma quickly changed the subject. 'We must try to save our money for Cup Day. The circus usually has a special performance for the Melbourne Cup,' she told Didi. 'Mr Wirth presents the winning jockey with a gold-mounted whip. We always try to be there. This year I'm putting my money on Everything Coming.'

It was easy to divert Sam. 'Then you'll be wasting it,' he cried, his dark eyes glowing with confidence. 'Hall Mark's going to win. You wait and see.'

'I suppose you think he's another Phar Lap?'

Sam's face fell. 'No horse could ever be as good as Phar Lap.'

'All I know,' interrupted Jamie in his best pretend-to-be-gloomy voice, 'is that I'm expected to work that night. Ferguson's asked me to take the evening shift.'

In one of her strange turn-abouts, Selma cried, 'Just thank your stars you've a job at all. Things could be as bad here as they are in the rest of the world.'

Suddenly, as if their interruption had been timed, four men dressed in dark shirts and coats came stumbling down the street, laughing and talking noisily amongst themselves. An overpowering smell of beer lingered about them.

They didn't acknowledge the two couples until they were almost on top. 'It's them Jews. From the circus.' And there, grinning nastily, was George.

Securely surrounded by his friends, he swaggered in front of Sam. 'My oath. What a cocky little bugger. Get in our way would you? How about me mates teachin' you a lesson?'

'What sort you reckon on teaching?' Jamie stepped out to protect Sam. From then on things happened too quickly to know who threw the first punch.

Within seconds, both Sam and Jamie were lying on the footpath with four men on top. And Selma, her voice shrill with fear, was screaming, 'Help, help. Someone help!'

Didi pushed her into a doorway. From there she uttered sporadic whimpers. These four men were bigger, more experienced at street fighting, but Jamie was giving two of them a bad time. So Didi ran, stumbling and falling, to help Sam. She jumped on to the men's backs, pushed, scratched and savaged them, trying to free him. Her weight almost useless, she was thrown off, and she landed on her knees, scraping one badly. Crawling along the pavement, she reached up, pulled at their jackets, yelled in the general area of their faces. The men pinning Sam to the ground took no notice. One reached over and, as casually as

153

brushing off an insect, pushed her away. She tore her coat as she fell and banged an elbow on the pavement. An agonising twinge, like an electric shock, ran up her arm.

Rasping breaths, the thump of flesh striking flesh, sounded clearly in the still night. Caught beneath two thugs, Sam didn't stand a chance. If only she could see his face. But they were on top. Instead she pummelled someone's arm, and hoped it wasn't his. Another arm struck out. She dodged, and wished she could see a little better.

They were getting the worst of the fight when she heard the sound of running feet, a cry of 'Stop... Hey, there. Stop. Break it up!' Heading towards them were two men in high-buttoned coats and helmets. Shrill whistles pierced the dark.

The thugs disappeared into the dark and left Didi and Sam sprawled alongside each other in the gutter.

'Thank you, officer.' Sam staggered up and began brushing mud from his clothes. 'They would've killed us if you hadn't turned up.'

From the tight looks on the policemen's faces it was obvious they weren't convinced. The shorter policeman began firing warnings as to what they could expect if ever caught disturbing the peace again. Meanwhile, licking a pencil, his tongue purpling like a lizard's, the taller policeman slowly and painstakingly took down their particulars. Sam, followed by Jamie, then Selma, spelt out their names and addresses. By the time Didi gave the same street name as the others, the policemen were looking so disgusted she was sure they would be locked up for the night.

It was Sam who finally convinced the police it was perfectly proper for all four to be living at fifty-four Mavis Road. 'It's a lodging house. In Carlton. The Finkelsteins

154

have only the best people as boarders,' he explained, forcing a semblance of gentility on to his dark foreign-looking face.

'Hmmmm.' The policeman placed his book in his jacket pocket. 'If these girls are as respectable as you say, you're to take them straight home, do y' hear? You've no right to be putting them in danger.'

Sam nearly lost his temper. 'But we didn't start anything.' A warning look from Jamie shut him up. The police were totally disinterested. Turning, they walked slowly up Aitkins street and disappeared into the dark. Selma's bitter comment later on was, 'They'd have taken the larrikins' side if they'd had the sense to hang round.'

With the police no longer there, Sam exploded. 'Fancy being blamed for that brawl,' he cried. 'I'm not going any further without a cup of tea.'

They walked along deserted city streets, their shoes clicking noisily on bluestoned lanes. Nothing stirred, until a shrill cry made Didi's heart jump. It was a stray cat protesting at the sound of their footsteps. They searched everywhere for an open cafe.

'Come on Sammy, let's go home,' Selma pleaded. At that moment Jamie caught sight of a small fish and chip shop, its door open and inviting. Tired and upset, they huddled inside for warmth, sat alongside a greasy bar sipping sweet milky tea, comfortable in the company of a few burly wharfies.

'We've got to start using our noggins.' For once Sam was serious. 'Next time we won't be so lucky.' He patted Didi's shoulder. 'That was very brave of you, Didi. I don't know too many other girls who would've joined in that scramble.'

'It was nothing. I didn't do much at all,' she said awkwardly. 'I've been meaning to take Tae-kwan-do lessons

155

for ages. They pushed me right off, you know.' But she reddened with pleasure at his praise.

'Tae-kwan-do? Women in America must be keen fighters.' All trace of cockiness had vanished from Sam's voice. 'You have so many different ways of doing things. So,' he reached into his pocket and produced a small gold coin which he flicked into the air, 'perhaps you can explain this.' He threw the coin unexpectedly at Jamie, who caught it, then he leaned over to take it back.

'You have some very strange money in America,' he said, handing the coin to Selma. 'Do read what it says.'

'One dollar. Australia. Nineteen eighty-eight,' Selma read, then stared at Jamie, her mouth open.

'And whose head is it?'

'A woman,' Selma scarcely dared draw breath. She held the coin up to the light. 'There's a woman wearing a crown. It says, Elizabeth the Second.'

In the bright light Sam's head seemed very square, very pugnacious. Didi swallowed nervously, but all Sam did was slip the coin into his pocket. 'I think you two have some explaining to do!' His voice was pleasant but firm. Jamie and Didi nodded. After the previous events of this evening, confessing would be a relief.

Three more cups of milky tea and still they sat on. The wharfies had left long before. 'I'm closing in five minutes,' the owner warned, wiping his bar with a greasy cloth.

'Come on, we've missed the last tram home.' Selma picked up her coat and gloves. 'Let's start walking.'

'I could sleep for days,' Didi sighed as they drifted out into the cold dark night.

'What I find amazing,' Jamie said, 'is that you believe us. You find our story credible.'

'We didn't dare say anything,' Didi added. 'We thought you'd think we were balmy, lock us away.'

'I collect coins,' Sam shrugged, 'so, the first thing I did was look. Then the rest fell into place.'

Jamie laughed. He laughed for a very long time. When he eventually stopped, he cried, 'You mean you knew all the time?'

'Of course.'

'How?' Didi demanded. 'How did you know?'

'The clothes you were wearing, the way you spoke. Your watch.' Jamie laughed ruefully. 'Also,' Sam reddened, 'you didn't strike me as a couple enough in love to run away together,' he added rather apologetically.

Didi grinned. 'I guess not. When we arrived here, we barely knew each other.'

'You're not Sam's cousin?' Selma asked. Jamie shook his head. Selma looked very disappointed. 'And I suppose you're not Jewish, either,' she added sadly.

'Grandma Molly used to say she had a Jewish grandfather on her mother's side,' Didi said hoping this would do. From the look on Selma's face she knew it wouldn't.

'And you really aren't married?' Selma went pink. 'To think, you've only had that tiny bed to sleep on.'

Jamie, more relieved than he could ever have believed possible, cut through her embarrassment. 'Sam and Selma, we need your help. If the fortune-teller's right, we must leave right away.'

'Of course.' Sam reacted as if this was the most natural thing in the world. 'Only, one thing.'

'What?'

'Well, two things really.' Sam ticked them off. 'First, I'd like to check King's Theatre for myself, see how things are, and second...' he paused. Didi frowned. What would he want? Waiting for his answer she heard an owl hoot ghoulishly in the dark recesses of the cemetery and the wind's bony fingers rustle the branches of the trees. She shivered violently. Someone had laid a shroud of reponsibility about her shoulders and it felt heavy and unwanted.

'In return,' Sam continued, 'I would like you to tell us something about the future. It seems a good businessman could use this information very well.'

They agreed. On the way home Jamie described areas of Melbourne which would escalate in value in the next half century, related bits and pieces of carefully edited information, such as when the Second World War would begin and end. There were inventions like plastic, television, microchips and computers to describe. Nuclear power, supersonic jets, men travelling to the moon, communication satellites...

Some of this Sam and Selma could scarcely believe. 'You mean one machine can complete a whole week's work in an hour?' Sam asked incredulously.

'I'd love to own a film machine,' Selma sighed with longing.

'Actually, tellie's coming soon,' Didi said, having recently completed an asssignment on this topic. 'It'll be invented in England, in a few years time.'

Sam scoffed at the idea. 'I wouldn't bother with one of those. I'd get fed up with watching. Think of the time we'd waste. But machines for housework, that will wash dishes, dry clothes, cook food in minutes? All our drudgery will disappear.' His swarthy face shone with approval.

'Most of this won't happen till I'm over seventy,' Selma cried sadly. 'I'll be an old lady when we next meet. If we ever do.'

This thought made her so miserable, Didi tried cheering

her up. 'Migrants will come to this country from every single continent in the world,' she promised. 'We've become a very multi-cultural nation.' But Selma didn't seem to appreciate this one bit. Instead, she was far more interested in the fashions of the future and began questioning Didi very closely on what her mother and Kate wore.

After a while Sam said doubtfully, 'You tell us about all the good things we can expect. What about the bad? Wouldn't we be better off being prepared?'

'Perhaps you should be bringing your family across from Europe,' Didi began, when a kick landed viciously on her shins. She yelped, before catching sight of Jamie's face. He looked furious. So she mumbled, 'Oh, I reckon we've told you most of it. Look, I'm terribly cold and tired. Could we hurry home?'

When they fell into bed, around four a.m., Jamie was grateful he'd fooled round in history classes. Given a choice, there was a lot about the second half of this century he'd rather forget. Nevertheless he sighed loudly when he heard sobbing from the other end of the bed. 'What is it this time?' he asked patiently.

'Why did you stop me? You're so unfeeling. Millions and millions of people are going to die in the next fifty years. You could prevent it. How will you live with that for the rest of your life?'

Jamie squinted at her in astonishment. 'What are you talking about?'

'The war, of course. Do you realise we're the only people in the world who know what's going to happen, and you stopped me warning Sam. If we tried really hard maybe we could prevent it.'

159

'What makes you think they'd listen? They'd be more likely to think we're nuts.'

'How do you know?'

'What about concentration camps, Hiroshima, Vietnam, Chernobyl, the Middle East?' he said dryly. 'You reckon anyone in their right mind would believe those will happen?'

She shook her head. But saying is one thing, feeling another.

'I know this sounds dead selfish but I honestly don't see what we can do. If we try and change things we'll never ever get home. Maybe that's what the Voice meant by saying it's dangerous here.' He pulled the blankets up with a jerk, and his toes stuck out near her face.

'We could warn people. Stop the war starting...'

He shook his head. 'It's too late. It's much too late.'

'What on earth are you talking about?' She propped her head on her arm and stared, honestly mystified. 'This is only nineteen thirty-three. There are six years to go before 'thirty-nine. Six years is a helluva long time.'

He groaned. 'It's beginning to happen right now. Can't you see? The whole catastrophe started ages ago. The Depression, all the things that led to it. They set it off. You can see that, can't you?' She blew her nose and he added glumly, 'You know, I reckon history's like a steam train. It chuffs along, but if you and I try and stop it, there'll be a collision, bigger than the one we know is coming.'

She shook her head. 'I can't believe our being here is accidental. What if we were sent on purpose, maybe to stop things happening?'

'You make it sound as if being here is logical,' he said irritably. 'I can't believe that. People always want reasons, want things to be clear cut. They're not happy unless black's black and white's white. What if there's no reason

160

at all for us to be here except an alien made a mistake? Like the Voice said?'

And he pushed his point home. 'I got over those sorts of expectations years ago. Life's all about luck.' He darted a look her way. 'Like being born into the right family!'

'Luck brought us here?'

'Well,' he shrugged, 'whatever it was, I'm sure we're not here on purpose.'

'You reckon anyone else could have landed here?'

'Probably. As I said, it's a matter of luck. Coincidence. You and me being in a particular place at a time when everything was right to bring us here.'

She glowered at him. 'What about your parents splitting up? Did you think that being born in the wrong sort of family was coincidence?'

Instead of getting hurt and angry, as she thought he might, all he did was laugh. 'Sometimes.'

She smiled, but her smile was quavery. 'I sure know what you mean. Sometimes I wish I was someone else. Do you ever feel like that?'

'Sure.'

'Like when?'

'Well... like the time my dad nearly killed my mum!'

'You're kidding!'

'Wish I was.' Her shocked face amused him. 'I nearly got the cops. Had to knock Dad out to stop him. It only happened once. Mostly they were very polite. Case history of a marriage. Weapon, politeness. Result, instant death.' His voice turned savage. 'They simply didn't talk. You know,' he added, 'one time they didn't speak to each other for months. And no one ever knew about it. Except me.'

'Hell.' She thought this through. 'How did they manage to share the house?'

'They sent notes to each other. Through me.'

161

'What about your sister?'

'Oh, Linda's smart. She'd got out long before.'

'Must have been fun.' She propped up her head to stare at him. 'Want to talk about it?'

'Not really. I'm only telling you 'cos it stopped me for ever from wanting to take on other people's problems. It's a thankless task, let me tell you. Anyway, I've enough problems of my own. Haven't you?'

'Yeah. I suppose so. All the same, maybe we could warn Sam, just a little?'

'There's no such thing.' He sounded adamant. 'You get in boots and all. Take whatever crap's served out, or keep your nose clean.'

She sighed resignedly. 'I suppose so. All the same, I feel guilty. I keep thinking we should be out there, warning everybody, stopping it all from happening.'

He glared at her. 'Didi Falconer,' he snapped. 'You're plain ridiculous. How can you, personally, prevent everything that's going to happen this next half century? You reckon you can stop it by yourself? Who are you kidding?'

There was silence. 'It's been a long day,' he said at last. 'We've got too much to worry about. Go on, get some sleep!'

'We should think it over. Let's talk more. Maybe tomorrow?'

'Sure, sure. Sure thing.'

'Hey,' he said, as she settled herself for sleep. ' I think you'd better sleep alongside me. We might be more comfortable.'

It was much later, as she began drifting off, that she remembered he hadn't mentioned the trunk, nor its contents, to Sam. And she wondered why not?

13. She'll Be Apples

AFTER A CRAMPED night on their tiny bed, they woke to a fine spring morning.

Didi felt warm and relaxed. The horridness of George and his friends, the fearfulness of the Voice were distant and remote. Lying ever so quietly, she watched budding branches wave about in the breeze, their shadows flicker on the ceiling above her head. It was hard to believe that in their own decade, over half a century in the future, those same trees were losing their autumn leaves.

Already up, Jamie was pulling on his jeans. 'Sam and me, we're off to check out King's Theatre.'

Didi propped on her elbows. 'Can I come too?'

Jamie shook his head. 'Sam wants to suss out the staff, check out their movements. I reckon it's easier with less people. Maybe we can sneak in.'

Didi pictured the projectionist's booth, shelves packed tight with canisters, hundreds of reels of film. She shuddered. 'I guess they have to leave the place sometime,' she said. 'It's Sunday. Things round here shut on Sundays.'

'That's why Sam wants to do it today.' Jamie worked at sounding confident.

'Is he planning a break-in?'

He wouldn't answer this directly. 'The place should be empty today.' Jamie buttoned up his shirt. 'Any other time's too dangerous. If the projectionist, or that bloke in the ice-cream suit, sees you and me again, they'll call the cops. The last thing we want is someone getting windy.'

She agreed, but a detail had nagged her all night. 'How do you know Sam won't tell anyone about us?'

He slid into his jacket. 'I'm surer of Sam than Selma. You know how she loves a gossip.'

'Like you said last night, we'd be real freaks, wouldn't we?' She panicked for a moment, but when Jamie left she forgot everything, gloried instead in being alone. Working her way across the bed, she stretched and stretched as far as she could go.

She was tired, tireder than she had ever been. Apart from last night's excitement, she had worked much of the previous week. Saturday too. No wonder she was worn out. People here worked long hours, yet she heard few complaints. Happiest when occupied, her new friends hadn't come to question what they did. After a depression she supposed, it was enough to know a meal was coming, have warm clothes to wear and a roof over one's head. And she had to admit they knew how to enjoy themselves, even if some of their ways were different.

What bliss it was being idle. Lying there, yawning, stretching her arms and legs like a kitten, she totted up the hours of her working week. Plus Saturday morning, they came to forty-nine. Hard to believe that a week ago she was someone else. Didi Falconer, schoolgirl. A shiver went down her spine. How easy life had been. And Kate, Tom and Jane? How little they had to do with her! Any chance of seeing them in the near future seemed quite remote.

Chasing the thought away, Didi decided it must be time to get up. They had stacks of dirty gear, no washing-machine or clothes dryer to help. Passing the tumbledown sheds on her way to the loo, she had seen the copper, noted that it was fuelled by wood. No point expecting Jamie, once he and Sam got back, to help. Yesterday, while helping her make their bed, he'd murmured, 'Gee, it's great being away from feminists.' Then, when she got mad, claimed he was pulling her leg.

Someone tapped at the door. 'Who's there?' She pulled on her jumper.

Selma, looking far too fresh to have been roaming city streets until four, opened the door and walked in. 'Mamma's arranged a bigger room for you and Jamie.'

Didi looked anxious. 'Hey, how much did you tell her?'

'What sort of a person do you think I am?' Selma seemed quite offended.

'You did say you wanted us to move rooms.'

'Don't be silly,' Selma sniffed. 'This tiny bed must be terrible to sleep on. Besides, I always keep my promises.'

She led Didi down the passage to their new room. One day it would become Jane's upstairs sitting-room. It presently contained two beds with high oak bedheads, two chairs covered in brown leather a little the worse for wear, a small rather ricketty table and a pretty wardrobe with candy-twist legs. From the window Didi looked out on to a patch of sparse grass, vegetables and chooks. If she stretched, made herself very tall, she could just see into their neighbour's yard. It was very quiet, very peaceful.

'Oooh,' she cried. 'This feels great.' She sank on to one of the beds in relief.

Selma remained grimfaced. 'Now, tell me the truth, Didi,' she asked in a no-nonsense voice. 'How old are you?'

There seemed little point in lying. 'Fifteen and a half. I'll be sixteen in February.'

'And you've been sleeping in that tiny bed with Jamie? Together?' Selma was outraged.

'It wasn't like that at all. I mean, he *is* Kate's boyfriend, isn't he?'

165

Selma walked to the window and peered outside to where a rooster was occupied with unmentionable activities. 'Surely,' her voice was choked up, 'surely, such talk's improper? Even in the future?'

Didi shrugged. 'Not as much as now. We talk about lots of things which you find...' she searched for the right word, 'embarrassing.'

'Does this mean women have lost all modesty?' Selma's face remained a mottled pink.

'I guess...' Didi said helplessly, 'I guess we don't think being modest as important any more. Not like you do.'

Selma blinked. Didi thought she might stalk off in disgust, but her curiosity won out. 'So, what is important?'

This was a tough one. Didi paused to consider. 'Having a decent career, being responsible for oneself.'

'What about love and marriage?'

'Oh, that's important too, but I guess it isn't as top of the list as it is here,' Didi said, annoyed to be apologising for her generation.

'So women are quite happy becoming dried up old maids,' Selma cried.

'You don't have to be married to make love,' Didi exclaimed. Why was Selma so obsessed with sex?

'What about unwanted babies? There's a girl I know who had to have an operation. She got septicaemia, nearly died.'

'Oh, is that all? We have the Pill.'

'The Pill?' Selma's eyebrows shot up. She sank on to a bed. 'What's that?'

This led to an explanation about hormones and fertility cycles. Didi was astounded at how little Selma knew about her own body. 'If you're still a virgin,' Selma demanded to know, 'how come you can tell me all this?'

'I learnt about the human life cycle at my last school.'

'At school? You learn this sort of thing at school?' Selma's voice rose so incredulously Didi felt sorry for her.

'Ahem.' she felt curiously inhibited. 'Just one thing before we go.'

'Yes?' Selma's hand was on the door handle.

'Where can I buy tampons?'

'What are tampons?' And when the question was finally understood, 'I'll get you some rags.' Selma's voice was low. 'Do you need them now?'

Didi shook her head.

'Tell me when it happens,' Selma whispered, 'and I'll bring them to you.'

'What do you mean?' Didi's voice emerged half-strangled. 'You'll bring me some rags?'

'Yes. Old sheets, pillow-slips, anything cotton. When we get the curse we rip them up for our use.'

'Yetch!' Forgetting Selma's feelings she cried, 'You mean I'll have to stuff rags between my legs? How do you get about?'

'I agree, Didi. Unfortunately, being a woman *is* very uncomfortable,' and Selma closed the topic.

Later on, telling Jamie the story, Didi said, 'Just imagine! I could have told her about gays, or PMT, or AIDS and having to use condoms.'

Jamie shook his head. It was his firm belief Selma wouldn't have known what condoms were. 'Anyway,' he added, 'by now she probably thinks our generation deserves whatever we get.'

As they moved their few things into the new bedroom, Didi talked to Selma about the revolution in women's lives.

'So,' Selma was smoothing her hair at the dressing-table mirror, 'your mother is in charge of a big office, does most of her housework and tries to be a good wife and mother.

Even with all this machinery your generation has invented, it sounds as if life's still harsh for women.'

Didi disagreed. 'But we're independent. We don't have to wait for a man to ask us out, or get married to leave home and live with a guy, or wait for a guy to buy us what we need. We've got full economic and political rights.' As she repeated the words Jane and her friends so often used, she wondered how true they were. Reviewing her parents from this safe distance, she recalled that she rarely saw Tom help. He claimed he had too much to do at the bank. Seen from Selma's perspective, Didi doubted if Jane's life was much easier than Mrs Finkelstein's, however there *was* the obligation to defend her own generation.

'Maybe it is a bit better,' Selma said dubiously, 'but it seems to me women still do too much, no matter where or when they live.' And her mother passing by with a large tin of beeswax polish seemed to back up this argument.

Didi protested weakly, 'It's not like that at all.'

But Selma had lost interest in the subject. Instead she demanded, 'Do you want me to show you how to use the copper?' Didi nodded gratefully.

They fed woodchips into the fire. When the water was warm Selma shook in Persil suds 'For a Whiter Wash', churning the witch's broth with a long stick bleached through years of boiling. As they were working Didi thought about something which was puzzling her almost as much as it did Selma.

There she was, absolutely free of her family by nearly sixty years, almost the age of consent, and sharing a small room with an attractive male. What was extraordinary about this, she supposed, was that she was doing nothing about it.

So why wasn't she?

Didi had few illusions that men did the chasing. Back in

Sydney she had watched too many girls set out to catch certain boys. And eavesdropping on the girls at St Anne's, long ago she decided they were a predatory lot.

Anyone would think she was frightened of losing her virginity. Or didn't like Jamie enough to set him in her sights. Picturing Jamie, his long legs and slim hips, his eyes the colour of the sea on a calm day, she felt herself flush. Well, that wasn't true. Her real reason for laying off was that Jamie was taken. He was, like a vacation, or tickets to a concert, booked. Jamie was Kate's. And though Didi sometimes hated Kate, often wished she lived with anyone else, it seemed rude to move in when Kate wasn't around to protect her property.

Not that Didi would be rejected. Jamie was a normal healthy male and Kate was currently inaccessible. It was Didi sharing his adventure, and his bed. Groaning softly, she threw more suds into the copper. Selma looked up from folding sheets but Didi was lost in thought.

What a waste. She liked Jamie a lot. And with their proximity, the step from friend to lover was small. Only last night she was woken by him edging her way, rubbing against her. Some instinct made her roll towards the crack between the bed and the wall. At the time she had assumed he was asleep and dreaming. But was he? If Kate discovered Didi had 'borrowed' her boyfriend, all hell would break loose. Look what had happened over the parrot earrings? No, for as long as they remained here she and Jamie would remain just good friends.

Meanwhile she should concentrate on the washing. They were barely started when Sam and Jamie returned to find the girls knee deep in dirty linen. 'Well?'

'Well what?'

'What did you find out?'

'About what?'

Didi threatened Jamie with the laundry stick. He ducked and pretended to be frightened. Then Sam came to her rescue. 'It looks as if we can get into the theatre next Sunday.'

'How do you know?'

Jamie slung his arm around Sam's shoulder. 'Here's a smart fellow,' he said. 'Do you know what happened? When we got there that bloke who sells ice-creams was mopping up from last night. I stayed outside in case he recognised me, but Sam told him that he was from the gasworks, and he was there to fix a leak.'

'On Sunday? In a theatre?' Didi was incredulous. 'And he believed you?'

'It was simple,' Sam told her. 'I said I was part of an emergency seven-day patrol to protect people from leaking pipes. Somebody had reported a funny smell coming from the back of the theatre. Then I looked about the place and said I would have to get back for more repairs.'

'So Sam asked when would be convenient and the fellow said any time but next Sunday as it was his day off and no one would be there.' Jamie smiled triumphantly. 'So that's when we'll go!'

'What if there's someone else around?'

Jamie looked apprehensive, but Sam just grinned. 'We'll think of something,' he promised. 'The place should be empty.'

'But that's only the start,' Didi cried. 'Then we have to show it. Reckon you can work the projector?' Something struck her as strange and she demanded, 'How come he believed that you were from the gasworks? You didn't have a truck or equipment to prove it.'

'I wore my work overalls and looked like I knew what I was doing.' Sam was becoming annoyed. 'Why else would I be there?'

'What if you were a burglar?'

'Whatever would give him that idea?' He was so horrified Didi didn't have the heart to tell him how this would change in the future.

'So that means,' Jamie concluded, 'we have until next Sunday to get things together.'

'I sure hope you're right,' Didi worried. 'Sure you remember that tune?'

'Stop panicking,' he said airily. 'She'll be apples.' Didi was not to know that privately, Jamie was equally anxious. Just a matter of getting into the theatre, finding the right film and running it. And bingo, there they would be, back home. Except...

Except for the squeamishness in the pit of her stomach. After dismissing the Voice as something to worry over later, her anxieties had returned. Doubly so. Icy warnings from a frozen universe. *'Neutralise error. This time warp is terminal. Return or stay for ever...'* And with this the memory of an indescribable cold, the bleakness of infinity, the memory of a distant star with cobalt fires.

They could predict so little. What if they broke in and couldn't find the film? What if they got the film rolling, Jamie played the music... and still nothing happened? They could be trapped for ever in 'thirty-three, their future ensured as their own grandparents.

As she threw pieces of underwear into the boiling water something new suggested itself, something so terrifying, her stick almost slipped into the murky depths. What guarantee was there the Voice would take them home? They could end up hunting kangaroos with the Aborigines, or in some frightening future as historical specimens?

A pulse in her head beat frantically. Surely they were better off here? At least they had set up home and friends, wouldn't starve or die of exposure.

171

I'll tell Jamie we have to stay, she thought. But right now didn't seem the right time.

Sam had vanished, not being one for 'women's work' as he put it, and taken Selma with him. To Didi's great surprise Jamie wrung out clothing as if he'd done it all his life. She mentally apologised for thinking him an MCP.

Once the clothes were boiled, they needed to be rinsed, dipped in blued water, then starched with a paste made from flour and boiling water. Finally, with everything strung on to a piece of rope hung between two branches, their underwear fluttering in the breeze, they went inside for lunch. There, they consumed huge helpings of roast mutton, baked potatoes and heavy treacle pudding.

Later Didi moaned as they lolled about the kitchen, 'I've got such an aching gut.'

'Too much heavy food,' was Selma's diagnosis. 'Come on. Let's go for a walk.' They strolled towards the Fitzroy Gardens where they collapsed on to an iron seat. They admired the spring flower display, the beds of daffodils, hyacinths and tulips. A brass band played rousing Sousa marches but Jamie, not wanting to attract any attention, resisted the urge to join in. Strolling home he took Didi's arm to help her across a road and Selma, ever vigilant, threw her a sideways glance.

'Wish I hadn't told her how old I really was,' Didi sighed. 'Now, for as long as we're here, she's going to mother me.'

What with a busy weekend, leftovers for supper, and work the next day, everyone felt flat that evening. Besides, it was one of the few Sundays nothing was playing at the Kadimah. 'We'll go next week,' Yankel promised Didi.

Didi smiled and nodded. If we're here, she thought wistfully. How confusing not to know when or where they might end up.

172

Sunday evenings, the lodgers flocked downstairs to listen to the Finkelstein's wireless. Crowding about the set they shouted the answers to a quiz show. So much snap and crackle made the questions hard to hear.

'What's a souffle?'

'Spell perspicacity.'

'How many legs does a spider have?'

'What's the name of the English cricket team's captain?'

'Douglas Jardine, Plum Warner, Harold Larwood,' Joe, Yankel and Sam screamed in unison. It took Mr Finkelstein's interest in games to sort out the right answer. The quiz show was followed by a radio adaptation of Noel Coward's *Private Lives*. Out in the street it was so quiet that Didi fancied even the wind was holding its breath. Sonia clutched her knitting to her like a lost lover. 'That was lovely,' she sighed.

'I'll bet you didn't know actors have to wear evening dress when they speak on the wireless?' Mr Finkelstein prodded Jamie's chest as he presented this interesting fact.

'Even though we never see them?'

This set Sam, Yankel and Jamie right off. 'How ridiculous!' Tears of laughter ran down their cheeks.

But Mrs Finkelstein liked things to be nice. 'Sam, your trouble is you haven't any class,' she scowled. 'Not everybody can be as prost as you!'

Sam glared at his landlady. 'What does *prost* mean?' Didi asked, amidst gales of laughter.

'Vulgar!' Selma stared defiantly at her mother and, in a very daring move, took Sam's hand and held it.

Sam was bolstered by this and his eyes narrowed. 'It takes more than clothes to make a lady.'

'Ben, tell Sam to stop arguing with me.' cried Mrs Finkelstein, managing to ignore the fact that she'd started the fight.

173

No one felt like joining in. Sonia began packing up her knitting, Joe stood up and Yankel closed the piano. Mr Finkelstein, pulling nervously at his ear, pleaded, 'Jamie, *please*, play your harmonica!'

Circus music, loud and furious. The *Poet and Peasant* overture danced next to 'Little White Lies' followed by 'La Paloma'. Gradually, Jamie built up the sound into a steady thumping blues which had everyone clapping, rocking and clicking their fingers.

A new rhythm alerted Sam. He sat up and looked knowingly at Didi. 'What's that?'

'Do you like it?' Didi whispered. 'It's real funky.'

'Funky? What's that?' His hand beat out 'Walk on the Wild Side'.

Didi giggled. 'Sexy and slow, and well, funky.'

But some of the lodgers, wriggling uncomfortably with this new syncopation, were relieved when Jamie broke into their favourite Charleston.

After Jamie and Didi had gone upstairs and were settled in their new room, Didi cried, 'I think Mrs Finkelstein's unfair. Why is she so mean to Sam?'

'She doesn't think he's good enough for Selma.'

'Why does he put up with her?'

'It's as much his fault as hers. You've seen how he baits her.'

'Still, it's rough on Selma.'

'I found out more about him. He comes from this real up-market family. They sent him to study medicine in Paris.'

'So why didn't he stay?' Perched on the bed, Didi was trying to get her curly hair to sit flatter, look less like a sea urchin's, more like Selma's.

'He was in with the socialists, got into hot water, and had to leave, pronto.'

'Oh. That's what happened to his nose. What's a socialist?'

'Someone wanting more say in running things.'

'Don't be a dag. That's democracy.'

'You're right.' His eyes twinkled and she was reminded of how good-looking he was. No wonder Kate got breathless and dithery when he was around.

'Is it something to do with communism?'

'Sort of. Socialists want everybody to share in things.'

'Oh,' she said thoughtfully. 'Sam used to be one. Selma called him a lapsed socialist.'

'Hmmm, he said something like that. Says he's fed up with failing when he tries to help other people. So he's going the other way. In the future he's going to become a big property owner.' Jamie was suddenly jolted by a memory. *'Owned half of Melbourne he did. Had an uncanny instinct where to buy property,' the pawnbroker had said.*

He was snapped back by Didi asking, 'Reckon he can?'

'Probably. He's pretty keen.'

She considered this. 'He's certainly different to anyone I know at home.'

'Oh, I don't know. My old footie coach Bob Gilligan, and my ex-piano teacher used to think along the same lines.'

'In what way?'

'They said the same sorts of things. Like you have to make the best of every opportunity that comes along.' He shrugged. 'That is, if you want to get on. They both work like fiends.'

Didi looked interested, so Jamie described these two men in some detail. In the telling she heard quite a lot about Jamie's past. About his parents' divorce, Liz's migraines, what life was like with one parent, how he worried about leaving her. When he finished she remarked,

175

'You've certainly had a lot happen to you. But I reckon you're lucky to have those oldies. All I've got is my family and these days we don't get on. There's Helene Schaeffer, of course.'

'Who's she?'

'Just my very best friend in all the world.'

'Aren't you lucky to have one.' She glanced up quickly but his smile wasn't mocking.

'Not really.' It was hard not sounding sullen. 'Not any more. Not when she's in Sydney, and I'm in Melbourne.'

'Makes it rough.' And then, wanting desperately to mention her name, he asked, 'What about Kate? Isn't Kate your friend?'

Didi looked away. 'Look,' she said earnestly. 'Kate's my sister, and your girl. I think we should lay off talking about her.'

'Maybe.' His smile was wry. 'But let's clear up one thing. Kate's a great chick, but we don't seem to be a team.'

'Oh?' she started to say. 'Could've fooled me.' But his hurt face stopped her. 'I thought you were going with Kate,' she said thoughtfully.

'Don't get me wrong,' he said hastily. 'I think Kate's great. I really do.' Then, more to his surprise than hers, it came out in a rush, 'We both want to go steady, but Kate doesn't understand I've got lots of commitments. My time's taken up with music. Know what I mean?' She looked up. To her astonishment he'd gone bright scarlet. Taking out the harmonica, 'Ain't Misbehavin' ' floated between them. *Savin' all my love for youuuu...*

'I thought we were going together?' said Kate.

'We are.' Even to himself he sounded harsh and uncompromising. 'But if you want to go to that disco, you'll have to go alone or take someone else.' He knew he was making an issue about one weekend but, he told himself, there was a principle at stake.

'I thought we were going together,' she repeated, her pretty face hardening. 'It's a bit weird you telling me to find someone else.' He watched her lips tighten, her green eyes blaze. For a minute there she looked very much like Tom.

Women! he thought, pulling on his jeans and shirt. All the same. Could never let things alone. 'We *are* going together,' he said, trying to hold his temper. 'But I already told you. The group's got a good gig Saturday nights. There's no way I can get away for a whole weekend.'

As if the whole thing was happening in slow motion, he watched her become furious. Then, naked under the sheet, she moved slightly, provocatively. He felt a fresh stirring. Did she know how much he wanted her? Ever since the previous weekend when they first met, he couldn't have enough of her. Touching, smelling, loving her. If only she wouldn't make such a fuss over a weekend.

'I don't see why you have to play every weekend.' She refused to meet his eye. 'It's not as though you're that desperate for money.'

He wanted to deny this. Wanted to admit he was squeezed for cash, needed the members of the band as mates, explain they made great music. Yet he turned away. It was the wobble in her voice which made him do up his shirt and pull on his jacket. How he hated weeping women. Because of Liz, he knew. In those last tormented months of his parents' marriage, he would lie in the next room, listen to Liz weeping with pain, feel utterly helpless.

He glared at Kate, then ducked off to the bathroom. When he emerged, Kate's kid sister, Didi, was sitting in the family-room.

'Hey,' she called, 'could you fix this tellie for me...?'

177

The harmonica repeated, *Savin' all my love for you...* It happened every time he found a new girl. No one understood how his time wasn't his own. Once you started with a chick she thought she owned you. Only this time, he told himself in a sudden burst of honesty, he was really keen. Somehow, Kate had managed to get right under his skin. And now he was blabbing to Didi. How pathetic.

Didi sighed wistfully and changed the subject. 'Which bed do you want?'

'I don't care,' he said easily. 'You choose.' While he experimented with reggae rhythms, Didi recalled her morning's conversation with Selma. In the end she summed it up with, 'I've decided they're hung up over sex.'

'It's probably more fun that way.'

They both giggled. When the light was out, Jamie said, 'By the way, Sam asked me what your name really is?'

For once Didi didn't mind. 'It's Eurydice. Jane and Tom conceived me on a tour of the Greek islands. When I was born Kate was two and a bit and it was too hard for her to pronounce, so she called me Didi. Pathetic, isn't it?'

'I don't know.' He turned off the light. 'I rather like it.' In the dark he told her more about his trip to the theatre with Sam. In return she mentioned her anxieties, and instead of pooh-poohing them as she half expected, he conceded they were real, for wasn't he having similar ones himself?

'So, we need to decide whether we stay here or we take a gamble on getting home,' was his summing up.

By now it was very late. He sounded tired, despondent. There was a long period of silence, so she knew he had dozed off. Knowing that tonight she could stretch out as much as she liked, she immediately fell asleep.

14. FIRED!

IT WAS A typical Monday morning. Grey, wet and depressing.

From the beginning nothing went right. First Didi woke with a hangover, as if they'd spent the weekend painting the town red and were now expected to suffer for it.

Then their tram was late. She and Selma ran like mad once they got off, almost missing the eight-forty start and a morning's pay. Mr Bent was in an evil mood. Foul, even for someone so normally bad-tempered. Madge, down with flu, had phoned to say she would be absent. Mr Bent saw any girl taking a day off as a personal affront.

'Miss Major!' Standing in front of his desk, she watched his eyes dart suspiciously around the room. 'You'll replace Miss Buxton during her lunch break.'

Could she handle pounds, shillings and pence? She brewed several cups of tea, delivered old Bent's messages around the store and worried. By the time she got back, she decided she probably couldn't.

Outside, the rain was coming down in a ceaseless monotone. Instead of their usual walk to the library, Didi and Selma ate their sandwiches in the tiny airless cloakroom. By the time she sat at the console, Didi was as nervous and irritable as an old cat.

179

At first things went smoothly. 'We're short on pound notes,' Mr Bent instructed, checking every move. 'Try and work around.' She nodded. Showed she understood. The first containers were easy to handle. A five-pound note needed change for four pounds eleven and sixpence. She sent back eight shillings and sixpence. Then came two ten-pound notes and one five-pound note for an article costing twenty-one guineas. Working out the sum on paper, she inserted three pounds nineteen shillings into the canister and remembered to add the receipt. Old Bent gave a sour congratulatory cough.

Didi breathed loudly and relaxed. That's when the trouble started.

Possibly it was a stroke of bad luck. Mr Bent had left her momentarily to check a badly written docket and Betty, whom Didi was relieving, was due back from lunch any minute. Didi was sent a five-pound note for one grey cardigan, which cost three pounds, four shillings and threepence.

Not trusting her mental arithmetic, she wrote it down. The change was one pound, fifteen shillings and ninepence. Rechecking, carefully placing the money in the canister, she sent it up the tube. It drew breath warily. Came a pause. Expelling air with a sigh, a note shot back. 'Ten shillings short,' it said. The handwriting was spidery and curlicued.

'I sent *three* ten-shilling notes, *two* two-shilling coins, *one* shilling, *one* sixpence and *three* pennies,' she replied.

The container returned, its tone peremptory, 'Kindly check your balance. You sent us two ten-shilling notes. Where is the third?'

Just then Mr Bent returned. 'What's this, Miss Major?' He picked up the notes.

'They've made a mistake,' Didi mumbled, wishing he'd

leave her to sort things out with the spidery handwriting at the other end.

'What do you mean, *they've* made a mistake?' Mr Bent's voice was icy.

'They're absolute idiots down there,' Didi snapped.

The atmosphere dropped. 'Hardly, Miss Major.' Mr Bent frowned and his mouth wobbled like plasticine. 'Perhaps you would kindly count the money in the change drawer in front of you?'

She counted the money. Then did it again. Each time, the balance was correct. 'See? I knew I'd sent them the right amount,' she cried pleased with her arithmetic.

Another canister whistled in. 'We are still waiting for the correct change,' it stated angrily.

Mr Bent picked up an orange ten-shilling note. Slowly he placed it in a canister and sent that along the tube. As he turned towards her she saw an unusual expression on his face. Mr Bent was smiling. 'Miss Major, we shall have to dispense with your services. We can't have a thief in the cashier's office.' The matter settled, he rubbed his dry hands briskly together and returned to his desk.

At first Didi didn't understand. 'Hmmm?'

He looked up, apparently astonished to find her still there. 'Just take your things and leave quietly.' Leaning over his desk, he studied a slip of paper.

Didi's jaw dropped. 'Mr Bent! Are you saying I've stolen the money?' Would someone rescue her? Had none of the others noticed something wrong? 'I haven't taken any money. Why would I take your money?'

At Mr Bent's disbelieving glance, she cried, 'Go on, search me.'

'I'd rather not make a fuss.' His gaze was fixed at a point above her head. 'If you just take your things and leave, I'll ask Foy's not to prosecute.'

181

Her eyes filled with angry tears. 'I'm no thief,' she shouted. Betty and Prue stopped what they were doing and stared, bewildered.

Selma rushed to her side as Didi, exploding with a terrible rage, screamed, 'How dare you call me a thief? Any fool can see they've made a mistake.'

Mr Bent rose to his full height and looked down at her. His tone was dispassionate. 'Really Miss Major, we would appreciate it if you left without a row.'

But Didi felt she had been ravished. 'Well,' she screamed, 'you can keep your shitty job. And,' she added before slamming the door in his face, 'You, Mr Bent, can get well and truly stuffed!'

The look on his face was worth it.

As she picked up her jacket in the cloakroom, she realised Selma was following her. 'What are you doing here?' she cried, still furious.

'You don't think I'd stay where they call you a thief?' Selma protested weakly.

It acted like a dash of iced water. 'Don't be silly,' Didi said grimly. 'It's too hard getting another job. No, you stay on here. I'll see you tonight.'

15. DON'T GET SICK

DIDI EXPLODED FROM the back of Foy's and marched in what she hoped was the general direction of Mavis Road. Hopping mad, she went over and over in her mind what she should have done.

Why hadn't she insisted on being searched?

She should have gone directly to the managing director, created a fuss no one would ever forget, proved she was no thief. But she was junior and new. Who would take her word against old Bent's? I'll bet he took the money himself, she thought darkly, though this was impossible, she knew.

Once clear of the city, she trudged on without looking where she was going. Passing a horse and cart stopped in front of a hotel she muttered, 'Old Bent's a sadist.' A blinkered eye winked in agreement. The horse was drawing a cart filled high with beer bottles. Imagining the crash, old Bent beneath a mountain of glass, made her smile. Forced to dodge a couple of drunks who came staggering out of the hotel, she nearly fell into a deep hole. Further along the pavement, workmen were moving wooden barrels, running them along thick ropes into vast cellars. The air was filled with the bitter-sweet odour of hops and malt. She looked around and realised with a jolt, that nothing was familiar. She was now in foreign parts.

The rain had stopped. A watery sun warmed the air, but

the gutters overflowed with mud and filth. Watching each step to avoid falling into slimy puddles where the bitumen was broken up, she walked by tiny cottages, workers' houses, lining the road. Their paintwork was grubby and peeling. What little iron lace-work remained was rusted through. Loose pieces of corrugated iron flapped in the wind. Some verandas were boarded in to make extra rooms. Others sat rakishly askew giving their houses an air of uncertainty.

Turning left, hoping to find something familiar, she cut through a narrow street and saw, on the next corner, a miniscule house transformed into a shop, its clouded windows covered in advertisements. She crossed the road and was about to enter and ask for directions, when a very fat woman stepped outside and began cleaning a rug. Something about the woman, maybe the angry way she held the rug, as if it was personally reponsible for becoming dirty, made Didi hurry on. Dust flew everywhere.

She passed houses so small they were no more than sheds opening straight on to the pavement. Looking in doorways, down corridors of peeling paper, she saw broken walls, torn lino, missing floorboards. Poverty became a stench, of open drains, leaking gas, rotting garbage. Skinny kids, noses dripping, sidled out of doorways, gazing blankly as she went past. Their mothers stopped gossiping only long enough to stare. Didi smiled politely, but her greetings were met by stony faces. First this street, then another and another. She kept turning left, convinced this would take her north to Carlton and home. The houses in this suburb were different to anything she had ever seen before. Didi supposed their occupants used whatever materials were available, whatever could be scrounged. There were shacks, lean-tos, composites of wooden crates, bits of iron, tarpaulin and odd timber offcuts. Their windows were covered with hessian bags instead of glass. That people lived here was obvious, for alongside each shanty was strung up two or more lines of washing. At one point, turning in a direction that she was convinced must lead to a main road, she passed places that were, at first glance, quite normal, then realised they were still incomplete. One side was properly built, the other a make-believe where wooden planks propped up walls of corrugated iron. The whole thing looked as if it had been finished off with sticky tape.

Plodding on, she wished she felt better. Not that she was frightened. On the contrary, this was more 'Explorers Unlimited'. Besides, she told herself, seeing this part of Melbourne's history, a part people usually preferred to ignore, was really very interesting. Anyway, getting lost was a distraction from thinking about old Bent and how she'd messed up that job.

She belched, and the taste of half-digested porridge and toast stayed in her mouth. A wave of nausea made her break out in a sudden sweat. Last January, when the Falconers were holidaying in a houseboat along the Hawkesbury, she had come down with a twenty-four-hour flu. Tom caught it straight after. Both of them were terribly ill, but all Tom could say was, 'Trust Didi to give me the runs. I expect she did it on purpose.' She remembered cringing at his sardonic humour. Now, looking back, she realised the sarcasm was probably unintentional.

And this felt exactly the same.

It's only a reaction to old Bent and getting angry, she told herself. Except that her bowel was twisting about like a lassoo. A lightning bolt of pain made her stagger, crouch and nearly faint. Clutching a fence to steady herself, she sank on to the pavement.

'What's up, dearie? You sick or sumptin'?'

185

She nodded, too sick to say anything. From the corner of her eye she saw a woman untangle herself from the fence, where she was talking to her neighbour. Wispy rags peeped out from beneath a faded headscarf. Taking Didi by the arm, the woman peered curiously into her face. 'You don't look too good, dearie.' Her smile exposed bare gums.

The black waves were unrelenting. Didi's hands slipped away from the fence. The woman pushed her head between her knees. 'Try that, love. It might help.'

She obeyed. Colic seized and shook her like a naughty terrier, a cold sweat drenched her. 'Where's a lavatory?' she murmured.

'Come on dearie, it's not the Ritz but you can use ours.' The woman helped Didi to her feet and took her into the house.

She was led down a corridor where walls wept and floorboards curled up in despair. Someone more alert would have stopped, appalled at the sight of wall-to-wall beds, tattered wallpaper, clothes and scraps of blankets flung everywhere. But Didi just managed to reach the outhouse in time, where she collapsed on the seat and allowed her insides to give way. Hoping the spasm would pass, she waited, and kept her eyes safely closed.

Feeling a little better, she looked round. Her sight adjusted to the dim light and she saw large black insects with shiny backs scuttle about. My God, cockroaches! Her legs jerked up from the dirt floor. What about the seat? Staggering up, she lifted each foot very carefully, and peered into the toilet. That did it. Retching and retching, she threw up again and again until there was nothing left except the bitter taste of bile. And then she groped her way through the low door and back into the house.

'Better, dearie?' In spite of the collapsed mouth and chin, the woman was younger than Didi first thought.

Perhaps a worn thirty. And this must be the kitchen. There was a bucket filled with dirty dishes and on the table, the makings of a scratch meal. The woman was drinking tea from a cracked cup. She wore, over a torn and dirty petticoat, a faded flowery coverall. A half-dressed toddler with a runny nose and a red-raw bottom was leaning on her knee. Catching sight of Didi he gave a low whimper, as if a normal lusty cry was too exhausting.

'Come on, sit down,' she was invited. 'Take the weight off your legs. How about a cuppa? Make your insides feel better.' Didi saw a small stove, something like a camp oven, with a blackened kettle on the top. 'You been with old Mother Ryan up the road?' The woman peered into Didi's white face.

Didi stared, confused. 'Why would I go there?'

The woman laughed uproariously, as if Didi had told a good joke. 'Lots of young girls go.' She smiled knowingly. 'The old cow makes 'em pay five pounds, but it's cheap for an abortion.'

Didi felt weak with horror and pity. She shook her head, and was in return handed a cup of tea. The liquid was sweet and strong. 'Now then dearie,' the woman said, 'where d'you live?'

'Carlton.' The toddler had fallen asleep in a corner, his naked bottom exposed to an unkind world.

'Carlton.' His mother eyed her thoughtfully. 'Stranger round these parts, are you?' Didi nodded. 'Well, you're not too far off. You well enough to walk?'

Didi handed back the cup and found she did feel better. 'Thank you so much,' she said awkwardly. 'I don't know what I'd have done if you hadn't been around.'

'Oh, you're just lucky I was out there chewin' things over with Nell.' Taking Didi out to the street, she explained how to get home.

On wobbly legs, her strength returning very gradually, it took Didi over an hour to get back to Mavis Road.

When she got in, her reflection looked like death. So she did the sensible thing and went to bed. Fortunately, Mrs Finkelstein was busy in the kitchen and didn't hear her come in. The last thing Didi needed was having to explain why she was home so early.

She dozed off immediately, but her sleep was restless, punctuated as it was by dreams...

Mr Bent was telling Selma he'd called the police... They came! The same men who rescued them from George and company. One waved a notebook with her name and address written into it. This time there was little doubt about her crime. She could expect less leniency. 'Making a pest of herself,' the policeman grinned, opened his purple mouth, then turned into a lizard.

She woke, and her sheet was wet through.

When Jamie came home he was astonished to find her there. 'Hey pal, what's up?'

She said, 'Everything.' And, to her great annoyance, after having planned to make the day into a great joke, she burst into tears.

'Hold on.' Jamie sat on the bed and gazed at her crumpled face. 'Don't get your knickers in a knot. Start at the beginning.'

'I got the sack,' she began mournfully.

'Yeah?' For some reason he didn't seem surprised. 'Is that all? I thought it was serious. What happened?'

Once it was told, much of her upset vanished.

'It's rotten luck. But don't take it personally,' was his verdict. This cheered her up, and when he suggested, 'Why don't you stay in bed? I'll bring up your tea on a tray,' she meekly agreed, snuggled further under the bedclothes and felt embarrassingly well.

188

Later, she tried to decribe the shanty town for him. 'Someone should try and do something. You should see how those people live.' Her head shook in dismay. 'I don't see how this government can let it happen.'

To cheer her up, Jamie performed a couple of his own compositions. With only half his mind on the music, he watched her closely as he played.

She was such a cat. With those narrow green eyes, wide cheekbones and fluffy hair. She acted like a Tabby but she resembled nothing more than a small, rather winsome Persian. He wondered what she would do if someone stroked her. Probably scratch!

And she, listening carefully, watching him loop those extra-long legs over the bed-end, was thankful that his great height, those extra years, were no longer such a barrier between them.

When Selma arrived home she came straight upstairs to check on Didi. The story, retold to the soft accompaniment of Jamie's harmonica, was embellished only a little.

As she listened, Selma grew crosser and crosser. 'That old crocodile Bent.' Her gentle voice became increasingly contemptuous. 'Ten minutes after you left, the Men's Department sent us a note saying they'd found the money. It had fallen into the back of the container.'

Didi shrugged. The sickness had purged her of anger. 'I reckon old Bent just didn't like me,' she murmured. 'Whatever happened, he'd find a way to give me the sack.'

'The girls are furious. They're going to report what happened to the general manager. Try and get you reinstated.'

'Well, be careful. I'd hate them to lose their jobs because of me. Anyway,' Didi added pensively, 'we mightn't be here after Sunday. There's probably no point bothering.'

As soon as it was said she could have kicked herself, for

189

Selma's smile switched off abruptly. 'I'll bring your tray upstairs,' she called, hurrying away to help her mother prepare dinner.

Much later, after Didi had eaten and was feeling considerably healthier, she was listening to Jamie playing some Beatles numbers... *Back in the US, back in the US, back in the USSR...* when he stopped in mid phrase to suggest, 'Why don't you come to the circus with me tomorrow? Donald keeps saying you've a job any time you turn up. It could be fun to work together.'

'Hadn't you better first ask if it's OK?' she asked, trying not to look too delighted.

'We've only a few more days.'

She beamed at him. 'I think it's a great idea.'

It would be fun to spend these last days working together. But now, now they were planning to get home, she found herself wishing they could stay a little longer. .

16. Too Scared To Get Close?

AT EIGHT IN the morning when they arrived, Wirth's Circus seemed half dead. Sam waved them on ahead. 'Jamie, you take Didi to find Donald,' he called. 'I'll check out our morning chores. We'll meet for lunch.'

Jamie knew Donald spent some of his nights in the dressing-room, so they headed that way. Though last night's performance had ended late, they found Donald already up and checking his equipment.

'Thought you'd rather work with us,' he said when Didi walked in, not in the least put out she had turned up without giving him some warning. 'Can't think of anything duller than working in an office.' He gave her a droll look and waggled his ears. She giggled appreciatively so he immediately introduced her to Miss Violet. From the pink velvet dressing-gown, collar trimmed with feathers, to the high-heeled mules on her feet, every precious detail told Didi that here was a Star.

Within minutes Didi was settled at the table, in front of her a large basket crammed full with clothes which needed mending.

Jamie had already left for the stables when Miss Violet doubled up with a violent coughing fit. It subsided, but left her very drained. 'How I wish this flu would go,' she murmured.

Donald was busy rubbing grease into some ropes. He frowned worriedly. 'You'd better rug up. That sort of flu can lead to all sorts of things.' His big head shook mysteriously.

'Like what sort of thing?' Didi asked.

Miss Violet flushed angrily. 'He means I might get tuberculosis. Because circus people lead such hard lives, they're always scared their lungs will suffer. And...' her voice rose accusingly, 'and they're too scared to call it by its proper name.'

'It's true.' Donald looked rueful. 'You know how superstitious we are.'

'Well, people do die from TB.' Poor Miss Violet had another coughing fit before adding, 'But this is just ordinary flu. Madame Zara is really sick but I'm fine.'

Didi looked at Miss Violet's sunken eyes, the dark hollows beneath, and asked, 'Why don't you go to the doctor? Maybe he'll give you an antibiotic?'

Donald looked up. 'What's that? What did you say?'

She'd done it again. Jumping up, waving one of Donald's socks as a distraction, Didi cried, 'You know, I'm getting really muddled. Did you want these darned in different colours?'

'Yes, they should look as strange as possible. Why don't you use the orange wool?' The awkward moment passed as Didi and Miss Violet, pulling out thread, beads, wool and buttons, exclaimed over the treasure trove in the sewing basket.

'All these bits and pieces are used when we make our costumes,' Miss Violet explained. She asked Didi to alter one of her dresses right away. 'I'll wear it tonight in the performance. What do you think?'

She held out a dress which had a low-cut bodice of silver lamé and a skirt made from lime-green tulle. The outfit was small enough to fit an undersized five-year-old. Didi cleared her throat. Not wanting to hurt Miss Violet's feelings, she said gently, 'It's very bright, isn't it?'

'It's terrible.' Miss Violet's calm voice might have been discussing the weather. 'I wear it with a red wig, orange socks and purple shoes. The effect, I assure you, is totally bizarre.' Didi grinned, but Miss Violet might have been talking about an outfit for the Melbourne Cup.

After Miss Violet went off, with much moaning and groaning, to a rehearsal, Didi took a pin and stuck it in her finger. On purpose. Perhaps that would remind her. Fancy telling Sonia she would be replaced by a machine. And now this. 'I'm such a fool,' she thought, but it was hard to keep her wits about her, the odd slip here and there inevitable. Fancy forgetting antibiotics wouldn't be available for years.

All this time Donald was tending his ropes, saying very little. Had he noticed? As she darned and patched she wondered if she should ask about her pay. Then decided she would do this for nothing, so grateful was she for this friendship. Still, they needed money. There was still Mrs Finkelstein to be paid before next Sunday.

Sunday! Her stomach contracted with fear.

To stop herself from panicking, to focus her mind on other things, she counted up the friends she had made. There was the Finkelstein household and the girls at Foy's, although she doubted she would see them again. And now there was Donald and Miss Violet.

Making friends in 'thirty-three was easy. She pondered the difference between home and here. Like a whiff, an odour of something unpleasant, came the faint reminder of 'Eurydice, Eurydice...'

'Why are things from the north like boxes?'

'Because they're square...'

Clenching her teeth, she chased the thought away, as if

it was a spider or a blowfly, and concentrated hard on her work. Half an hour later Donald left the room and went off to rehearsal.

The morning passed so pleasantly Didi couldn't call this work, not with Donald instructing her to take it easy or she might damage her eyes, and Miss Violet keeping her company between rehearsals. Curious about circus life, she asked Miss Violet. 'Do you practise a lot?'

'Of course. Our acts are dangerous if they're done badly. It's so easy to pull a ligament or strain one's back.'

'How many hours practice do you do each day?'

'It varies.' Miss Violet permitted herself a little smile. 'Anything from a few hours to all day if we're setting up a new routine.'

Didi considered this answer while she threaded a darning needle. She was astonished at the amount of work the clowns did. At the performance the other night their act looked spontaneous, a bit of fun created on the spot.

'What's it like living with a circus?'

Miss Violet shrugged a tiny shoulder. 'I've been here a long time. You know, I love the smell of sawdust.' She raised a finely plucked eyebrow and added, 'Sometimes when I'm in bed, I think it would be delightful to own my own home, small and cosy. I imagine how nice it would be to wake in the same place each morning.'

'Yes, yes,' Didi chimed in. 'You must get fed up with travelling.'

'Then I realise how boring it is,' Miss Violet continued, 'to be always in the same place, everything safe and predictable.' She held up tiny wrists. 'So maybe I have sawdust instead of blood in my veins. Besides,' she added darkly, 'in the circus I'm somebody. Out there, let's face it, I'm just another midget.' With this, she burst into gales of laughter. Overcome by a new coughing spasm, she collapsed on the couch, where she lay choking and spluttering until falling at last into a restless sleep.

Didi watched over her with a mixture of sympathy and trepidation. There had come a new fear...

'Jamie, you're not allowed to get sick,' she announced when they met by the river for lunch. 'Do you realise how dangerous it is for us here, away from modern medicines? What if you get sick?'

They were watching coal barges, half-submerged by their cargo, float down the river. His eyebrows shot up. 'Why would I get sick? Anyway,' he grinned, 'would you miss me? I'm just the pest who fell into 'thirty-three with you.'

'What do you mean?' She stared into his laughing face. 'I thought we were mates?'

He smiled reassuringly. 'Course we are. Actually,' he mused, 'these few days with you have been ace. Since I've been in Melbourne I've made heaps of friends, but none are chicks. You know,' he said thoughtfully, 'I've never had a close friend who was a girl. Probably because back home I went to an all-boys school.' With this astonishing admission he began unwrapping his sandwich.

'I thought you knew heaps of girls in the city,' she said suspiciously. 'Anyway, what about Kate?'

'Oh, I'm really keen on Kate,' he admitted. 'But that's different. Sex gets in the way. There's no way I can see Kate as just a good mate.' He took another bite before saying, 'To tell the truth, I've taken out lots of girls, but after I stop seeing them, we never stay close friends. Not that we hate each other or anything,' he added hurriedly. 'But I can't say anything that pops into my head, not without worrying they'll get uptight. Mostly, I'm really careful. I reckon girls play too many games.' Thinking over what he had said, he frowned and added. 'To be perfectly honest, I'm not sure I really understand women.'

She nodded violently. 'That's just how I feel about men.' They both laughed. She added rather daringly, 'I wonder if we're all that different?'

He stopped half-way through a mouthful. 'What do you mean?'

'Well, we want the same things. Like knowing your friends like you, and having someone you can really trust. Being able to ask them for help if you're in trouble.'

'And knowing they'll be there,' he interrupted. 'Can't argue with that.'

'So you see, in the end gender doesn't matter. It's the other things that count.'

Jamie agreed. Polishing off his sandwich, he produced the harmonica from his back pocket and began cleaning it with a linen napkin. Didi started on her own lunch. Half-way through, she asked, 'What about your sister? Didn't you learn about girls from her?'

'Linda's nine years older than me. Having her round is like living with a bloody-minded aunt.'

Trying not to show too much curiosity, Didi waited until he put the harmonica back in his pocket. 'The most important thing in my life is my music. If I'm not thinking about music, I'm playing it. The harmonica and the piano. Now there's the flute and the clarinet and I want to start playing the oboe. I have lessons three times a week. In between, I do stacks of practice. You know,' he said thoughtfully, 'I keep thinking I should take a weekend off. Be more like other people. Each time I try, I feel half of me is missing. If I don't play some music every day I get withdrawal symptoms.'

'Like you're into drugs?'

He grinned at the comparison. 'Yeah, sort of. Anyway, on weekends I play with this group. They're called The Window Displays. They're very good,' he said earnestly. 'I figure they're good enough to hit the top of the charts. The women are there, but none of us has time for 'em.'

He stared moodily at the river. A few seagulls searching for scraps came daringly close and pecked the grass in front of him. 'And there's school and loads of homework. Friday and Saturday arvos I play footy. Got to keep fit.' He looked up and smiled. 'I ask you, where do I fit it all in? I talk to the girls at school.' He shrugged. 'But somehow, it never seems to last for more than a few weeks. In the end they get fed up because I'm never there for long enough.'

This long speech left him breathless.

'What about Kate?' she asked. 'Where did you meet her?'

'Some guy brought her to the pub where we play.'

His gaze flickered across the river, recaptured the pub's smoky atmosphere, the strobe lights beating to the rhythm of music amplified to a physical presence of its own. Hard to believe it was only last week. Surely he'd known Kate for ever...

He was ordering a beer from the bar when his attention was caught. She was laughing. With her head thrown back, her neck arched gracefully. He thought of a Beethoven sonata, a Mozart aria, a Bach fugue.

He stared hard at the heart-shaped face, wide-set eyes, and delicate mouth. Under the bar lights, her hair, like autumn leaves, formed a halo around her head. He couldn't remember what she was wearing but it was black and tight. Whatever it was, it looked great. Kate turned. His eyes met hers and she smiled.

That was when he knew he was hooked.

He became aware Didi was staring and said, 'Oh, I don't

know about me and Kate. She wants things her own way. Anyway, I don't think she's as keen as me...' His voice trailed helplessly away.

'You've got to be kidding,' Didi laughed. 'I reckon she's real gone. When you came home... I've never seen her look that way.' Suddenly protective of Kate's interests, she cried. 'You know what your problem is? I reckon you're too scared to get close.'

There was an ominous silence.

Jamie laughed mirthlessly. 'For the first twenty years my mum thought my dad was really close. Then, last year my dad pissed off with someone else.'

'Look, I understand,' she said in her most adult voice. 'Having watched your parents split could turn you off any relationship.' At the sight of his angry face she stopped short.

This time the silence lasted. 'How's that for pop psychology?' he growled at last.

She flushed. The crimson seemed to rise from her very toes. 'I'm sorry, I didn't mean to sound clever. It popped into my head. Anyway...' desperately trying to square off, 'my dad's given me loads of hang-ups, really.'

'What about your mum? You never say much about her.'

'Oh, she keeps us together.' Perhaps the break from home had helped, but suddenly she saw her family in a fresh light. 'No. That's not true any more. She's very involved with her job. And Dad takes up heaps of time. What with Kate doing her final year I get really jealous. There's nothing left over for me. All the same,' she sighed, 'I guess she'd never get any sleep if she had to worry for me as well as Kate.'

'Exactly,' he nodded. 'What about the men in your life?'

'There aren't any.' He looked disbelieving, so she added, 'There was this guy in Sydney. We moved to Melbourne and that was that. Actually,' she admitted wryly, 'it was no big deal. We used to smile at each other in class but we never went out or anything. What with Kate being so pretty, she gets all the men.'

He looked up at her. 'Yeah, does she? Well, I happen to think you're just as pretty. But in a different kind of way.'

'What?' She laughed incredulously. 'Me, pretty? You're having me on. I'm short and fat. My hair sticks out everywhere and my nose is too small.'

'And you've got a great shape. Lucky you.' His tone was quite matter-of-fact. 'I really like your eyes. Has anyone ever told you you're a Persian? Persian cat, that is.' His mouth was back on the metal grid and 'I've Grown Accustomed To Your Face' drifted across the water and on towards the city. 'Anyway,' he added when the melody was finished, 'you've got it all wrong. There's lots more to being pretty than how you look. It's what you're like inside. The way you enjoy music and worry about the people we've met. Coping with this crazy thing that's happened to us. Besides,' he grinned, 'you've got an ace smile.'

'You don't have to be nice to me.' Then, in spite of herself, she smiled.

'There. See?' Leaning her way, he said, 'It sort of lights you up inside.'

She laughed out loud, and he joined in. Then, looking up, they saw Sam coming towards them.

As they walked back to Wirth's Park, Jamie practised arpeggios and scales and Sam quizzed Didi about her new job. He wanted details of what she'd done that morning. When she mentioned how sick Miss Violet seemed he interrupted to question her on medicine in the future. She told him as much as she knew about antibiotics, organ transplants, in-vitro fertilisation and genetic engineering. He asked enough for her to need a degree in medicine for accurate answers. She wished she knew more, but he seemed satisfied with what she had to say.

During dinner all three had stories about the circus to relate. Selma was openly peeved. 'There I am, counting change all day, putting up with old Bent, while you lot are having fun,' she complained.

'Tell you what,' Sam suggested, 'why don't we go tomorrow night? We could watch a performance from the wings. Selma, why don't you meet us? We can have a picnic tea.'

'Great. Let's do it,' Jamie cried, and even before Selma finally agreed, it was all decided.

Later that evening Didi asked Selma if she might see some of Rachel's work. Selma took Didi to her room, opened a wardrobe and held out a dress. She asked, 'What do you think of that? Isn't it gorgeous?'

Didi agreed. Under the harsh centre light, the delicate beading glittered with an opalescent shimmer and the flowers looked almost real.

It was very late. Thanking Selma, Didi left for her own room, feeling more bewildered than ever. To Jamie she said, 'It's definitely not the same.'

Squatting on his bed, concentrating on a Cole Porter medley, he refused to take her seriously. 'Oh, come on. It has to be. Anyway, it's probably faded.'

Didi had crawled under the blankets. Glaring at the top of his head, which was all she could see, she cried. 'I'm absolutely positive that's *not* the dress I found in the trunk. Mine was wool, this one's satin. Anyway, the other fitted me. This one's too small.'

'You sure? You didn't try it on.'

Didi scowled obstinately. 'I just know it did.'

Much later, she concluded that, except for colour and size, Rachel had sewn two identical dresses. Struck by another thought, she resisted the temptation to nudge Jamie awake. Why didn't he mention the trunk? Even last Saturday, even after admitting to Sam and Selma that they were from the future, he remained secretive on certain issues. Was there some disadvantage in them knowing more? Something she hadn't thought of? As for that dress, she would tackle Selma the very next day.

That night Jamie had a curious dream. Curious because some of it had already occurred, nor was this the first time he'd dreamt it. The subject was a conversation which had taken place over a year ago. In this dream, everything remained exact and true to life. He and his father were standing on the Major's property by the dam. Bill Major was staring at the water, checking the level. 'If it doesn't rain soon,' he said shaking his head, 'I'll have to sell off some stock.'

Jamie wasn't paying too much attention. Bill was always griping about the property, rambling on about expenses. Suddenly Jamie heard his father saying, 'Your mother and I...' There was an awkward pause, 'I'm sure you know your mother and I haven't been getting on too well these last few years?'

Jamie kept silent. He had no intention of making this easy. At long last his father said, 'So we've decided to separate. Your mother is moving to Melbourne. She tells me you intend living with her.' Bill's deep-set eyes, so much like Jamie's, gazed plaintively at his son. 'Sure that's what you want?'

201

Not daring to look into his father's face, Jamie studied his feet.

'What sort of a career do you think you're going to find in music?' Bill's voice rose. 'We've a big property here. You know Linda and her husband aren't interested. I'm fifty-three next birthday. One day I'll be too old to run this place and I'll be forced to sell. Have you thought about what you're doing?'

Up to this point the dream recorded exactly what had taken place. Jamie knew this for sure. This was the point where he tried to explain the importance of music to his life.

In reality Bill had stalked off and refused to listen. Jamie was left feeling angry and upset, guilty that he wasn't the sort of son Bill wanted. But this dream was different. In this dream Bill was saying, 'My boy, I understand exactly what you're doing. I'll stand behind you all the way.'

If Didi had woken and looked over at the other bed, she might have noticed a small smile of triumph on Jamie Major's face.

17. THE RECKONING

IT WAS SUCH a glorious gold and green morning, the question of the dress quite slipped her mind. On the tram, Jamie beside her, Sam and Selma seated opposite, Didi felt such a spurt of happiness, she almost laughed aloud with joy. Wasn't she the luckiest of girls? Only a week after believing herself to be the loneliest person in Melbourne, she was surrounded by good friends and on her way to an unusual and interesting job. Everything around her shone with an extra intensity. Even the copper pennies they paid the conductor sparkled in the fresh morning light.

Reviewing her fellow passengers, she watched how some shielded themselves with the morning paper, others slept, or stared vacantly outside. On the whole, they looked tired and bored. No one seemed to be having any fun. Was it the same back home? Sobering to think she had never really noticed.

Meanwhile, with his usual indifference to the people around him, Sam was crooning Gershwin's, *I was so young, you were so beeauutiful...'* in her direction. Once, she might have been embarrassed and asked him to stop. But then once she had worried about being accepted by girls whom she secretly despised. Now she could only marvel at how she'd changed.

Jamie jumped off the tram before it came to a halt. 'I'd like to spend these last few days wandering about,' he called to her. 'Just looking at things.'

'We never got to the country,' Didi added, rather wistfully. 'And it's so close.'

Sam was trying to persuade them to stay. 'I could take you to an artist's village next week?' Didi beamed. Everything was wonderful. The sun, the crowd, even Foy and Gibson's sitting dourly on the corner. If only she could bottle up the morning, as if it was a perfect apricot or peach, and keep it with her for ever.

Meanwhile, Selma, who had been listening rather disapprovingly, went hurrying off towards Foy's. They waited until her small figure disappeared, then sauntered on their way. Jamie mused, 'I rather wanted another look around the city. All those old buildings still here. No one bulldozing them down.'

'Not as yet.'

'There's twenty years before that happens.' Followed by Sam, he sprinted into the distance, dodging two draughthorses harnessed to a truck loaded with beerbarrels standing outside Young and Jackson's. When Didi eventually caught up, Sam was explaining that not only was the notorious painting of the naked Chloe hung here, but there was no way a female could go inside without starting a riot at the very least.

Their arrival at the circus coincided with the trainer, Mr Harry Moolley, persuading his charges to enter the Hippodrome. The sight of three elephants lumbering along brought the friends to an abrupt halt.

'You know,' Sam decided. 'I reckon Mr Moolley looks more like a lawyer or an accountant than an animal trainer.' And Harry Moolley did seem absurdly fragile against the bulk of his huge playmates.

'Oh, I don't know,' Didi mused, 'he's got a long nose and big ears.'

Jamie chuckled and Sam remembered to check the time. 'Ferguson'll have a piece of us,' he cried as they went racing off. Didi looked about. Making up her mind, she sidled noiselessly inside. Three white-and-red striped wooden tubs had been placed in the centre of the ring. A great deal of talking, coaxing, stroking of heads and sensitive trunks was taking place, but she watched the elephants climb laboriously one by one on to the top of a tub. There, teetering dangerously, each animal took turns in raising a right front foot and balancing on the remaining three. Finally, holding up the right back and front leg, they managed to stand upright on only two.

The finale was spectacular. Clambering simultaneously on to the tubs, the elephants lifted their front feet, then held them out in a gigantic ring-a-ring-a-rosy. Forgetting she shouldn't be there, Didi clapped furiously. 'Come and meet baby Jessie,' Harry called, having noticed her creep in. Relieved that he wasn't annoyed, she clambered over the wooden seats and walked on to the ring.

One by one the elephants were introduced. 'This here's our Princess Alice. She mothers the babies. And this is Jessie.' Princess Alice lifted her trunk and trumpeted a greeting. When she stopped, and they could hear themselves think, Harry brought over the last animal. 'This lady's called Bessie.'

'They seem very intelligent.' Didi stroked Bessie's sensitive trunk. 'How come these are all girls? Don't you use males in your acts?'

'Male elephants are too hard to train.' Pulling out a large handkerchief Harry coughed politely into it. 'The bulls get very cantankerous. They don't like learning tricks, but the ladies love the attention.' Close up, Mr Moolley was as weatherbeaten as an old shed. Lines like wooden beams criss-crossed the skin around his eyes, and his teeth and fingers were oranged with nicotine. As he talked he continued to stroke Bessie's ears and trunk with loving gestures.

Didi asked, 'How did you become an elephant trainer?'

'I've worked with animals since I was old enough to crawl.' At twenty, wanting to see something of the world, Harry told her, he'd left East Gippsland, gone to Melbourne where he'd boarded ship as a sailor. This got him to America where his knowledge of horses gave him a job at a private zoo, training exotic animals. Then he'd met up with the great Barnum and Bailey who had taken him on tour.

'We travelled most of the year, north to the Rockies and as far south as New Mexico. Barnum and Bailey's always used female elephants. The ladies are lovely but the males get real moody.' Pushing Jessie gently away, he gave Bessie some attention.

Harry going on about masculine moods reminded Didi she was late. The last thing she wanted was Donald to think poorly of her. She ran all the way to the dressing-room, settled in, and was working on a sequined and appliqued jacket before Miss Violet drifted by. 'Hello darling, I think I'm on the mend,' she said huskily and looking up, Didi saw the circles under her eyes had lessened.

'Great. How's Madame Zara?'

'Still sick.' Miss Violet wrung her hands. 'So sick, you wouldn't believe. She's not right in the head.' Miss Violet circled the air with her finger. 'She's got funny notions. She doesn't sound at all like herself. The doctor thinks she's got meningitis. That's a brain sickness. He thinks there's a chance she might die.'

206

Didi's heart plummeted. Her marvellous mood vanished. Were she and Jamie, in some peculiar way, responsible for Madame Zara's sickness? The Voice! Whichever way they turned there was the Voice, it's intrusive presence a reminder of its own grim prophecies. Picking at the jacket, she asked, 'What sort of notions?'

Miss Violet turned away and wouldn't answer. Didi threaded a needle with orange wool. Changing the subject she said, 'I've been watching Mr Moolley rehearse the elephants.'

'Marvellous, aren't they?' Miss Violet fitted a cigarette into her long holder and settled down to chat. The room filled quickly with the smells of good perfume and Turkish tobacco. She stitched and patched and darned and Miss Violet read aloud from the paper. 'The Theatre Royal are closing down in November. They're putting on *Maid of the Mountains* as their last performance. Wirth's won't be here anymore, but you should go and see it.'

'Yes,' Didi said sadly. She pointed to the pile of mending. 'I should be finished this by tomorrow afternoon.'

'Clever you.' Miss Violet's eyebrows arched. 'Fancy getting through that awful job so quickly.'

'Oh, it's nothing,' Didi protested, 'I really like sewing.'

Miss Violet's eyes widened. 'Yes, well, domesticity's not exactly my line.' And setting off to light the spirit stove to make tea, she forgot what she was doing, and disappeared towards the rehearsal room.

This was Didi's second morning with the circus and Donald trusted her enough to leave her alone. At one point, she got up to tidy her hair and a stranger looked out of the mirror. Someone with green cat's eyes and a snub nose. Someone who seemed older than fifteen. She smiled, the stranger smiled back and she saw a round face with an appealing glow.

Settling back, she thought about Jamie and herself, about some of their conversations. What great mates they had become. What a shame, once they got home, that this would be hard to maintain. 'Once we get home...' She repeated the words aloud. However hard she tried to plan ahead, her mind refused to settle on anything beyond next Sunday. As if next Sunday was the end of her world.

Wouldn't it be great being home again?

But her mind veered off course. Impossible to imagine being back in her room with the posters of INXS and Rick Astley. And the family. Back to being Kate's stupid little sister, Tom making fun and Jane being too busy for her. Nobody realising how much she'd changed.

All this effort to get into that old theatre. Doubts divebombed her like magpies in early spring. She shooed them away, began fitting a sleeve, tried concentrating on the armhole.

The thoughts refused to go away.

Once they broke in, even got that film running, who was to say that they would return? Even if she and Jamie did manage to get away, what if they ended up in a different century or planet? Remembering their arrival, remembering the icy tones of the alien Voice, Didi shivered. What if, instead of arriving home, they were asphyxiated? Or their bodies disintegrated into separate molecules? There was an episode in *Star Trek* where this happened. They could be stranded for ever on some alien planet.

'We must make every effort to get back,' Jamie insisted every time they talked, as if these words were magical and could ensure their safety. To Didi they had a hollow ring. Sooner or later, she must make a decision. So she did. In spite of the Voice's awesome warning she decided it was wisest to remain right here.

At lunchtime, she hurried to the stables. Jamie was brushing Queenie, using strong circular strokes to give her coat its wonderful burnish. Watching him soothed her panic. 'Isn't she beautiful?' Jamie called. 'No wonder she's called the Wonder Horse. She's a proper queen of the circus.' Didi ran her hand over the satin neck. The horse turned her head. Didi drowned in the soft brown eyes.

'See?' he cried, plaiting the mare's tail. 'She recognises her admiring public. Only then did he think to ask, 'What's up?'

Didi jumped. Remembering they had planned to meet by the river, she said, 'I've decided we're being silly.'

'Yeah? In what way?'

'You know. All this business about getting home.'

'Maybe.' He slid the brushes and curry-combs into their containers. 'What do you mean?'

'Well, I reckon we ought to stay here with Sam and Selma. We're used to it already, and... it *is* OK, isn't it?' She paused. How to explain her instinct that things must go wrong? 'All the risks, starting with breaking into that theatre. If we get caught we're in big trouble. And even if we do find the film and the time warp, we could end up in some horrible place. There's no way we can be sure we'll get home, is there?'

'All the same,' he shrugged, 'you heard the warning.'

'I know, I know.' Her hands and knees shook with fright. Was it their fate to never get home, to stay here for ever?

His gaze was unblinking. 'Want to try Madame Zara again?'

'What's the point? She'll say she doesn't remember a thing. Anyway, I don't think we can. Miss Violet says she's terribly sick. She's got meningitis.'

'You're kidding. You can die from that. It's really dangerous without antibiotics.' Then, the same thought striking him, he cried, 'You don't think we had something to do with it, do you?'

'How could we?' she asked helplessly.

They made their way outside. 'What I'd like to know is,' her tone was wistful, 'what's so bad about staying here? Seems to me the real danger is trying to get back. How about we ignore all that stuff and stay on?'

He frowned. 'What about the risks? The Voice knows we don't belong, that we're strangers.' He mimicked the alien tones, '*Return or stay forever. This warp is terminal. Cancel error.*' And back in his normal voice, 'I reckon we're asking for trouble if we ignore its message. Anyway...' He went bright pink.

She knew what this meant. Turning on him she cried, 'You only want to go back because of Kate. You couldn't give a stuff about me.' They stared at each other. At that moment Didi really hated Kate.

'That's only partly true,' he agreed weakly. 'But that's not my main reason. I really have to leave because of the music.' His tone was very apologetic. 'You see, I need to get back home to play my music.'

'What do you mean?' She couldn't believe her ears. 'You play music here. You play all the time, don't you?'

'It's not the same thing. I know what's written later on. There are too many new instruments, synthesizers, computers. If I wanted to use them, and I do, I'd have to pretend to invent them myself. I can't do that. I wouldn't know how. Anyway, it would distort the truth. I reckon something would stop me. It just won't work. Anyway...'

'Yes?'

'I don't think we're meant to stay,' he finished abruptly. 'Something will happen to prevent it, just you wait and see.' Glancing at her unhappy face, he added desperately. 'It doesn't mean we can't still be mates.'

She shook her head. 'You just wait and see. It'll be too hard.' They walked outside, wrinkling their eyes against the sudden light. Seagulls circling above called out raucously, making fun of their problems. Sam was hurrying towards them. The river beckoned, and the sun shining on its banks coloured them an intense vegetable green.

Jamie took her arm. 'Let's talk it over later. We can make up our minds then. OK?' She shrugged and agreed. She didn't much like his conclusion, but sharing things made them easier.

The afternoon was uneventful. Selma was to meet them at Flinders Street Station on the dot of five-thirty. They were running late.

When they arrived she was already there, waving a wicker hamper in their direction. 'Look, Papa's brought us our tea.'

Sam peered inside. 'Meatballs, chopped liver, bread rolls, two sorts of mustard, potato salad, coleslaw, an apple pie and cold tea. That's OK. Now, what did you bring for the others?'

Selma swung the basket, Sam ducked. Didi called indignantly, 'Hey, that's my joke.' Jamie produced two bottles of drink and they strolled towards their favourite picnicking spot.

Soon, black clouds came rolling in, blocking out the sunset. 'Hadn't we better get moving?' Selma asked uneasily. 'There's a storm heading this way.'

'It's too nice to rush.' Jamie was throwing crusts to the seagulls who were swooping, bickering over the scraps.

They were half-way through their meal when the light suddenly faded. The birds rose as one, flew twice around their heads, then took off. Sheet lightning flickered. They were wrapping the last scraps of food when heavy drops of rain began falling.

The eye of the storm was directly above. One lightning flash, exposing their faces in a black-and-cream relief, was followed by an extremely loud thundercrack, loud enough for Selma to give up all pretence of being brave. She gave a little shriek. 'Come on, let's get out of here.'

Earlier, Donald had suggested that they watch the show from the back of the stage. Not only would it offer a different perspective, there was the added bonus they could get in free. Now they ran towards the mustering area. A figure slipped out from behind the side door and Selma, already terrified, screamed with fright.

It was George. In the intense glare of another lightning bolt hate lines seemed to slice his face into three. 'What're you doin' here?'

Jamie saw red. Without pausing long enough to count, 'Twenty, nineteen, eighteen, seventeen...' or breathe deeply, 'in through the nose, out through the mouth,' or use any of the self-control exercises he knew so well, he let swing. George tumbled into the dirt and Jamie, still seeing the world in an angry haze, not checking to see how badly George might be hurt, opened the door for the drenched girls to enter.

The big room was crowded with familiar faces. Once they were inside, Jamie stood rubbing his bruised knuckles and Selma looked faint. Sam broke the silence. 'He'll be waiting for us. We ought to stay here tonight.' He was very calm. 'He'll probably get his mates. They'll be looking for us.' Considering the circumstances, he sounded amazingly matter-of-fact.

'Don't get yourself in a knot. I can handle him.' Was it only Didi who heard the dismay in Jamie's voice? Stalking off, towering above everybody, getting as far away as possible from his friends, he hunched into a seat and glowered into space. Didi started to follow.

'Don't,' Sam said sternly. 'Don't. Give him time to cool down.'

From the other side of the room she watched Jamie take the harmonica from his pocket, hold it to his mouth, but couldn't hear what he played. She sat and waited for him to cool down. There was nothing else to do.

No one took any notice of them. As the time for the Grand Parade drew near, the atmosphere was chaotic, both in the dressing-rooms and the assembling areas. The acrobats were beginning to limber up, flexing and stretching their muscles, carefully easing their way into suppleness. One slip on the wires and they were in trouble. Some of the clowns, not the little ones who performed with Donald or Miss Violet, but big ones, part of another group, were smothering their faces with greasepaint and arguing.

'Caine Carrington's my choice for next Tuesday.'

'The nag who won the Caulfield? Hasn't a hope.'

'There'll never be another Phar Lap. Greatest tragedy in the horse-racing world.' This clown was made up like a mad baby with an oversized dummy hanging from his large bib.

'Me? I'm putting my money on Ragilla.'

Uniformed riders were marshalling the Brumbies into line. A buggy, with the signs of the zodiac painted on its side, was waiting to be drawn by Shetland ponies. Monkeys would hold their reins. Right now those monkeys were knotting their neck chains around each other and getting in everyone's way.

On the ringmaster's signal, the Panatrope blared out the opening bars of 'Under the Double Eagle'. A few seconds later an immense crack of thunder, like God's final curtain-call, rolled overhead. The music creaked downwards and stopped.

All the lights went out.

The crowd quietened. Then the anxious cries began. 'What's happened to the lights? Turn 'em on, bring on the lights.' The whistles, shouts and catcalls started.

Outside, things were worse. Shadowy figures, both animal and human, began blundering round, tripping over, getting in each other's way. The monkeys, frightened out of their wits, set up a sort of nervous yapping. This startled the horses into whinnying and pawing the ground. A dog barked hysterically. The sound was taken up by others. The noise rose to fever pitch. Someone must get hurt. It was unavoidable in such a tiny space. Where were the lights?

Convinced she was about to be trampled to death, Didi froze. Then came the faint sound of Jamie's harmonica, the notes growing louder and louder, at last ringing out with 'The Battle Hymn of the Republic.'

Glory, glory hallelujah,
Glory, glory hallelujah,
Glory, glory hallelujah...

It took some time for the hubbub to die down. The well-trained horses were easily calmed, the clatter of metal-shod feet quickly stopped. Except for a poodle with a neurotic whine, the dogs gradually, very gradually ceased barking. One of the monkeys kept up a nervous chatter. Didi heard a trainer's voice calling, 'Come on, settle down. Down there Magnus, stop being a silly boy.'

'Hush.'

'Quieten down.'

'Everything's fine.' Jamie's harmonica moved into the lull with, Click go the shears, boys, Click, click, click...'

Gradually, as trainers continued to sooth and hush, people found matches, lit them. Pinpricks of light appeared and shadows grew into monsters. The music moved towards the passage and was now inside. Some whistlers held out determinedly, but the catcalls were dribbling to a close.

214

'Shhh. Stop that noise.' The voice sounded official. People obeyed. Didi held her breath. She followed the music as it travelled up from the doorway and along the timber seats until it finally floated up to the rafters.

Once a jolly swagman
Camped by a billabong
Under the shade of a Coolabah tree...
Voices picked up the chorus... *Waltzing Matilda,*
Who'll come a-waltzing Matilda with me?

The lights came on abruptly. Everyone sighed with relief. And there was Jamie, a small figure in the middle of the ring. The Panatrope started up, the music slightly discordant as always, and someone started clapping. The solitary clap swelled into thunder. The audience, the staff, even the monkeys joined in to thank Jamie and his harmonica. Everyone cheered and applauded until their throats hurt and their hands were sore.

18. AFTERWARDS

AFTER THE SHOW, everyone made a great fuss. Mr Phillip Wirth thanked Jamie for having saved the circus from possible tragedy. He had done them a great service and they were very grateful.

How pleased and proud they were. How easy it was to dismiss George, his friends, the inevitable retaliation. Looking back, how rash they'd been. Wouldn't Jamie becoming a hero further antagonise George?

Once the performance was over, Donald and Miss Violet invited them to stay for supper. Donald opened a bottle of vintage port he had been saving for a special occasion. Miss Violet produced a rich fruit cake which she cut into thick slices for everyone.

Donald owned a splendid record player and, according to Jamie, a stunning collection of seventy-eights. There were recordings by Fletcher Henderson, Duke Ellington, Louis Armstrong and the great Beiderbecke. They foxtrotted and tangoed, Didi and Jamie a little less expertly, to the music of Paul Whiteman and Benny Goodman. Other artistes heard the music and appeared carrying armfulls of provisions. And, although everyone seemed to eat and drink non-stop, the food and liquor never ran out. By the time the small grandfather clock, which Donald boasted had been carried right round

Australia, struck midnight, just about every person belonging to the circus had crowded into Donald's rooms.

Finally, Sam persuaded Miss Violet to sing.

Don't know whyyyyyy...

There's no sun up in the skyyy...

Stormy Weatheeerrrr,' she breathed, her voice husky against the sound of Jamie's harmonica. When she finished, the audience, a motley looking lot in theatrical costumes, stage make-up and street wear, clapped furiously and demanded an encore.

Blueee moooon,

You saw me standing alonnnne...

Without a dream in my heart,

Without a love of my own.

Listening to Miss Violet's breathy contralto, wondering how long it would take to find 'a love of her own', Didi glanced over at Jamie. He was looking woebegone, and with a sudden pang, she realised he was missing Kate. It made her feel rotten. Jamie was too nice a person, too good a friend to stay miserable. Forgetting all about herself, she prayed he might get home soon.

Thus it was well after midnight when they gathered up their bits and pieces and headed for home. Which isn't to say they were ignoring George entirely. But with the excitement, the wine, the late hour, they dismissed Didi's suggestion to camp on Donald's floor. Forgetting that originally it was his idea, Sam argued, 'If we don't get home the Finkelstein's will panic.'

'Hiding isn't going to help.' Jamie said cheerfully. 'They'll turn up sooner or later. I'll just have to lie low and stay alert.'

Didi shivered. Knowing it useless, nevertheless she urged, 'There's no point looking for trouble. Let's phone the Finkelsteins and stay on here.'

'Can't,' said Selma abruptly. 'We haven't a telephone. Can't afford one.' Having forgotten this, Didi was embarrassed. How long would it take for her to remember where she was?

The storm had washed the city clean, but the streets were very dark. What little light they had came from the moon which, after flirting behind a fan of clouds, hid for the rest of the night. Everything went pitch black.

Nevertheless, they strode along, crossed the river, chattering loudly, with arms linked in a show of solidarity as they headed north towards Carlton and Mavis Road.

As they passed the cemetery, Didi barely dared breathe. She listened intently to the click of their heels striking the pavement, the wind in the trees, the hiss from a night animal. Further on, the isolated laneways were familiar. Hadn't she walked them every day for over three months?

Nothing happened.

Jamie and Sam relaxed. The tension faded but not their voices. 'There was once an Irishman, a Scotsman and a Jew,' Sam began, and although they had heard the joke a dozen times, their laughter ripped through the still night.

As they were about to turn into their street, only half a dozen houses from home, there came a sudden rush of footsteps. Shadowy, figures appeared from behind. 'We'll get you, you Yid-loving bastard.'

'Run Selma! Didi, run!'

'Get those girls outa here.'

Someone hit Didi with a solid, heavy object. It landed heavily on the side of her head, then glanced off. If it hadn't, she might have been killed, for whoever wielded the instrument was stronger than her and meant business. The pain was excruciating. She heard somebody, possibly herself, give a harsh scream. Colours swirled... Then the blackness descended.

Getting beaten up was an experience she had read about. It was something that happened to other people. No one had reported how rotten she would feel.

An eternity passed between gaining consciousness and prising open her eyelids. She was lying on cold, rough pavement. The ground kept moving about as if she was at sea. Her vision swirled and eddied. She crept on to her knees and nearly blacked out again from the pain. Moving carefully, concentrating on one knee after the other, she reached the gutter. There, she vomited up the fruit cake, the wine, everything she had eaten and drunk that night. She ran a tentative hand through her hair. There was a nasty lump as big as a duck's egg on her head. Very gingerly, she tried to assess the damage. It was hard to do, for her hair was matted and her fingers sticky.

But at least she was alive.

Realising this, she felt fractionally better. Only then did she remember the others.

She found Sam and Jamie close to where they had been attacked. Both lay still. Then, groaning and moaning and dripping blood all over his denim jacket, Jamie got to his knees. But Sam was as limp and lifeless as a doll. Didi's heart gave a terrible lurch. Staggering to her feet, she stood over him.

Sam was dead. She just knew he was dead.

Jamie, white as chalk, except where he was stained by his own blood, felt Sam's pulse and called, 'Come on Didi. He's still breathing. Help me get him home.'

Didi looked up and down the street. Mavis Road had never seemed so deserted.

In their weakened state, frequently stopping to catch their breath and mop up Jamie's poor nose, they managed to half-drag, half-carry Sam towards the house. Never more welcome, the portly figure of Mr Finklestein appeared, still in his pyjamas and led by a distraught Selma. 'We shouldn't have moved him. We don't know whether he's got any broken bones.' Didi couldn't stop her voice from rising. 'I'm sure we shouldn't be moving him. We could be making things worse!'

'Don't be ridiculous,' Jamie scolded her back to reality. 'We can't leave him on the street. What if they come back?'

With Mr Finkelstein's silent help, they lifted Sam through the front door, up the stairs and laid him on his bed.

Throughout all this, Sam's eyes stayed closed. Didi kept insisting, 'We might be making things worse,' for this piece of first-aid knowledge was stuck in her mind.

'Joe's gone for the doctor,' said Mrs Finkelstein bustling about with bowls of warm water. They sponged Sam's face and head, cleaned off as much mud and blood as they dared without shifting him about too much. Selma and Mr Finkelstein stripped off Sam's torn and muddy tweed suit, replacing it with his own pyjamas. Mrs Finkelstein was ready to take on every larrikin in town. 'If I could get my hands on those gangsters... those anti-semites...' Didi knew this was no empty threat.

Any other time Didi would have found the idea of Mrs Finkelstein as a law enforcer amusing. But not with Sam lying motionless, his skin a strange grey, the right side of his face red raw.

They settled Sam into a position resembling comfort. Only then did Didi admit how much her right arm ached. She knew the bones were intact for it moved easily enough, but she was badly bruised.

It was an hour before Doctor Gottliebson arrived. A

short, rotund man whose thick glasses made him look like a lemur, he stared with annoyance at the lodgers milling outside, at the family huddled inside. Then he lost his temper. 'I want everybody out of here,' he roared. 'This isn't a party. We've got a very sick young man in this room. As for you,' he scolded Didi and Jamie, 'you should be in bed.'

'Please,' Jamie protested. 'Please, I'm his friend. Please, can I stay?' His face was swollen, his head ached like mad, but these were nothing in comparison with Sam. It was all his fault. Why wasn't it him lying there immobile? Whichever way he looked at it, it was his rotten temper which had brought Sam to this pass. His bloody, rotten temper. Why wasn't it him instead of Sam?

Jamie wished he was dead.

The doctor growled like a demented possum, then relented. Didi went to clean up, but the others stayed with Sam. Holding each other's hands for comfort, Jamie and Selma watched Doctor Gottliebson examine Sam, pause every so often to check out a particular spot. Meanwhile, the other lodgers waiting outside barely dared breathe. Doctor Gottliebson felt Sam's head, shone a small light in his eyes, then gave his verdict.

'Concussion,' he growled. 'He's badly concussed. A few broken ribs and a great deal of bruising. He's lucky he wasn't more badly injured.'

Later on, upstairs, he examined Jamie's nose and looked at Didi's head and arm. 'You're very lucky,' he said, packing up his stethoscope. 'Not a broken bone amongst you. Next time you won't be so fortunate.' He seemed almost disappointed it wasn't right now. Shutting his bag, he added, 'That young man ought to be in hospital. I'll look in tomorrow morning. If he's still unconscious we might have to move him right away.'

19. Help!

THE MORNING AFTER the attack Doctor Gottliebson arrived very early. 'Frankly,' he scowled. 'It worries me he's still unconscious.'

Doctor Gottliebson's huge eyes were opaque pools where patients could drown their problems. The family held its collective breath as he examined Sam. In the end he decided, 'He needs professional nursing. A hospital. They'll watch out for blood clots.'

Jamie was horrified. 'Hospital!' It was the first thing he had said to anyone since the night before. 'What will they do there?'

'First they'll X-ray him.' Doctor Gottliebson wriggled his plump shoulders. 'After that? Let's wait and see.'

Jamie started to object, but Doctor Gottliebson was very persuasive. Convinced that this was merely a further step in the series of disasters he'd begun the night before, Jamie didn't argue long. Besides, Mrs Finkelstein, having complete faith in the doctor's judgement, quickly talked the others into agreeing.

The ambulance arrived shortly after. Her borrowed clothes having been splattered with blood and mud, Didi was back in jeans and T-shirt. Catching sight of her, the driver raised a disapproving eyebrow. Didi shrugged it off. She stood watching Sam's still figure being lifted out of bed and carried down the stairs. As he was strapped into the ambulance the driver noticed Jamie's bruised face. 'What happened to you? Had a run-in with the rent?'

To Jamie's surprise the man seemed mildly sympathetic.

Selma was permitted to ride to the hospital with the patient. Before Sam was carried away, Jamie stood for a long time studying his closed eyes and grey face. Seeing him so still, it was hard to realise this was the same flamboyant fellow he liked so much. Perhaps Doctor Gottliebson was right. Perhaps hospital was the right place for Sam, after all.

As Sam and Selma were driven slowly towards the city, Didi and Jamie hurried after them on foot. When they reached Lygon Street a tram rattled past. The driver stopped, picked them up, then deposited them close to the hospital. They arrived in time to watch Sam being lifted out of the ambulance and placed on to a trolley. The three friends followed his unconscious body into the crowded lobby and waited as Selma gave the receptionist Sam's full name and age. Didi tried to help Selma fill out the complicated admission form, but she wasn't much use. What the hospital wanted to know—things like Sam's parents' names, where he was born, his occupation, what diseases he had suffered from as a child—were obscured by distance and time.

This completed, two orderlies rushed the trolley, Sam stretched helplessly on it, down a long dark corridor.

They kept up with the trolley as it was trundled into an elevator. They slowly creaked to the first floor and stopped with a jolt. The doors rumbled open. The orderlies pushed the trolley into the corridor. It clattered around a corner before disappearing behind a set of swinging doors. 'No visitors permitted outside visiting hours,' said the nurse in charge of Ward Seven. She directed them to the bench outside. The door swung shut in their faces.

They sat down to wait. Two men dressed in white coats with stethoscopes hanging from their top pockets emerged from the ward, deep in conversation. Selma took the opportunity to slip inside. Before anyone could stop her, she dodged a tea-trolley, ran up the aisle and touched the Sister's starched sleeve. 'Please let me stay. I promise I'll be quiet as a mouse. If Sam wakes up he won't know where he is and he'll be terribly upset.' Jamie and Didi heard her voice rise above the squeak of trolleys, the murmurs of the patients and nursing staff.

The nurse shook her head. Hairs from a mole on her chin pointed accusingly. She said, escorting Selma outside, 'Visiting hours are between four and four-thirty each day. Visitors are not permitted at other times.' Directing all three to read the list of rules pinned up on the wall, she rustled away.

At the top of the ward doors were two small glass windows. If they stood on tiptoe, the girls could just glimpse the foot of Sam's bed. After a while Selma tired. She perched on the end of the bench and stared blankly ahead. Didi tried finding ways to comfort her, but her mind was blank. Phrases came... They seemed trite and useless. Anyway, why not wait for the visiting hour? What difference could it make to Sam if they were there or not? Rubbing her eyes, which stung through worry and lack of sleep, she brooded over what it might be like to wake up in an alien room surrounded by old men coughing up phlegm.

Nurses and doctors hurried past. No one spoke to them, nor did they speak to each other. As the hours stretched endlessly, Jamie recollected Sam's befriending them, cajoling the Finkelsteins into putting them up, the circus into giving him work. Didi twisted the sapphire ring around her finger and thought about Sam's sense of fun, his amazing generosity, his plans to marry Selma and start his

224

own business. Sam had the energy and drive to be successful. Had this been spoilt?

Gazing at Selma's impassive face, she thought how she had never admired anyone so much before. She could only guess what Selma was feeling, but with her whole life hanging in the balance, her friend remained calm and composed, at least on the surface. Only the extreme pallor of ivory skin, the dark rings under her almond eyes, hinted at her inner distress. That and Selma's eyebrows. They needed plucking. A stupid detail, but they proved how quickly things could deteriorate.

Concentrating on Selma, she had quite forgotten Jamie, and started when he got up. He was staring in at the ward, trying to see round corners. He sat down. She studied his swollen, sore face. She thought she had never seen anyone look so depressed. If Sam doesn't recover, she told herself, Jamie will feel totally responsible, and what then? She willed Sam into opening his eyes. Apart from sharing the vigil there was nothing else she could do.

If Jamie stretched to his full height, he could see through the windows to the end of Sam's bed. Unable to remain still, he walked round and round the narrow corridor, studying the worn lino and the dirty kalsomined walls. Each time he peered inside the ward, there was no sign of Sam's beige blanket having shifted, no hint his legs could move. If only it was himself lying there. If only he was dead. That way he wouldn't be going through all this.

The doors swung open. Two orderlies wheeled out a trolley, Sam on it.

Selma jumped up to stare into the greyish white face. Sam's eyes were firmly closed. Didi followed the trolley into the elevator. 'Where are you taking him?' she demanded.

'He's off to X-Ray.' As the door closed she heard an

orderly say, 'Bluey says Caine Carrington's a dead cert for the Cup, so I'm putting five bob on the nose.'

Didi scowled disapprovingly, but Selma was too engrossed in her own misery to register what was going on.

When Sam returned, they sprang up to study him. He was still unconscious. They settled back to their vigil on the bench.

When lunchtime came round, Didi decided someone ought to take charge. She announced that they needed something to eat and drink. Selma and Jamie rose obediently and followed her out of the hospital into the street. A block away they found a small cafe where the tables and windows were draped in matching flowered chintz. 'What do you want?' she asked.

Both Jamie and Selma shook their heads. 'It won't do Sam any good for us to get dehydrated,' Didi said firmly, and when the waitress came over she asked for a large pot of tea and some sandwiches.

Jamie said, 'Fat lot of good we've done Sam so far.' Staring at his leaden expression, Didi had a sudden desire to shake him.

'It's not doing Sam any good you blaming yourself,' she pointed out. 'You know George was just waiting for someone to lose their cool. He was dying for an excuse.'

'I didn't have to be the one to give it to him, did I?'

'But you did. And if you hadn't, it would've been me. Remember how you dragged me away the other day? If you'd let go I'd have punched his stupid face into mulch.'

Jamie's face lightened. Didi searched for an appropriate parallel. 'Remember how the First World War started? Someone got assassinated. Everyone knows that wasn't the real reason. It's the same for us. George and his mates were looking for an excuse. They were sure to find something sooner or later,' and she added, 'you're just feeling guilty.'

226

To Didi's surprise, Selma came to her aid. 'She's right,' she said tiredly. 'Joe and Yankel said exactly the same thing. They've been waiting to get us. They've waited for months. Jamie, you mustn't feel too badly about this. If it had happened the other way, if Sam had lost his temper and you were hurt, I know he wouldn't be blaming you.'

She stood up and headed for the toilets. 'I don't think she realises how I feel.' Jamie's voice rose. 'I keep thinking of all the things Sam did for us when we got here.' He broke off. Didi could think of nothing to say.

'There's no point keeping on blaming yourself,' she tried at last. 'It was just bad luck.'

He took no notice. 'My bloody temper. It's always got me into trouble. And now look what I've done. It's my fault Sam's in there. I'm some great mate, I don't think.' His eyes were red and watery.

'I still reckon George would have got us in the end,' she persisted, but he glanced away.

When their food arrived Selma managed one sip, then pushed her cup to the side. Jamie shook his head. Didi looked at the soggy sandwiches and felt slightly ill. She paid the bill and they walked back to the hospital.

They found the Finkelsteins waiting outside Ward Seven. One look and Selma's iron will broke down. Mrs and Mr Finkelstein rushed to console her. Watching tears roll down their faces, Didi expected to be embarrassed. Instead she felt envious. It must be very nice to have parents who didn't mind showing their feelings. Not that Tom and Jane wouldn't worry as much as the Finkelsteins if something happened to her or Kate, not that they wouldn't respond with an equal amount of love and care, but their way was different. More controlled. She tried imagining Tom in tears and shook her head with disbelief. Did that mean he didn't feel as strongly as other people?

227

It led her to thinking about Jamie, about the subtle change in their relationship. Only a few days ago he was offering help and advice, like the big brother she didn't have. Now it was her turn to look after him. The tilt made her slightly uncomfortable. Would he forgive her, later on, when he was more himself?

They left the Finkelsteins, wandered down the corridor and sat on the stairs. Jamie repeated dully, as if there had been no break in their conversation, 'I'm a great mate, I don't think.'

Such guilt became too much to bear. 'I've never heard such crap,' Didi exploded. 'You've been a great mate to me. I'll bet Sam thinks so too. Just you wait till he wakes up and tells you himself.'

Jamie blinked. All day long he had wondered what he should do if Sam remained in the coma. Apart from feeling personally responsible, Jamie liked Sam, liked his ebullient personality. His was the most active mind Jamie had ever come across. He recognised Selma's intelligence and determination, but she was a little too volatile for his tastes. She made him slightly uncomfortable. He had no such reservations about Sam. Sam was interesting, brave and resourceful. How wasteful that his spirit might have been quenched. Brooding along these lines, Jamie felt himself become leaden, dulled.

Squatting on the stairs, he wondered what on earth was going to become of them? If they returned, if Sam survived and lived a prosperous and long life, it was sobering to realise that Sam would be an old man when he and Jamie next met.

And what about his own family? In a strange way Liz's break-up wasn't dissimilar to this. Jamie couldn't forgive himself for causing a friend to be hurt. In the same way Liz would never forgive Bill for finding another woman. For

228

eighteen months he had hated Bill for ditching Liz. Now, discerning that his father had grabbed a last chance for happiness, Jamie found, to his own surprise, his anger evaporating.

Picturing Liz as he last saw her, her tall bony frame and light brown hair so like his own, he wondered if she really expected him to live with her next year. Considering her ambitions for him, it was unlikely. Perhaps it was time he started believing what she said. She might like being alone, like the freedom it gave her. Staring round at the hospital's scuff-marked walls, seeing them as if for the first time, Jamie felt someone had just lifted a dead weight from his shoulders. He felt free.

Visiting time was at four. Only then were they permitted into the ward. With Sam lying so quiet and grey, they thought they might go mad with grief. This waiting was hardest to bear.

Visitors came, paused by other patients, chatted of this and that, spoke loudly so old ears would hear and understand. A bell rang at four-thirty. Bustled away, Selma, Jamie and Didi returned to their seat in the corridor. Mr and Mrs Finkelstein went home. Tragedy may have struck, but the other lodgers still needed their dinners.

Selma smiled wanly. 'When Sam gets better we have my parents' permission to get married,' she told them, then hid her face in Didi's T-shirt. They were too preoccupied to hear the lift doors open or to see Donald and Miss Violet advancing along the corridor. Dressed in a bright red coat, matching velour hat with black osprey feathers and very high heels, Miss Violet was dressed as if she was going to a party. Donald, in a black-and-white chequered three-piece suit, green tie and black Homburg, was equally spectacular. With their arrival, Didi noted a marked increase in the number of hospital staff drifting through the corridor.

Having bought Sam the biggest bunch of carnations he could find, Donald was furious when refused permission to see Sam. He ranted about hospitals being no better than prisons, while Miss Violet, blowing smoke from her Turkish cigarettes, did her best to smother the smell of disinfectant.

Amid their noise and chatter, Didi discerned a genuine concern for Sam. She was deeply moved. What marvellous people. Circus folk suffered from fluctuating seasons, being hurt, or put off when they got too old, but they were so big hearted. She wanted to hug them, but didn't dare.

Donald had a great deal to report. Word had got out about the attack. It seemed both the artistes and the hands at Wirth's were in an uproar. The men promised retribution if the culprits were found and the women were equally vengeful.

Ignoring the eyes peering through the swing doors at them, Miss Violet said, 'We're so sorry. Are you sure there's nothing we can do to help?'

Selma smiled weakly and shook her head. It was wonderful having their friends rally around, but what could anyone do?

'Why don't you go to the police?' Donald demanded. 'Why should those thugs get away? Surely you can think of something they could use as evidence?'

They looked at each other and shrugged. There was no question who was guilty, but George would be bound to have a good alibi. Selma said, 'It was dark. We didn't see their faces. There's no way we can describe our attackers.'

'You must have some idea,' Miss Violet insisted, but Jamie and Didi were quite adamant.

Donald said, 'I've a message from Mr Wirth. He said to tell you the circus will pay all of Sam's medical bills.'

Selma smiled faintly. 'Please thank him very much. When Sam wakes he will appreciate it very much.'

Miss Violet waggled her head in sympathy. Murmuring reassuring words, promising to return the very next day, Donald and Miss Violet got up to leave. Miss Violet stopped in front of Didi. Didi felt small arms encircle her, and the next minute they were hugging each other.

When the resident doctor came past on his next round, Selma grabbed his arm. 'Please,' she pleaded, 'can you tell me what's happening to Sam Cohen?'

'His X-rays have yet to be processed.'

'Isn't there anything else you can do?' The resident's expression became glazed as he hurried off.

A little later there was a rustle and Doctor Gottliebson was standing in front of them.

'Have you got any news?' Their desolate faces made the doctor gruffer than ever.

He blinked twice before answering. 'The X-rays show no bone damage or blood clots.'

'Thank God.' Jamie collapsed with relief.

Selma looked puzzled. 'Then,' she asked, 'why is he still unconscious?'

'I honestly don't know.' Doctor Gottliebson's scowl condemned the medical profession. 'But we're doing all we can. The nurses are applying foments to his face and head. The swellings are coming down. We'll have to wait for nature to cure him.' And he added resolutely. 'When the patient is strong and healthy like Sam, it shouldn't be too much of a problem.'

They nodded and settled back on the wooden bench to await further developments.

20. THE RETURN

BY SEVEN, WHEN the night nurses came on duty, they had been sitting outside Ward Seven for ten hours. At long last a pretty blonde nurse, young enough to be a little less hardened than those on day shift, took pity on their woebegone faces and beckoned them inside.

They stood next to the iron rails surrounding Sam's bed and stared at him in dismay. He seemed sicker than ever. In less than twenty-four hours his face looked like old parchment, his body fining down to mere skin and bone. In a sort of silent complicity they avoided looking at each other until the nurse returned.

Then Selma found enough courage to ask, 'Please, let me stay here tonight?'

The nurse was about to refuse, but something in Selma's expression stopped her. She made a show of shepherding Jamie and Didi outside before hiding Selma behind the curtain which surrounded Sam's bed.

Back in the corridor Jamie and Didi stared blankly at each other. 'Come on,' Jamie said at last, 'let's get out of here.'

They clattered down the stairs, through the foyer and out the front door. On the pavement they paused to breathe in the night air and looked about hesitantly. Then Jamie turned right and started walking.

232

It was interesting, Didi thought, as they crossed the road and headed towards the centre of the city, that Jamie was following the same route they travelled their first night in 'thirty-three. Only this time things were different. Tonight she wasn't walking several paces behind him. Tonight they walked abreast, like two people who knew and liked each other. And recollecting that she had shorter legs and couldn't keep up with his long strides, this time he remembered to fit his step alongside hers.

The street lights came on. A cable-tram, carrying home the last of the bank clerks and shop assistants, rattled past. A breeze rose, whipped round corners, flapped at torn pieces of newspaper lying in the gutter, billowed out a beggar's coat like a balloon. The empty city, the scraps of paper and garbage being carried past by the wind, a broken-down cart someone had left in the gutter, reminded Didi of being homeless and hungry. Destitute. They passed a window display. Didi didn't bother to look. Instead, heading west, they turned left at the post office, where the clock said it was seven thirty-three. They took another turn past a pub advertising three-course business luncheons for two and sixpence.

And as they walked it seemed to Didi that the things which plagued her before, things which had seemed so important, like settling into a new city, making new friends, coping with Kate and Bill, were now irrelevant. Certain issues which once bothered her paled into insignificance in the face of losing Sam, confronting Selma's grief, perhaps never getting home to her family. They strode further along Swanston street, turned right into Bourke, and she slipped her small hand into Jamie's. For a moment it seemed that joining her hand to his connected them like computer terminals.

At the first slight pressure Jamie glanced down, his look

233

softened, almost guaranteeing that, one way or another, everything must work out in the end. Neither had slept a wink the night before, yet she saw his eyes were still sea blue, his musician's hands still strong and muscular. The feel of his skin on hers was very comforting. Until recently, the only other person who knew her likes and dislikes, her strengths and weaknesses had been Helene. And now there was Jamie.

There were so many aspects of him to explore. To begin with there was the music. There was always the music. She pictured him with the harmonica, then the piano, could hardly wait to hear him play the clarinet, flute and oboe.

His bond with Kate was harder to understand. That was because she, Didi, was ignorant. In spite of all her reading, she couldn't imagine what it was like to link her body with someone else's and make love. The act made her wonder. Not the process, she had read enough to know the mechanics, rather what went on at the time in a person's head. Only a fool wouldn't admit that sex made all the difference. She was no fool, only sorry that her lack of experience set her apart. In this she was worse off than Selma, for at least Selma knew who her future partner was.

Well, Kate should be relieved Didi had decided not to 'borrow' her boyfriend. She glanced up and smiled. That bit was hard. Particularly as Jamie was such a spunk and she liked him a lot. There was a narrow line, she understood, between involving oneself romantically and staying good mates. When they got back, for it was too frightening to think they mightn't eventually get home, she would see how this mateship developed. At the back of her mind still lurked the fear that, once Jamie was back with his own group, he might view their friendship with embarrassment.

With these thoughts running through her mind she

nearly charged into him. Jamie had changed direction, was turning up Russell Street, was standing alongside King's Theatre. There was a billboard. Two sets of eyes peered at it incredulously.

By Popular Demand. For One Night Only.
On Our Selection
directed by KEN J HALL.
with
BERT BAILEY, Fred MacDonald, Dick Fair.
Heading an All-Australian Cast.
TONIGHT'S PERFORMANCE begins at 8.15.

There were sketches. Of Dad and Dave. Of Dad and Mum in the car. Of two young people with their arms around each other.

It took Jamie ages to find his tongue. 'We have to go.' He listened to himself as if someone else was speaking. 'This is it. If we don't go now we'll never get back. Ever.'

'Sure.' Didi hesitated only a second. 'But what about Sam? Can we leave while he's sick? Shouldn't we wait a bit longer?'

Glancing down, Jamie saw his hands were trembling and slid them into his pockets. He said, 'This is our last chance. If we don't go now, we'll probably never get home. Besides,' refusing to meet her eye, 'if we miss this chance, Sam mightn't be around to help us break in and maybe we won't get another.'

Didi studied Jamie's grim face. She whispered, 'The post office clock said seven thirty-five. It means we've still time before it starts. Let's get back and see how he's doing.'

Turning, they narrowly dodged a waif emerging from the shadows behind. 'Watchit mate,' he shouted, his carton of matches spilling on to the pavement. They raced off, headed towards the next block and darted through the hospital entrance.

'Excuse me,' the nurse at the reception desk cried, 'you can't go in there.'

They dashed across the foyer down the long dark corridor and up the last flight of stairs. By the time they stopped, gasping for breath, in front of the doors which led to Ward Seven, Didi had a stitch in her side and was bent over with pain.

Jamie's face dropped. Selma had vanished. Then he remembered she was inside. 'Come on then.' He pushed open the swinging doors. Several sets of rheumy eyes watched them tiptoe towards Sam's bed.

They peered around the curtain. One look and Didi's heart sank. Sam was still unconscious, but Selma was there, still seated beside the bed. Her head was on Sam's pillow.

Jamie stole up to the side of the bed and stared intently at Sam. Was it wishful thinking or did his skin look less parchment-like? There was only one way to find out.

His hand crept into his hip pocket. Perched on the side of the bed, he placed the harmonica near his mouth and began to play. He had thought to start with circus music, something like 'La Paloma', 'The Merry Widow Waltz' or the *Poet and Peasant* overture, but he remembered the music he had heard in the Finkelsteins' kitchen. So one of Yankel's Russian folk songs floated tentatively across the bed. *Otchi chornya...*

A slight movement caught his eye. He stopped playing for a second and stared. Did one of Sam's eyelids flicker? He saw Didi watching Sam intently, as if she intended writing a report on every twitch, and Selma's eyes seemed to bore right into Sam's skull.

'Try something else, Jamie. Play something else,' Selma ordered without looking up.

Jamie needed little encouragement. He had begun Mozart's *Rondo Alla Turc*, when someone wrenched the curtain aside. A voice, sharp enough to cut through any nonsense, cried, 'What's going on here?'

A nurse, not the one who had let Selma wait inside the ward, but another, this one older, more severe looking, her hair completely hidden by the starched veil and wearing steel-rimmed glasses, was glaring into the cubicle. 'This is a hospital. What do you think you're doing?'

Selma grabbed her by the arm and gestured towards the bed. 'Ain't Misbehavin' ' rang clearly through the ward. Almost on cue, Sam's eyelids fluttered, his head turned towards the sound, his lips moved imperceptibly. Forgetting everything but her patient, the nurse rushed towards him, and Selma, who had managed to stay dry-eyed since her parents left, burst into floods of tears. 'Sammy, Sammy!' She collapsed on to the bed, stopping Jamie in mid bar. Everyone, even the nurse, was beaming with relief.

Only after things had settled down, after the nurse had agreed that it had done Sam a great deal of good to see them, that they could stay another five minutes but certainly no longer, did Jamie remember the film. He placed his hand on Sam's. '*On Our Selection*, Sam. It's playing tonight. We have to go. You understand? It may be our only chance.'

Sam nodded weakly. He closed his eyes and seemed to fall asleep. He looks so frail, Didi thought. But at least he's alive. And conscious.

She looked at Sam's hands, the dark hairs on the back, the squarish fingers. At the moment they seemed too pale and limp to belong to Sam. Wondering if her own looked any different, she glanced down and saw the ring. On an impulse she slipped it off and pressed it into Selma's palm.

Selma knew what this meant. 'I know you have to go,'

she said at last. 'But I'll find a way to contact you.' They gazed at each other and the sad expression in Selma's eyes made them seem larger, darker than before. Thinking, 'It's true, hearts really can break,' Didi stared at Selma. She took in the curly hair framing a pale face, the tired patches beneath her eyes. She had never seen Selma looking so pretty. They hugged. When Didi straightened up her cheeks were wet. 'You'd better go right away,' Selma insisted, embracing Jamie.

Didi had difficulty stifling a sob. 'How will we know if Sam's OK?'

'I'll find some way of letting you know,' Selma promised. 'Now hurry, or you'll miss your chance.'

Jamie held out his harmonica. 'When Sam wakes,' he instructed, 'give him this.'

Selma was horrified. 'But you can't give this away.'

Jamie shook his head. 'You don't understand. I'm not giving it to Sam. I'm lending it until he gets better. If we don't come back, ask him to leave it somewhere, somewhere he thinks I'll find it. That way I'll know you're OK and maybe I can find you.'

Selma took the harmonica and placed it under Sam's pillow. Another quick hug, and Jamie tore Didi away. They ran. Ran past the rheumy-eyed old men and the astonished nurses, sped through the ward and out the swinging doors. The elevator being far too slow, they flew back down the stairs, turned left into the long corridor and dashed out of the foyer as if their lives depended on it.

It took only five minutes to get back to the theatre. Small globes strung over the entrance flickered invitingly. The foyer was ablaze with light, but empty. Didi stopped in front of the ticket box and peered inside. It was deserted. They were too late. There was no way they would get in. They would never get home.

She stopped dead. Her shoulders slumped forward in despair.

'Come on Didi,' Jamie called impatiently, 'you can't stop now.'

'It can't work, Jamie,' she cried, the terrible truth dawning on her, that it was far too late. Now she was sure she wanted to go home, and they would never make it. Nothing could get them away. They had forgotten. Without the harmonica it was hopeless. This could never work. They were stuck in 'thirty-three for ever. It was as the Voice had predicted. They *must* have the film and the music. Only this magic combination would get them back to their own decade. 'It won't work, Jamie,' she cried, waiting for him to stop and turn.

Jamie refused to listen.

Two strides and they were in front of the entrance to the auditorium. An usher appeared before them. Was this the same lad they met before? The dirty white suit seemed. familiar. 'Tickets please?'

Jamie grabbed Didi's hand. Brushing the boy aside, as if he was made from straw, he pulled her into the smoky auditorium.

'Hey, you can't walk in without tickets,' the usher called. 'What d'you think you're doing? Come back here or I'll call the manager.'

Jamie was moving ahead, dragging Didi alongside, running down the aisle searching for seats.

Two were empty in the second row from the front. Stopping, being pulled over people's feet, knees, she tripped, fell over handbags, umbrellas, heard people swear, the usher cry, 'You can't stay here. I'm calling the manager.'

Up on the screen, well above the disturbance, a white-bearded bloke was saying, '*I worked hard and honest, living on dry bread, harrowing me bit of wheat in with the*

239

brambles...' Jamie pushed Didi into a seat. She hit her right hip so hard she swore.

'Such language.'

'Sit down!'

'We can't see!'

'Well, I never...'

'Would you mind not talking during the film?'

In the dim light Didi saw that Jamie's eyes were closed. He was concentrating furiously. His lips were pursed. Music, a thin wavering, whistling sort of music, was emerging from his mouth.

'*But I never lost heart for one single moment...*' She pummelled his arm so he would listen. 'It won't work,' she cried. 'It's useless without the harmonica.'

The old man up on the screen was saying, '*But me spirit was never broken. Even when the cattle had perished and died before me very eyes...*'

Why wouldn't Jamie listen? She screamed at the top of her voice, 'Can't you see it won't work? You need the harmonica!'

Someone switched on a light. Didi closed her eyes, squeezed them shut against the glare, and a familiar voice, a very familiar girl's voice demanded, 'Why are you two sitting in the dark? Hey, you look like you've been asleep..

'*This is the Midday Movie.*' To Didi's intense relief someone turned the light right down, switched the sound off.

Didi stared wildly about. She was back home in the family-room.There was Jamie, seated next to her, blinking rather stupidly into the distance, with Kate standing over him.

Kate was looking rather annoyed.

240

After Kate and Jamie had left to go to an evening's rage, and Tom and Jane had returned from their stroll through the Botanic Gardens and were in the kitchen cooking dinner, Didi crept downstairs into the cellar. She turned on the light, looked around at the shadows that had loomed so forbiddingly earlier that day and smiled. The cellar was comfortably familiar, better lit than she remembered. Even the air seemed fractionally warmer.

She walked unhesitatingly to the trunk, pulled out the blankets and laid them out on the floor. A plaid of orange and two shades of brown. The colours were bright. Apart from the worn pile they might have been woven yesterday.

The clothes lay underneath.

Didi took her time unpacking the underwear. She counted each piece very carefully. Then there was the skirt and the jumper. They were clean. Every trace of mud and blood had been removed.

Probably for its protection, the navy woollen dress had been folded and placed beneath the rest. Didi held it up, shook it out, then held it up again. She paused to admire the sequinned hibiscus flower pattern on the bodice.

A sudden thought and she felt inside, felt where someone might have hidden something in the pockets, listened for a crackle.

And there, right inside, was a folded piece of yellowing paper. On the outside, faded but still readable, was her name...